Handle With Care

Handle With Care

Nice meeting you this weekend. Happy fishing & reading! Patrice

Patrice Wilton

The characters and events portrayed in this book are fictitious. Any similarity to real persons, living or dead, is coincidental and not intended by the author.

Originally published as a Kindle Serial, July 2013

Published by Montlake Romance
P.O. Box 400818
Las Vegas, NV 89140

ISBN-13: 9781477848906
ISBN-10: 1477848908
Library of Congress Control Number: 2013911418

Dedication

First of all, I would like to thank all the men and women who have valiantly gone to war and fought for freedom. All of you are the true heroes of my story.

I would also like to show appreciation to the incredibly wonderful Wounded Warrior Project, which I learned about during my research. For more information on this organization that assists and supports our wounded warriors and their families, please see

http://www.woundedwarriorproject.org/.

On a personal note, I would like to thank my fabulous agent, Pam Ahearn, and everyone at Montlake, the brilliant editors, and the author's team, who are marketing gurus.

I would also like to welcome the latest addition to my growing family—my fourth granddaughter, Andrea Wilton. Love to her and all my extended family.

EPISODE ONE

CHAPTER ONE

Shane Dawson surveyed the boardwalk, his grip on Major's leash tight. The pup pulled, eager to join the steady Saturday stream of joggers and skateboarders. The temperature of the slightly damp air hovered in the mid-sixties. It was only mid-April—not yet tourist season—and Belmont Beach in Southern California bustled with perpetual energy. Probably not the best spot for training a dog, but Shane's time was severely limited, and so was the pup's.

"Come on, Major, let's go." He adjusted the length of the leash, not wanting to give too much. The problem pup immediately bit the rope and tugged. Shane shook his head but couldn't stop the grin. "Let go. This isn't a game. You know the rules."

The golden lab ignored him and playfully growled around a mouthful of leash. Shane muttered, "Don't do this. You buck the system, you're labeled a screw-up for life. Trust me, boy; I know what I'm talking about." He knew the words were useless and that the misguided animal would learn by making his own mistakes. Just as he had. But he aimed to make sure the price wasn't too steep.

"Look, you learn this, you can be a 'hero dog.' It's a really big deal. Don't you want that? Helping folks out, making a difference?" He leaned over and took the leash out of Major's mouth. "Just behave. You know what you have to do. Walk. Halt. Heel. And fetch things when I tell you to."

Major gave up the game of tug-of-war, looking around for something of more interest. They crossed the street successfully, entering the fray of people. He knew the dog didn't have a mean bone in his body but just needed discipline—and time to be a puppy. But that wasn't in his cards. He was being trained to help the wounded warriors recently returned from war, but so far Major didn't get it.

Any dog could be ordinary, but Major had a chance to be so much more. He was smart and knew all the basic obedience skills, except he liked to play more than he liked to work.

Shane couldn't blame him for that—he'd spent most of his life doing the same thing. After graduation from high school, instead of going to college he and a buddy had hitchhiked to California to become surfers and make action films. When that didn't pan out, they'd joined CAL FIRE, the California Forestry and Fire Protection department, and he became a medic, while his friend flew choppers. With close to 6,000 wildland fires per year, they never lacked for action.

Both men had relished the excitement and danger, but after several years on the job, Shane had wanted more. Exactly what, he wasn't sure—but something bigger than what he was doing. So he took online college courses, concentrating on science and pre-med, figuring one day he'd want a promotion from being an ambulance driver. He'd been close to getting his bachelor's when he hit a major bump in the road, setting him on a wild detour.

An attempt to blow up Disney World had been miraculously thwarted, and the children and families lived to see another day. But Shane couldn't shake it off. After 9/11, nothing seemed right in the world. The religious fanatics in the Middle East were bringing their bombers and prejudice to his turf, threatening the core of American civilization. He refused to sit by and do nothing. The following week he joined the army, eager to take the fight to Iraq.

Major sniffed the air, straining against his restraints, but Shane yanked him in. Discipline could be learned; it could save lives. "Whoa, take it easy, little guy. Remember the rules: Walk, don't run."

After a few more tugs, the pup trotted along beside him. Major held his head high, his mouth slightly open, his nostrils twitching, as he took in his new surroundings. He wagged his tail and seemed to have a perpetual sappy smile on his face.

Too friendly, the trainer said, and gave the dog a month to shape up or be shipped out. Shane, as a volunteer for the Wounded Warrior Project, had offered to take the dog for a couple of weeks, to see if he could teach him the importance of service.

"Now, I'm going to unleash you for a minute." He stooped over and looked the dog in the eye. "This is your big chance here, so don't blow it." He patted the dog on the head and unhooked the leash.

"Remember who you are. A military dog, enlisted to give service. Now make me proud." Major gave Shane's bionic hand a lick and then trotted along beside him.

Shane wiped his i-limb on his T-shirt and noticed a few curious stares. He was used to it now and almost proud of the realistic appendage, but it made other people uncomfortable. The mechanical hand, with its lifelike fingers controlled by electrical signals, was highly functional, unlike the old C-shaped pinchers (he'd had one of those, too). He knew he was damn lucky to get an i-limb courtesy of the military, and not because he was a war hero, either. Let other people call him that. He knew the truth, and had to live with it too.

He'd been a medic in Iraq, and on his first mission he'd been captured and tortured by the Iraqi forces. After six months of daily beatings and being forced to patch up their wounded, Navy Seals had miraculously crept into the enemy camp and released him. He'd spent many months in hospitals and rehab and had been given several prosthetics, yet miserable son-of-a-bitch that he was, he'd not been in an appreciative mood. Nothing could fix what ailed him or take away his deepening despair. Tormented over losing his limb, worried about his future—or what he considered his lack of one—he hadn't wanted to live anymore.

If it weren't for his best buddy, Brent, and his family connections, Shane'd still be a bitter, broken-down vet, drinking himself into a slow death and living off the streets. They'd guided him toward the Wounded Warrior Project, where, after a few ups and downs, he'd cleaned up his act. Found something to believe in again.

"Come on, Major. Let's finish up. You're doing great, and I've got to get to work."

Major sat then and growled a warning. Shane looked up just in time to see a young boy on a bike weaving through pedestrians, right toward them. A frantic woman rode behind, apologizing and calling for the kid to slow down. The boy noticed Shane and veered left at the same time that Major attempted to get out of the way.

Shane winced as the boy—he figured the kid to be about five or six years old—flipped over the handlebar and landed chin down on the hard cement. His mother skidded to a stop, lost her balance, and toppled off her own bike. The boy howled, and Major, eager to give comfort, licked the kid's face.

Shane pulled Major back and clipped the leash onto his collar. "Hey there," Shane said, dropping to his knees and touching the kid's shoulder. "I'm a medic. I can help."

The woman, eyes flashing with anger and worry, reared up on her skinned knees. She pushed him aside. "Step away from my son. I'm a doctor, and your dog was running loose."

Technically, her kid had run over his dog, but now wasn't the time to split hairs. "He's not my dog. I'm just training him," Shane replied, while mentally cataloguing obvious injuries. The chin was bleeding a lot and might need a stitch. "Doctor trumps medic," he said and scooted out of the way.

She ignored him and concentrated on her son. "Josh, let me see your face. Does it hurt anywhere else?"

The boy lifted his eyes, tears spilling down a scratched cheek while blood dripped from his chin. "My arm hurts, Mom."

"Oh, honey. Let me take a look." Her efficient moves were part doctor and part mom before she released a sigh and pressed a kiss to a clean spot on the boy's forehead. "I'm sorry, sweetie, but you may have dislocated it." She glanced at Shane. "I didn't bring my cell phone. Could you call an ambulance, please?"

Shane whipped his phone from his pocket, glad to be of service. Major scooted closer to Josh, sneaking in a face lick. "You got it."

She took off her lightweight pink top and pressed the soft inside of the fabric to Josh's chin. Without her jacket on, Shane could see the curve of her full breasts. Hardly the moment to be appreciating her physical attributes, although she had plenty; he chastised himself and quickly glanced away.

"He may need stitches," she muttered. "And he definitely will need his arm examined."

Shane ended the call and stood, scanning the boardwalk, as impatient as the mother for the EMT to show. "They have a vehicle nearby. It'll just be a few minutes."

"Thanks." She focused her attention on her son, stroking his hair while keeping the once pink and now red jacket in place. Calm, collected, but definitely loving. "You might miss a day of school, but otherwise you'll be fine. You're so brave, Josh. Shh, it's okay, now."

Shane didn't think the kid was so brave, as the more Mom sympathized, the louder Josh bawled. Major howled in unison, accompanying the boy in a pitiful duet. Eager to distract them, Shane lifted his bionic hand, flexed his mechanical fingers, and began to make scratching motions in the air. Then he wrestled it down with his good hand.

The boy stopped the hysterics with a hiccup. Wide-eyed, he whispered, "What *is* that? It's so weird."

"It's a bionic hand, and you're right," Shane told him. "It is weird. The stupid thing has a mind of its own and acts out all the time. Especially in public. It's so embarrassing."

The kid giggled and shot a look at his mother. "You're not supposed to say 'stupid,' is he, Mom? It's a bad word."

Shane glanced at the pretty woman cradling her son, and cocked an eyebrow. "Stupid? Since when?"

"Oh, some time ago." She eyed his prosthetic, and some of the earlier frost left her turquoise eyes. "That's a pretty cool hand. I haven't seen one before."

He held it out for her to see. "Yup. It's an i-limb. Top of the line." He grinned. "Call me lucky."

"I didn't say that." She frowned, and her eyes met his. "What happened?"

He kept the facts short. No one was interested in his hard-luck story, and he had to keep it light for Josh. "Got my hand chopped off in Iraq."

Josh made a face. "Eew! Bet that hurt."

"I'm sure it did"—he gave a careless shrug—"but I passed out. Don't remember a thing."

The boy's eyes grew even rounder. "Really?" Not waiting for a reply, he glanced at Major. "Your dog is licking my leg. Can I pet him?"

"Probably shouldn't." With reluctance, Shane pulled the dog away. "He's training to be a hero dog."

"What's a hero dog?" the kid wanted to know.

"I thought you were kidding," Doctor Mom said.

"They help our military who've come back from war with missing limbs. The dogs become their companions and are trained to fetch and do household chores. Like open doors and closets. Some dogs even do laundry."

"Wow, Mom. Could we have one of those? You hate laundry."

She glanced at Shane and managed a small smile. "No, Josh. Others less fortunate than ourselves need these highly skilled dogs a whole lot more than we do."

The boy's cheeks turned pink. "But what if I broke my hand or my wrist? Then could I have one?"

"You haven't broken anything," his mother replied and ruffled his hair. "Good try, Pumpkin."

"Don't call me that. It's a baby's name."

"You're still my baby and always will be." She tickled him, and tried to sneak in a quick kiss, but the boy wasn't having it.

Josh attempted to push himself up but grimaced painfully. "Is that why you have this dog?" he asked Shane. "Does he do things for you?"

"No, I can function on my own." He flexed his hand, knowing Doctor Mom was listening to every word. "Major isn't behaving as well as he should. He'll be kicked out of school if he doesn't stop jumping on people. Like today, he got in your way and made you fall off the bike." Shane gave the kid an out.

"Wasn't his fault. I was going too fast and couldn't steer right. He won't get in trouble, will he?" The boy's eyes filled with tears once more, this time the empathetic kind.

"No, not for that. I agreed to help train him because he's smart enough to be a service dog, but he's just too friendly."

"That's a hard life for a dog just the same," the boy's mother said, and for the first time she looked directly at him.

He felt a jolt of awareness shooting through him.

Eyes the color of the Caribbean Sea and just as deep and fathomless. A man could get lost in them. She had a cute, upturned nose and soft, kissable lips. Not that he wanted to kiss her or any woman. He didn't have the time or the inclination to romance someone and preferred the simplicity of a one-night stand. Not that he'd had one of those in a long, long time.

When he'd first been treated at Walter Reed, an old girlfriend came to visit. He'd glimpsed the pity in her eyes when she looked at the ugly stump, before she'd turned away. To spare her any more pain, he'd told her that he'd met someone else when he was overseas. She'd left in a hurry, glad to get away. He was in a much better place mentally now, but dating was far from his list. He had important things to do, like finishing his pre-med courses and getting into a good school. Hero dog training was just another he'd added to his list of responsibilities.

"Have we met before?" he asked, his eyes searching her face. He could swear he'd seen her before. The hospital maybe?

"No, I'm sure we haven't," she answered, looking down the boardwalk. "Where are those medics? What's taking them so long?"

He was about to call to find out, when he spotted them weaving their way toward them. "Here they are."

"About time."

He nodded in agreement. The last thing he needed was a visceral attraction to a beautiful woman. No woman, no matter how pretty, would deter him from his solitary path.

CHAPTER TWO

Shane watched as the medics arrived with a stretcher and eased Josh onto it. His mother held her son's hand, comforting him with light touches and soothing words.

Now that the boy had medical attention, Shane glanced again at the mother's face. She had removed her visor and he could see her more clearly. "I have seen you before. I'm sure of it."

She gave him a quick, dismissive look. "No. I remember people and faces."

"Maybe I've seen you at the hospital," he answered stubbornly.

"Most likely," she replied, climbing into the back of the ambulance, alongside her son.

Her unfriendly attitude irritated him, and made it that much more important to make his point. "The Long Beach Memorial. That's it." He grinned, smug now that he'd remembered. "You're in ER, right? My unit works out of that hospital. I just started a month ago."

"Right." She darted a glance in his direction. "Can you take care of our bikes? Just get them to the hospital, and someone will take it from there."

He wanted to tell her what she could do with her bikes, but then guilt settled in. Their nice day out had turned into a real bummer. "Sure thing. It's the least I can do." He gave Josh the thumbs up. "Good luck, kid." To make the boy smile, he took hold of Major's paw and wiggled it to wave good-bye.

He watched the ambulance pull away, then glanced at the bikes, unsure of how he'd transport them to the hospital. He looked around for assistance and saw a skateboarder fly past, grab some old lady's handbag off her shoulder, and race down the boardwalk.

The lady stopped, her hands to her chest in disbelief, and shouted, "Thief!"

Shane unleashed Major. "Go! Stop him. You can do it."

The dog took off, and Shane rushed after him. His lungs were aching by the time he caught up with them. Major had the scruffy teenager on the ground, fifty pounds of drooling, growling dog keeping the boy in place.

"Back down, Major." The dog lay down but kept his eyes trained on the young man. What? Seventeen, with a scruff. Hard times, maybe.

"Let me go," he said, his eyes shadowed.

"You're not going anywhere," he told the kid, patting Major on the head. "Good job." He turned his attention back to the thief. "Give me the lady's purse."

"Make me." The kid stood up, and brushed himself off. "Keep that dog off me, or I'll sue."

"You're a thief," he replied. "How can you sue?"

Kid shrugged, still acting tough. "Why not? It's America."

Shane rocked back on his heels and crossed his arms. "So you think you can take a woman's purse? Not following the logic."

The teenager grimaced. "Fine. Take the old lady's bag." He tossed it in Shane's direction. "I'm outta here."

"Afraid not. The woman has a cop with her, and they're right behind you."

The teenager's eyes flashed with fear, but he turned his head and laughed. "See if they can catch me."

Shane knew he was about to bolt and get away. A part of him recognized the pain in the teenager, but another part wanted justice for the innocent woman. He stuck out his mechanical hand and made contact with the young man's chest. "Not so fast. This is a bionic weapon, and I'm special ops," he lied. "You don't want to mess with it or me."

The boy glanced down, and his youthful pink cheeks lost color. His cocky attitude slipped some too. "You can't... didn't do anything."

"Yes, you did," the lady said, having arrived with her armed escort.

Major had the purse between his teeth, and wagged his tail. The woman bent down to retrieve it, but the pup thought it was a game and tugged.

"Drop it, Major." Shane picked up the bag, handing it to the lady. His eyes met the teenager's. "An apology is in order."

The law officer stepped between them. "I've got this." His eyes scanned Shane, head to toe, pausing at the hand, with a nod of respect. "Thank you, sir."

Pale as milk, the teen blurted, "I needed the money." He glanced at the lady. "Sorry." He looked it too. At being caught perhaps?

"You're under arrest," the officer said and put the young man's hands behind his back to handcuff him.

"What did you need the money for?" Shane asked, searching the boy's face.

He shrugged. "Haven't eaten today."

"When was the last time you did eat?"

"A couple of days ago."

The officer looked at the woman, clutching the bag tightly in her hands. "You want to press charges, ma'am?"

She looked at Shane and back at the youth, her prim mouth pursed in thought. "I have a grandson your age. Ran away from home. Are you a runaway?"

"No, ma'am."

"I'll need to call his parents," the patrolman interrupted. "What's your name and number?"

"Won't do no good," the teen said belligerently. "I haven't seen my family in weeks. Dad threw me out. He won't want to see me now, anymore than he did then."

The lady looked at Shane, who shrugged. What happened next wasn't up to him. As he looked closer at the thin adolescent, he saw a kid warring within himself over good and evil. Not committed to crime. Yet.

The officer cleared his throat. "Well, if you haven't got a place to sleep, I'll have to take you into protective services. How old are you?"

"I'm seventeen. I can fend for myself."

"You wouldn't be lying about your age, now would you?" he questioned. "Let me see some I.D."

"I left my wallet at my friend's house." He lifted his chin, defensive. "I've been takin' care of myself. Dad's messed up all the time; callin' him won't do no good. Mom left last year."

"I won't press charges," the woman decided, looking at the bewildered policeman.

Shane pulled out his wallet and handed over a twenty. "Use this for food, not drink. And if you have some spare time, here's a card where I help out sometime. You ever hear of the Wounded Warriors?" he asked. "They're always looking for volunteers to help the men and women who've come back from war. You think you've got troubles, you ought to see them."

The police officer looked uncertain. "I really should take you in, but somehow I don't think you'll be better off." He looked the youth in the eye. "This is my beat and I'll be looking out for you. Don't ever let me catch you doing this stunt again."

"I won't. I promise." He gave them a shy wave. "Thanks."

The three of them watched the boy skate away.

Shane turned to the police officer. "I have another problem you might be able to help me with." He told him about the bikes and how he needed to get them to Long Beach Memorial.

"If I had a car, I would drive you," the woman said. "Thank you for getting my purse back."

Uncomfortable at being in the spotlight, Shane shifted from one foot to the other. "It was Major, really." He positioned the lab at his feet.

The officer patted his chest. "I'm Donald Masterson, ex-Marine. I can drive you and the bikes there myself. Got the SUV today. Normally it's the patrol car, but it had a flat."

"You, young man," the older woman declared, not done speaking, "were very brave." She pointed to his hand. "And handicapped!"

"This?" Shane flexed his bionic fingers. "This is no handicap, ma'am." With a John Wayne grin, he turned on his heel. "Over here, Officer."

"Why'd you do it?" the officer asked. "Give the kid money."

Shane sighed, realizing how far he'd come and how far he had to go. He gave a careless shrug as he thought about the kid's fears. "I've walked a mile in his shoes."

~

When Lauren and Josh arrived at the ER, the receptionist rushed them in right away. "What happened?" Betty asked. The plump, grey-haired former nurse assessed the situation in seconds.

"Josh fell off a bike. Face wound needs a stitch, maybe, and his arm's hurting."

Josh's eyes filled with tears, though he hadn't so much as sniffed inside the ambulance. "I think it's broken. I might need a bionic arm."

Lauren bit back a laugh and exchanged an amused look with the receptionist. "We ran into a war vet, and he had an i-limb. I've heard about them but not actually seen one until today. Pretty cool, actually."

Betty's calm demeanor helped Lauren keep it together too. It was so hard, watching her son go through his first ER visit. "Well, kiddo," Lauren said, "let's get you examined, and if we can't fix your existing arm, we'll order up one of those new gadgets. How's that?"

"Thanks." Another tear ran down his cheek. "Mom? Do I still have to be brave or can I cry now? It really hurts."

She put her arm around his waist and gave him a hug. "Oh! Honey, I didn't mean that you couldn't cry. Being brave is getting through the pain, that's all." Lauren knew very well about that. Her eyes filled as she worried she wasn't letting her son be a child. "Am I too tough on you? You're only six. Cry if you have to."

As if sensing she wasn't just talking about a cut on his chin and a hurt arm, Josh set his jaw. "I'm the man of the house."

Uncertain, she ruffled his strawberry-blond hair. "That you are."

Josh had lost his father when he was three years old, and Lauren had had to raise him as a single mom. It hadn't been easy. She'd been grief stricken and so, so angry. The man who killed her husband had two prior DUIs, but he'd been allowed behind a wheel. Why not just give him a shotgun and a license to kill?

"Lauren?" She glanced up to see Dr. Knowles standing in the doorway. "You can bring Josh in now. Face first, then some X-rays."

After Dr. Knowles stitched up Josh's chin and the X-rays were done, they finally left the hospital. No fractures—but a badly sprained elbow would keep Josh's arm in a sling for weeks. Unfortunately, hours in the hospital, in addition to the pain, had made her son a little short tempered. He needed routine to be at his best. What had happened today was outside her control.

He kicked the sliding glass door when it didn't open fast enough.

Instead of yelling, she put a protective arm around his shoulder. "Josh, I'm so proud of you, hon."

"I want a cheeseburger and a milkshake. Can I have a milkshake?"

McDonalds was a treat, and he'd earned one. "We'll see. It's getting kind of late and..."

He immediately stopped walking. "I want McDonald's!"

Careful to control her own temper, she took a deep breath, prepared to attempt to reason with a tired, injured Josh. A headache started at both temples. His temper tantrum was cut short by the blaring ambulance pulling up to the emergency entrance. The man they'd run into, or over, this morning, slid out from the passenger side.

He seemed startled to see them. "You two still here?" He glanced at Josh's sling, then his chin. "I wondered if you'd need a stitch. Nothing broken?"

"Naw. Just a sprain. Hurt really bad, but I'm not a crybaby. Am I, Mom?"

"No, you're SuperKid."

"Did you get your bikes okay?" he asked.

"Yeah. We did. Thanks." She shielded her eyes from the bright sun. "I'm sorry if I was rude to you before." She took in details she hadn't noticed before. His confident manner, great smile. Wise eyes.

His partner called out, "I can use a hand back here."

Shane's tanned cheeks darkened. "Gotta go. We have a patient with heart problems."

"Well, don't waste time talking with me." She smiled to take the sting out of the words and walked Josh over to the cab they had waiting.

"I like him," Josh stated. "Can he be my new daddy?"

CHAPTER THREE

"Now, why would you ask such a silly question?" Lauren outwardly stayed calm while her pulse leapt with apprehension. What if he'd heard Josh say that? She didn't dare look back, so she slid next to Josh and quickly shut the door. "Sixty-three Carleton Lane. Thank you."

"Because everybody else has one, and I want one too."

"I know that, honey, but what do I always tell you? We don't need anyone else. You've got me and Julie. That's like having two parents." She pulled the twenty she always kept in her keychain for emergencies from the pouch, knowing it should be plenty to see them home. No cell phone, no credit cards. What had she been thinking leaving the house so unprepared? Josh wanted to ride his bike—that's what.

"No, it's not the same at all." He shifted away from her. "You won't even let me see Gary anymore. Why can't I see him, Mom? Why not? He's my friend."

Realizing the importance of the issue to Josh, she took a deep breath and stayed calm. "I told you, honey. He's not with the Brothers for Life organization anymore. I don't know why."

She didn't want to tell Josh the truth—that she didn't trust Gary. There was nothing concrete, no evidence of misconduct, but it had worried her when she'd seen the way he looked at her son. She had taken him out of the program, refusing to take chances with his safety.

"I don't care," Josh said. "I still want to see him." His eyes filled with tears. "Doesn't he want to see me?"

"I'm sure he does. How could he not? You're the coolest, most wonderful person I know."

A small smile crept on his face. "You're just saying that 'cuz I'm your kid. You have to like me."

"I don't just *like* you. I love you to the moon and back. It's you and me, kid. We'll always have each other."

He sulked, not letting go, which worried Lauren a little. Because Josh had ADHD, he had a tendency to obsess over things, and she certainly did not want him obsessing over Gary.

Josh thought about it for a minute and then asked, "If I can't see Gary, what about this other guy? He was super cool. Can I see him?"

Lauren was glad when the cab pulled up in front of her house. "We're home now, sweetheart. We can continue this conversation some other time."

Josh rolled his eyes. "Yeah. Like never."

She paid the driver and helped Josh out of the car. He winced when he moved his arm.

"Has the medicine worn off? You need more, kiddo?"

"It hurts. And I don't want to wear this stupid cast."

"It's not a cast. It's just a sling, and it helps mobilize your arm. When we get you inside, you can lie down and we'll ice your elbow."

"I don't want no ice. It'll hurt."

Once the door was opened, Josh marched into the family room off the kitchen and plopped down on the sofa. His face was glum. "Stupid dog made me fall off my stupid bike."

She ignored his repeated use of the word "stupid" and said instead, "How about if we turn on *SpongeBob* or *Scooby-Doo*?"

"Don't want that. I want *Power Rangers*, not a dumb baby show."

He always wanted to see either that or *Teenage Mutant Ninja Turtles*, but she preferred him to watch something that didn't involve fighting. Which, of course, explained why he was demanding it now.

Lauren could see he was heading for a meltdown, so she turned on *Scooby-Doo*, hoping he'd soon forget about the other. "There. You love this show. Watch it, and I'll get you some juice to take your medication with. Then we can ice the arm. You heard the doctor. He said it had to be done every hour or so."

"No way." He kicked the coffee table.

"Please, don't do that." Lauren went into the kitchen and found the children's Tylenol. She poured some juice, hoping he'd take it before the pain ratcheted. She returned to the living room and held out the glass. "I'm sorry, sweetheart. I know it hurts. This will help." She had the chewable pill in her other hand. "Here you go. Wash it down with your juice."

He turned his head, refusing the drink and medicine. "No! It tastes bad."

Frustrated, but knowing he was even more so, Lauren counted to ten. "If you don't take it, the pain will be worse."

His jaw set. "You take it. I don't want it. Chewables are for babies."

"Not true. It's for little boys and little girls too." She popped one in her mouth. "See. It's even good for me." She handed him the glass of juice. "Take the pill, hon. You'll feel better if you do."

He did as he was told, and she was glad that mini-crisis was over.

"Do I have to go to school tomorrow?"

"No, honey." She kissed the top of his head, loving him so much it scared her. "Not until you feel better. In a day or two."

"Can you stay home with me?"

"You know I'm supposed to work. But Julie can come in early and keep you company until I get home."

"I want you." Josh rubbed his eyes and looked ready to cry. He had to be exhausted, but she knew better than to suggest a nap.

"I took an extra day off last week to go to your school's sports day. I can't take another. And you love Julie."

He shifted his bottom, moving to the far side of the couch so he was out of her reach. He pouted for a few minutes; then a thought occurred to him, and he bounced up with excitement.

"If you go to work, maybe you'll see that guy again. Then he could be my friend. You could ask him, couldn't you? Maybe he'd like to take me to a Dodgers' game. Brad is going with his father, and we could all go together."

"Oh, honey. I can't ask him that. I don't even know him."

Josh stood up and kicked a chair. "You don't care about me. All you ever do is work, and you won't even ask that guy to take me to a ball game. You are so lame."

He stomped off and slammed his bedroom door.

Lauren left him alone, knowing that he needed his own space to calm down and that anything she said would only upset him more. It was unfair for him not to have a father like "everyone" else, but she couldn't miraculously bring her husband back to life. As much as she wished she could. If only she could rewrite the script, maybe her darling Jeremy would have made it home safely from the office. They'd had an argument that morning, and she had continued it when he called from the car on his drive home. If she hadn't distracted him, he might still be alive. Sure a drunk driver had weaved into his lane, but if he hadn't been arguing with her on the hands-free device, he might have seen the other car and diverted in time.

It was their final conversation and the burden of that was something she'd carry in her heart forever. To make it up to Josh, she cherished and pampered him, and tried to be both mom and dad. Just short of spoiled, Josh was a good kid, even though he could be difficult at times.

She knocked on his bedroom door, then opened it. "I'm sorry about today, Sweetpea. We always have so much fun on our Sundays together, and going to the emergency room with a sprained arm was certainly not in our plans." She ruffled his hair. "Won't you keep me company? Come out and watch some TV until dinner time."

"Okay. But can I skip my bath tonight?"

"Yes, I suppose so." She put an arm around his tiny shoulders as they walked to the living room. She handed him the remote. "Here you go, hon. You can watch Mickey while I start dinner."

"I don't want Mickey. I want *SpongeBob* instead."

"Your choice. Just use the remote to go up or down; you know how." She had the parental controls on the cable, so she felt comfortable letting him surf the channels. She went into the kitchen and had just taken the chicken out of the freezer, when Josh called to her.

"Mom! Mom! Come quick. It's the guy with the funny hand."

She hurried back into the living room to see the handsome young medic's face on the local news channel. "What the heck? Why are they interviewing him?"

"I don't know. But there's his dog!"

Lauren sat down to listen to the broadcast. His name was Shane Dawson, and she heard how he and his dog had chased down a skateboarder who'd run off with a lady's handbag.

"That must have happened right after we left," she told Josh, with a surprised look. "I thought our boardwalk was safe."

"It is, thanks to Major. Maybe they'll let him be a hero dog now."

The journalist made it out to be more than it was, and Shane looked bored by the interview. His answers were brief, and he denied that he was any sort of hero.

"Just in the right place at the right time," he said.

He smiled, and she smiled at the TV, remembering how he'd tried to distract Josh with humor, using his devilish grin and quick wit. Now that her concern for her son was over and she had time to reflect, she could admit that he'd been attractive and funny, and she hadn't been very nice to him. There'd been something behind his eyes, some inner pain or a deep secret that he carried inside. She recognized it, as it mirrored her own.

CHAPTER FOUR

The following day, the guys at work kidded Shane about the news report, calling him "our local celebrity, the war hero." He laughed and joked right back, but the fact was, he hated any discussion about his past. He'd lived through it once, and it wasn't a place he cared to revisit.

The eager reporter had dug up some background facts on him. Discovered he'd been to Iraq and that he'd been held captive by a guerrilla group for months. She even gave details about the Navy Seals sneaking into the enemy camp and carrying him off and the firefight that ensued. Thankfully, she hadn't followed up the story about the next year of his life. Doctors, hospitals, rehab, and a piss-poor attitude.

The only upside to the brief report was the mention of his volunteer work with Wounded Warriors, giving the program some much-needed publicity.

But this didn't make him a hero, that's for damn sure. Truth was, he rarely slept more than a few hours at a time, scared of his own nightmares and random nighttime sounds, like a dog barking across the street. He was more coward than hero.

"Got a call, Shane." Rick Turner, colleague and friend, poked his head around the corner. "If you can stop preening long enough, we need to help some bugger that fell off a ladder after he touched a live electrical wire."

"Crap." Shane set aside the textbook he was reading.

"What's worse? Getting electrocuted or breaking your back?" "Let's hope the correct answer is 'none of the above.'"

~

Shane and Rick arrived on the scene within minutes and found the forty-year-old handyman sprawled on the floor, next to the massive chandelier he'd attempted to install. The homeowner had called EMS as soon as the man fell from the ladder.

They assessed the situation upon entering. The injured man had no obvious external head injury and attempted to sit up. Shane approached, while Rick brought out the backboard they'd use to transport the victim.

Shane knelt beside the man as Rick positioned the backboard. "How're you feeling?" he asked. There was no apparent physical injury, but the man was pale and had difficulty breathing. "I need to see if you've suffered an electric shock. Any numbness, impaired vision, loss of consciousness?"

While Shane asked questions, he and Rick maneuvered the man onto the backboard. Rick applied a cervical collar to keep the man's head in position. The injured man's eye had turned black, which indicated head trauma.

The homeowner and his wife, both elderly, were standing next to the dining room doorway, clearly distraught. "His name is Dave Fisher," the homeowner said, "and he's been awake the whole time. Said his arm was numb and he can't see clearly."

"We'll take good care of him," Rick replied as they carefully carried the unlucky carpenter toward the door.

Shane and Rick secured the patient in the back of the ambulance, and then Rick got in the driver's seat. The trip was less than ten minutes, but Dave Fisher went into respiratory arrest, and Shane had to initiate CPR before they reached the hospital.

~

Lauren returned from her coffee break and overheard two of the nurses talking about the new medic. It seemed everyone else had been aware of his comings and goings, except her.

"He has the dreamiest eyes," said Margaret Hornsby, a curvy woman with red, shoulder-length hair. She sighed and touched her well-endowed chest.

"Who has?" Lauren asked, as if she didn't know.

"Shane Dawson. He was here a few minutes ago, dropping off a patient, and I swear, my heart nearly stopped." She fanned herself. "He asked me some questions in the oh-so-nicest way, and when he smiled, I damn near came in my pants."

"Margaret!" Lauren tried not to look shocked. She knew all about Margaret's dating habits and how she met strange men in bars. She didn't approve, but neither did she want to be a prude.

"Well, it's true." Margaret's face was flushed. "I think he's sweet and sexy."

Trish, a pretty brunette, grinned. "Not only does he have bedroom eyes and a dreamy smile, but the cutest tush."

"Really?" Lauren pasted on a smile and put her hands on her hips. "Well, I'm sure we could sit and chat about his charms all day, but don't you ladies have anything better to do?" She sugar-coated her voice. "I'm sure you must have some patients to take care of. The last I looked, this was a hospital."

Margaret rolled her eyes. "Come on, Dr. Reynolds. He's only been here for a couple of weeks, but he's a darling to everyone. He remembers the nurses' names and their children's too. How can you not love a guy like that?"

"Okay. I get it. He's the sensitive type, not the modern-day alpha male. That's all very nice, but we need to keep our libidos in check. We have an ER to run."

Trish shook her head. "If he doesn't get your motor running, then you need a new one. Speaking of which, when was the last time you had a date?"

Lauren stiffened. "My love life is not open for discussion."

"That's because you don't have one." Trish looked at Margaret, who nodded in agreement. "We think the world of you, Dr. Reynolds, so I'm saying this for your own good. The hospital can't be your life. Your son needs a dad, and you need someone to love."

"No, I don't, and my son and I get along fine on our own." Lauren did not want to have this conversation. Talking about Josh not having a father always upset her. Already her stomach was churning. "You both know what happened when I dated that guy last year. Josh got attached and then Ron took a hike. I can't chance him getting hurt again."

"What about the Brother for Life program?" Margaret asked. "Didn't he meet someone nice there?"

"No, that didn't work out." Lauren sighed. "Actually, it was a bit of a disaster."

She walked away, effectively ending the conversation, but the guilt lingered. Of course her son longed for a father. Recently, that was all he talked about.

For the next few hours, the ER was nonstop action. There was the boy who'd swallowed a small plastic toy; another child who arrived with suspicious bruises and a broken arm; and a young man who'd sustained multiple injuries when he lost control of his motorcycle and hit a telephone pole.

There was a brief lull around four, and Lauren actually had a few minutes to herself. She scarfed down a sandwich and a coffee, and when she returned to the ER, Shane was wheeling in a frail woman.

"Her name's Eleanor Barnes," he told her, "and she's having difficulty breathing. I gave her an IV, but she's still in a lot of pain."

As if to prove it, the woman collapsed in a prolonged coughing spasm, and her face turned crimson. At the end of it, she was weak and shaken, gasping for breath.

Lauren took over and Shane assisted. Once they had Mrs. Barnes stabilized and an orderly had wheeled her away, she gave Shane a brief smile. "I heard you were in earlier today." She stuck out her hand. "I'm Lauren Reynolds, by the way. Sorry, I didn't introduce myself before."

"Shane Dawson." He nodded. "I looked for you earlier, but you weren't around. I wanted to ask about Josh. How's he doing?"

"He's not a happy camper, but I let him stay home from school today. His nanny will find ways to amuse him."

"Major says he's sorry for getting in your way. He made it up yesterday by catching a crook."

"Yes. I heard that on the news."

He looked down at his feet and hunched up his shoulders. "That was a bunch of B.S."

"I think the reporter had a thing for you." She smiled. "So do the nurses, by the way."

"They're just being nice to the new guy on the block." He lifted his eyes. "So how'd you know I was here?"

She felt a direct hit when his heavily lashed brown eyes met hers. She wouldn't call them "bedroom sexy"; they were too intense for that. "Penetrating" was a more apt description. She felt as though they could reach deep inside her and discover her inner secrets.

Feeling vulnerable all of a sudden, she folded her arms across her chest. "The nurses were talking about you. Listing your charms, as a matter of fact."

"Oh, yeah? What kind of charms?"

He flashed his cocky smile, and her stomach jumped. No sweet wonder the nurses got a little weak in the knees. The guy oozed sex appeal without appearing to even try. Good thing she'd been so preoccupied yesterday, or she might have noticed it then. Not that she liked flirty men—she'd had more than her share of them as a grieving young widow.

"Let's see." She hid a smile. "Oh, I remember: they liked your tush."

He laughed. "Not exactly what I had in mind, but hey, a compliment's a compliment."

"So, on the news report I heard you mention the Wounded Warrior Project. I know you train dogs. Do you also help with that organization?"

"I visit vets and try to mentor them like they did for me. We're getting ready for a weekend up at Monmouth, end of May." He grimaced. "Five miles of mountain biking. I'll have to get in shape for that."

Without meaning to, she slid her gaze over him, taking in his broad shoulders, muscular arms, and trim waist.

"Your shape is fine," she said a little too sharply. Then she added, "It's a wonderful thing you're doing."

"Least I can do. They saved my life, made it worth living again."

She frowned, unsure what it was about him that unsettled her. "You're an interesting man, Shane Dawson." He certainly did seem to have his heart in the right place. Just a young man, probably a few years younger than herself, she'd guess, and he spent so much of his time doing good deeds. She wondered if he'd be willing to do one more.

"Thank you." He gave her a quizzical look. "I think."

Although she'd rather stick a pin in her eye than ask for a favor, for Josh's sake she swallowed her pride. "Josh has been pestering me about you. He thought you were funny when you did that thing with your hand."

"Yeah." He made a face. "It always gets a laugh."

"Look, this is kind of awkward, but I promised my son that I'd ask." She fought the urge to cringe. It was only a request. He could always say no. "Josh is going to a Dodger's game with his friend and the friend's father, and he'd like to have someone to take him."

Shane didn't answer right away.

"I didn't want to ask," she said quickly. "Don't worry about it." She licked her bottom lip. "It would mean a lot to him, but…." Her mind raced through the possible problems a one-time boys' night out could create. Josh would be thrilled to death, but afterward he'd be even more frustrated than he was now. She really needed to find a way to distract him from his daddy fixation. Perhaps, if he needed a man in his life, he could hang out with Brad and his dad more, or some other friends.

Shane ran a hand through his hair. "You're not married?"

"No, I'm widowed."

"I'm sorry." He ran a hand over his jaw. "Doesn't he have an uncle or anyone else in his life that could step in?"

Lauren's spine stiffened. "No. Or I wouldn't have mentioned it to you."

He folded his arms, then dropped them by his sides. Opened his mouth, shut it again. Lauren held her breath. Say no, she silently pleaded. Say no.

"When is it?" he finally asked.

"You can say no," she said hopefully.

"I'm asking which day. I might be busy."

"Of course you might be." She fidgeted with her hands. "This is really a very bad idea. A boys' night out will only fill his head with more notions of what he can't have."

"Up to you, but I owe Josh something for spraining his arm."

"No, you don't. It was an accident." She smiled, feeling somewhat relieved. "Look, I'll just tell Josh that I asked, and you said you're sorry, but you have other plans that day."

"What day is it?" he asked, his eyes nailing hers.

"Next Friday. It's a night game. But I'll find someone else."

To avoid the intensity of his stare, she began tidying up medical supplies.

"Look. I want to do this, all right?" He stepped in front of her. "I might have to rearrange a thing or two. Let me see if I can work it out."

"Really?" She glanced up at him, surprised. "This is an awful lot to ask from a stranger, and it's really very kind of you, but you don't owe him or me anything."

"Josh doesn't have a dad, and it's the least I can do. Call it payback."

The tightness in her chest disappeared, and her shoulders relaxed. She managed a small smile. "Thanks."

~

At home, Lauren didn't mention Shane, but Josh brought it up right away.

"Did you see him, Mom? Did you ask?"

"Yes, honey. He brought a patient in, and after we took care of her, I had a word with him."

"You did? Awesome! You're the greatest mom in the whole wide world!" Josh jumped up to give her a hug, and accidentally knocked over the enormous Lego building he'd been working on. It must have been an all-day project, with his arm in a sling.

"Josh, he hasn't given me an answer yet. He said he had to see if he could clear his schedule." She bent over to kiss his cheek. "I know how much you want this, and I don't want you to be disappointed if it doesn't work out. I could always go with you."

"I know. It's just that everybody else has a dad."

She bit her bottom lip, her breath catching. His comment sliced right through her, as it always did. "You have me." She smiled, blinking back tears. "You're my whole world, sweetheart."

"But I want to be like other kids, Mom. I want to have a dad too."

He'd only started asking for a father in the past few months. Around the time she stopped letting him see Gary from the Brothers organization. She wondered if Gary had given him the idea, but it didn't matter who or why. He was now obsessed with wanting a father. "I'm so sorry, baby."

"That's okay, Mom. We'll find me a dad—don't worry."

"Oh, hon. You have me and Julie and two sets of grandparents. For now. One day I hope you'll have a father too." Unfortunately for all of them, her parents lived in Phoenix, and she and Josh only saw them a few times a year. Her in-laws had moved to the west side of Florida and rarely came to visit. She didn't have any brothers or sisters, so they weren't any little cousins running around. They were pretty much on their own.

"Can it be soon? I want a real dad to do stuff with."

"Okay. We'll put that on my shopping list."

~

The next day Shane delivered a patient to the ER and then checked to see if Lauren was working. He found her standing outside a patient's bay, making notes on a chart.

He walked over to her and said in a low voice so he wouldn't be overheard, "I'll do it."

She jumped in surprise and quickly turned to him. "You mean the ballgame? Friday night?"

"Yup. I managed to rearrange my schedule." He glanced at Rick, still talking with another doctor about the patient they'd brought in, to avoid looking at her. "I know what it's like not to have a father."

"You do?"

She tilted her head to look at him, and he noticed, once again, how pretty she was. Until the accident on the boardwalk, he hadn't really seen her. How had he missed that sleek, shiny hair, the glow of her skin, the little mole above her lip? Now, he wondered what it would feel like if he ran his tongue over it.

"Shane, you grew up without a father?"

He nodded. "He walked out when I was three, and eight years later Mom remarried. So I know how Josh feels."

She touched his arm. "This means so much to him. I can't thank you enough."

"No big deal." He stood close enough that he picked up a scent. She smelled like gardenias. He wondered if it was perfume or shampoo. Then he stepped back, effectively shutting off his senses. Didn't matter that she was pretty. Didn't matter that he hadn't been with a woman since....

"It is to me."

Her eyes were shining, and she looked all flushed and excited. He gritted his teeth. The last thing he wanted was her damn gratitude. He didn't know what he wanted, but it wasn't that. "Well, I've got to get going. More lives to save," he added lightly, poking fun at himself.

She smiled. "Would you like to meet him at the game or pick him up?"

"Depends." He shifted his feet, wishing she would stop looking at him like he was the answer to her prayers. He had no answers, not for himself or anybody else. "Where do you live?"

"Not far from where we ran into each other. Our home is a few blocks off the beach."

He gave it a moment's consideration before committing. "My condo's pretty close. What time should I be there?"

She pulled out a pad and scribbled down her address and home number. "Six?"

"Sounds good."

He took off before she got all gushy and embarrassed both of them. It was plain to see how much this favor meant to her and how important the night was to her son.

Shane felt good about helping out, but he had to ask himself—was he doing this to cheer up a fatherless boy or trying to score points with the kid's mom?

When he got home from his shift, he took Major out for a walk along a nature trail. They were trotting along nicely until Shane stumbled over the lead. He unleashed the pup so he wouldn't keep tripping over him, and just then a raccoon shot out of the bush. Major gave chase.

"Major, stop! Heel!" When the dog ignored his commands, Shane had no choice but to run too.

He was sucking air in open-mouthed gulps by the time Major gave up on the raccoon and loped back. He wagged his tail and butted his head against Shane's leg.

"You want me to pet you?" Shane gasped. "You're a very bad dog."

Major licked his hand, and Shane sat down on a large boulder next to the path and gave him a hug. He took a deep breath and mopped his brow. "Sit down, boy. Let me get my wind back. I'm not as young as you." He petted the dog. He took a moment to get his breathing under control, then spoke softly. "You have a nice house to sleep in, good food every day, and me to keep you company. I wasn't that lucky. No. I spent a whole year living on the streets. Woods too, just like this one."

He looked into the dog's eyes. "After I lost my hand, I went into a major funk. Got really screwed up in the head. Couldn't hold a job, not that I spent much time searching. I was too busy trying to drink my sorrows away." The dog whined and put his head in Shane's lap. "Yeah, I was a miserable son of a bitch. A real head case. Didn't care if I lived or died."

He kissed the dog's head. "What I'm trying to say to you, is that you need direction, Major. You got to be more than you are, a better dog, so to speak. You have to focus and set your sights high. You and me—we're two of a kind. We weren't born to be a hero, but we have to fight to become one. I'm willing to try. How about you?"

Major got on his haunches and tugged on Shane's sleeve. "You want to go home?" He stood up. "I hear you, buddy. Let's get some grub and a warm bed."

As they headed back, his thoughts returned to Doctor Reynolds, raising her son alone. She was much too young to be a widow, and too darn pretty. Being an ER doctor, she probably didn't have time to meet men and date. Heck of a thing for the boy. Growing up without a father was not easy, not by a long shot.

Going to a ballgame with the boy was the least he could do.

CHAPTER FIVE

Shane had had a helluva day. A dead battery in his Jeep made him late for an exam. He'd missed fifteen minutes, which made him rush through the questions and doubt his answers. He was an undergrad at UCLA, and it was too expensive to flunk out. If he failed this— no, he couldn't think of failure. He had to pass with honors and get into a great medical school. Nothing else mattered.

By the time he'd finished the exam, he had a massive headache, and then he got stuck in traffic on the way home. Now he was late picking up Josh, and Lauren would probably be thinking the worst.

God, but she was a looker. Her chin-length, chestnut-colored hair looked silky to the touch; she had classic cheekbones, a cute upturned nose, and blue eyes that could be cold as ice or warm as a sunny day.

He figured he knew which expression he'd be seeing when she opened the door.

Once he located her house, a nice-looking bungalow with a fenced-in backyard and flowering bushes and plants in front, he parked next to a Cadillac SUV and rang her doorbell.

He heard Josh yell, "He's here, he's here!" before the kid opened the door.

"Hi, Josh. Sorry I'm late, but I got stuck in traffic."

"That's okay." Josh grabbed his artificial hand and pulled him into the house.

Shane stood in a large open room that must have originally been a formal living area but was now converted to an office and playroom. Bookshelves lined two walls, and standing in front of them was a mahogany desk with a leather chair. The front of the room had a big bay window and had been sectioned off with children's furniture and Josh's toys.

"We're in here," Lauren called from the back of the house.

"Come on," Josh said, leading him past French doors and into the family room.

Shane noted one overstuffed sofa and two comfortable chairs that faced the large plasma TV. "Hey, everybody," Josh shouted. "This is Shane. I don't know his last name."

"Dawson. Shane Dawson."

"Hi, Shane. Glad you could make it." Lauren took his arm and introduced him to Kevin Henderson and his son Brad.

He shook hands with Kevin, a tall, fit-looking guy, who studied him with curiosity. "I've been hearing all about you. War hero, huh?"

"No, I'm certainly not a hero." He hated that title. What did it mean, anyway? "No more than anyone else who served."

"No need to be modest. Lauren was telling me how you got captured in Iraq and lost your hand." Kevin nodded to the i-limb. "She seems to think you're quite the guy."

His tone was rather sour, which should have been a welcome change from the fawning some people did, but Shane sensed a faint and puzzling hostility from the other man.

"That's not what I said," Lauren protested.

"Close enough," Kevin answered, and Shane saw a look pass between them.

Feeling awkward, he looked around to see where Josh had disappeared. He and the other boy, about Josh's size but with darker hair, were lying on the floor, playing a game on an iPad.

"Well, I'm sure Shane doesn't want to sit around and discuss his war stories. Right?" Lauren smiled at him. "Kevin has the tickets, and he's offered to drive. Is that okay with you?"

"Sure. Easier than taking two cars." He stood there, feeling like a second wheel, and wondered why the heck he'd agreed to come. If Kevin and Lauren were such good friends, why didn't Lauren just go to the game?

She grabbed Josh's jacket and helped him into it, careful not to jar his arm. After a big hug, she said, "Hope you all have a wonderful time. Go Dodgers!"

The two boys ran through the house and outside, the screen door slamming behind them.

"Too bad you can't come along," Shane said, glancing at Lauren's flushed face. Why was she all pink cheeked around this guy? Wasn't the man married? Maybe he was, but looking for some action with the grieving widow? Or he might be a single dad, too. Wouldn't that be convenient?

"No, thanks," she said. "I'm going to enjoy a night by myself. Watch a movie or read a book."

Kevin stepped close and whispered something for her ears only. She smiled and dropped her eyes, like a girl on her first date.

The skin prickled on the back of Shane's neck, and he asked himself what the hell his problem was. It didn't matter if they were sleeping together or not. He had no personal interest in Lauren. He was doing the kid a favor. Payback, remember?

But why had she asked him to take her son to the ball-game? Why not let hot-to-trot Kevin be surrogate dad for the night?

Kevin talked about himself all the way to the game. A lawyer in some big firm, someone had given him the tickets. Premium seats and complimentary parking too.

The stadium was packed. Once they found their seats behind home plate, they returned to the concession stand for hot dogs, French fries, and water for the boys.

The game started off slow. The pitchers did a better job than the batters, which meant nobody was doing much scoring. Ho-hum for the spectators, and the boys were getting antsy.

During a break in the play, Shane slipped out. He returned a few minutes later with two large bags of popcorn and two new Dodgers caps for Brad and Josh.

The Dodgers were trailing by two for most of the game, but when Andre Ethier hit a home run with the bases loaded in the eighth inning, the crowd jumped to its feet.

Josh reacted like the rest of the hometown fans, jumping around and screaming with excitement. In his wild exuberance, he knocked his bag of popcorn over someone seated one row ahead.

The man, wearing a San Francisco Giants' hat, jumped up as popcorn rained down on him, knocked over his beer, and swung around to face Josh. Seeing the size of the boy, he unleashed his fury on Shane. "Can't you control your son?" he snapped. He stood up and turned, gesturing to his wet jeans. "Kid made me spill my beer. Got half of it on my pants."

"I'm sorry," Josh whispered, turning beet red. "I didn't mean to do it."

"I have popcorn down my neck, my jacket. Now I'm wearing the beer too," the man grumbled. "Even my shoes."

"I'll buy you another beer." Shane waved to a girl selling beer in the aisle and stuck out his wallet.

"I don't want a beer from you," the man said. "These kids have been a royal pain in the ass. They've been kicking the back of the seats and yelling in my ear all night, and you've done nothing to stop them."

"Back off, buddy," Kevin said. "This is a family event, and the kids are having a good time. Let's leave it at that."

"I'm sorry," Josh said again, looking terrified.

The burly man was still on his feet, and he leaned toward Josh. "If you kick the bottom of my chair one more time, I'll—"

"You'll do what?" Shane said. He stood as well, shielding the two boys with his body. "Don't threaten these boys. We're all here to have fun."

"What did you say?" The man's bulbous nose grew redder as his temper soared.

"I said to leave the boys alone."

"Listen, you." The guy grabbed Shane by his jacket. "You need to teach your boy some manners."

"And you, sir, have had too much to drink."

"Like hell I have!" He glared at Shane. "Damn ass punk."

"Calm down, both of you," Kevin snapped. "Take your seats before we're thrown out."

Shane locked eyes with the man. "Kid said he was sorry, and I offered you a beer. That's the best we can do."

"Go to hell," the man said and slugged Shane.

Security guards surrounded them in seconds. Kevin tried to explain, but tempers had flared, and the incident got out of hand. Other fans and Giants supporters tossed around insults, and a few more punches were thrown. Within minutes, all of them were escorted out of the stadium.

Kevin didn't say a word, but his body language spoke volumes of his displeasure. He marched the boys to his SUV, and as they climbed into the back, he turned to Shane.

"Why couldn't you just let it go? You've ruined the night for the kids."

"I'm the one with the black eye." He stuck his good hand in his pocket and took a couple of calming breaths. He wasn't pleased with the way Kevin was shoving the blame on him. He'd done nothing but defend the boys.

Josh jumped out of the SUV and threw himself at Shane. "I still like you, even if nobody else does."

Shane ruffled the boy's hair. "Sorry, kid. But that guy was a bully and a loser."

EPISODE TWO

CHAPTER SIX

Shane wanted to tell Lauren his side of the story before Kevin did, but never got the chance.

"What happened to your eye?" she asked the moment he stepped inside.

"He got into a fight," Kevin said. "The other guy started it when Josh accidentally knocked over his beer, but Shane didn't know enough to back away."

"That's not exactly the way it happened," Shane spoke quickly. "The guy got lippy and wanted to bully the kids."

Lauren looked from one man to the other. "That doesn't explain a black eye. Who threw the first punch?"

"He did. The guy had had too much to drink," Shane said, "and he wouldn't accept our apologies. I didn't strike back, but things got ugly."

She frowned. "Josh, why don't you boys go play in your bedroom while I make coffee for Shane and Kev." She waited until they left, then turned to Shane. "This night meant a lot to my son. How did this get so out of control?"

"The guy grabbed my jacket and threatened your son." Shane thought he'd shown remarkable restraint under the circumstance and had behaved admirably. Yet she was giving him grief. "I protected Josh. Sorry, if you don't see it that way, but I did what I had to do."

Kevin snorted. "Yeah, like get us thrown out."

"You got thrown out?" Lauren asked, her brow wrinkling.

"We weren't the only ones," Shane said. "Some other people got involved. Security came and cleared us all out." Shane felt like a kid in front of a schoolteacher, and he resented having to explain his actions. She should be thanking him instead of shaking her head with annoyance.

"Was Josh in jeopardy?" She glanced at Kevin. "Was this bully picking on the two boys?"

"He made a couple of comments, but if Shane hadn't stepped in, he'd have backed off." Kevin lifted his chin in Shane's direction.

Lauren turned her blue-eyed gaze on Shane. "Thank you for protecting him, but I'm just so sorry that the night ended on such a bad note." Her gentle voice made it worse. "Poor Josh. This meant so much to him."

Kevin smiled, and Shane wanted to punch him in the eye.

"Me too," Shane said, chin in the air. Without another word, he turned and left.

All the way home, he cursed himself for being an idiot. He should never have gotten involved. He didn't need to play big brother to some kid, or score points with his mom. He had enough on his agenda. Between his part-time job, his UCLA courses, and studying for the MCATS, the last thing he damn well needed was to feel sorry or responsible for some kid.

~

Lauren watched for Shane at work, but with shift changes and the general busyness of the ER, days passed before she saw him again. When she did, she pulled him aside and asked if he could meet her for a cup of coffee.

"Not interested," he answered flatly.

She grabbed his arm. "I want to apologize to you, and you need to hear what I have to say."

He shrugged. "I don't need to hear anything. It's over and done."

"Let me be the judge of that." She tilted her head and looked at his eye. "Ouch. I'm sorry."

"You didn't hit me." His lips turned up in a half-smile.

"You took the punch to protect my son." She grimaced. "And I didn't thank you properly. Please have dinner with me after my shift."

"You've already apologized, and I accept. No need to prolong it over dinner."

"No dinner then, but will you meet me for coffee? There's something I want to discuss."

"Okay. Coffee. What time?"

When they reached agreement on the time, he nodded and left. Lauren returned to the busy ER, wondering if what she was about to propose to Shane was a sensible idea. She'd given it serious consideration and had decided the gain outweighed the risk, but because she was a cautious person, it wasn't surprising that she was having second thoughts.

After her shift, Lauren waited in the cafeteria, sipping a bitter black coffee and wondering if he would show. She half-hoped he might not, as she dreaded the conversation that lay ahead.

Shane strolled in and a warm flush spread inside her. She jumped out of her chair to greet him. "Hi. You made it."

"Yeah." His face wasn't friendly. "I have a few minutes."

"Perfect. I can't recommend the coffee, but I'm happy to buy you anything you want. The apple pie looks good."

"Coffee's fine."

When he had his, he followed her back to the table and sat across from her. "So, what's this about then?"

She licked her lips, keeping her eyes on her cup. "Josh is really upset about the other evening. He thinks you hate him, and he says it was his fault you all got thrown out of the game."

"It wasn't." He looked around the room. "The guy was a bully. His team was losing, and he took his anger out on the kids."

"You defended him, and I should have taken your side." She gave him a quick glance. "I'm so sorry, Shane. Thanks for taking care of my son."

"No big deal. The guy was an idiot." He took a sip of the hot coffee, and spat it out. "Damn. That's hot."

"I should have warned you."

"That would have been nice."

She smiled. "Now I owe you another apology. First a black eye, now a burnt mouth. Forgive me?"

"It's nothing." He pushed the coffee away.

She leaned across the table and touched the bruise gently with her fingers. "You did me a favor and got this in return. I wish I could make it up to you."

"You can," he answered with a grin. "Stop touching it. It hurts."

She winced and sat back in her chair. "Oops. Sorry." She picked up the salt and pepper shakers, moving them around to avoid looking at him. "Thanks for the hat, too. Josh hasn't taken it off since."

"Figured the boys needed a souvenir, but as things turned out, this was not a game to remember."

"Yeah, well, he still enjoyed himself." She ran a finger up and down her coffee mug, delaying her next request. "Look, Shane, there's no sense in me beating around the bush. I need to ask you something, and feel free to decline. I don't want to pressure you."

"More ballgames?" he asked, raising one brow.

"More than that." She looked at him. "Here's the whole story." She took a deep breath. "I had a relationship with a guy about a year ago, and it didn't work out. Josh moped for a long time afterward, wondering why Ron wasn't coming around anymore. Anyway, thing is, I found him a mentor from the Brothers for Life program." She took another sip of her coffee, then pushed the mug away. "That didn't work out either."

"It's a good organization. Why didn't it pan out?"

She lowered her voice. "I had a funny feeling about this guy. Nothing I could prove, but my instincts were telling me something wasn't right."

"You think he was a molester or something?"

"Not sure, but I didn't want to find out." She licked her lips. "Josh wants a dad so bad, and he'd been begging to see Gary again."

"And of course, you can't let him."

"Right." She couldn't look at him. "Josh has ADHD. He's very impulsive and becomes fixated on things." She cleared her throat. "And I'm afraid he has now transferred his feelings from Gary to you." She darted a quick look at his face. "This is embarrassing for me to admit."

"No problem." Shane scratched his jaw. She noticed the slight stubble on his face. Normally she didn't find that appealing in men, but it suited his California surfer good looks. "I can probably get away one day this week."

She shook her head. "That's not where I was going." Lauren looked directly into his eyes, noticing as she had before how they seemed to change color. One day they could appear brown, and the next day they'd be green. "Actually, I have a proposition for you. I wondered if, maybe, you could be, like, a big brother to my son? Just a few hours a week?" She bit the bottom of her lip. "I realize that's a huge commitment, and so I'd like to pay you."

"Pay me?" He scowled. "What do you take me for?"

"It's not an insult," she assured him. "It's more of a business arrangement."

"Well, put like that, I'm not interested." He got up to leave.

She put a hand on his arm, stopping him. "Why? You already agreed to see him once this week."

He sat back down. "Because I want to, not because I'm getting paid."

"Okay." She swallowed hard. This would mean so much to her son, that her own emotions were on overload. She had to suck back tears. "I'll keep my money, but will you spend some time with Josh?" She knew it was a terrible imposition, and he had every right to refuse.

He toyed with his coffee for a minute. Glanced around the room, taking his time to make a decision. "On one condition."

"Anything."

"I want something from you."

"What?" When he wouldn't meet her eyes, she sat up straighter. "Please don't tell me you're asking for sexual favors." She laughed. "Kidding, of course."

"I would hope so." His face was stern. "Truth is, I'm brushing up on some of my pre-med courses, preparing for MCAT. I could use a tutor."

"Really? That's wonderful." She thought about his time restraints. "How do you manage it with your job?"

"No social life." He said it so matter-of-factly, she knew it had to be true.

"Of course I'd be willing to help you. Delighted, as a matter of fact." Relief washed over her, easing most of her tension. "Then I wouldn't feel so darn guilty asking you to spend time with my son."

"So? Do we have a deal?"

"We have a deal." She gave him a warm smile. "What are your plans? Going into research?"

"I'm not sure what I'll specialize in, but I want to help the thousands of young men and women returning from war." He ran a hand through his sandy hair, mussing it up. "I've enjoyed being a medic, but I want to do more."

"Whatever you decide, I'm sure you'll do well. From everything I hear, you're great at what you do."

"Thanks, Doc. I intend to be." He lifted his i-limb and opened and closed his life-like fingers. "I'm not going to let this hold me back." He added, "Obviously I can't tackle some of the simple tasks people take for granted, but I've learned how to work around them."

"When I watch you work, it's hard to believe you wear a prosthetic. And you have a natural gift with the patients.

You're so at ease." She smiled. "So, how's the course work going?"

"I'm holding my own, but not top of the class either."

"Do you have time to mentor? Josh will take up some of your valuable time."

"I'll make time." He didn't smile. "I want to get into a top medical school. So yes, this agreement works for both of us."

She stood up. "Good. I'm glad we can help each other."

He stood too. "When can we start?"

"Josh can't do much yet, but I could start tutoring you anytime." She looked into his eyes, almost giddy with relief. "Let me know when."

"I will, Dr. Reynolds. That's a date."

CHAPTER SEVEN

Margaret Hornsby cornered Lauren the moment she entered the ER the next day. "I saw you having coffee with that sexy medic last night. What's up, you sly fox?"

"Nothing's up. Not between us, anyway." Lauren licked her lips. Why did talking about Shane make her uncomfortable? Because the other nurses thought he was hot? That must be the reason, because she certainly had no interest in him. Zero. If she wanted to date, she'd find someone older, more settled, not someone who had years of medical school looming ahead of him. He shouldn't be thinking of dating either.

Lauren knew Margaret was digging for information, so she told her what she knew. "He told me he's hoping to get into med school. He's a few credits shy of a degree, and he's taking the remaining courses at UCLA and studying for MCATS. He wants to work with vets like him. Isn't that something?"

"What about his hand? Will that be a problem?"

"No, I'm sure it won't. People with disabilities aren't so limited anymore. Besides, hand transplants will eventually be more common than prosthetics, and he'd likely be a perfect candidate."

"Wow." Behind Margaret's round, pink-framed glasses, her brown eyes sparkled. "Two hands. I've imagined having one of them running over my naked body, but think what he could do with two." Her rosy cheeks flushed brighter and she giggled.

"I choose not to," Lauren replied dryly.

"Oh, Dr. Reynolds, you're no fun at all. If you don't have sex, can't you at least dream about it?" She put one hand on a plump hip and pretended to fan herself with the other. "I'm getting hot and bothered just thinking about him in my canopied bed. I'd like to tie his wrists to the bedposts. . . ."

"Enough. I don't need the details, please." Lauren didn't want to envision Shane and Margaret—or Shane and anyone—having sex. Her stomach tightened at the mere thought. "What about John Sullivan? Why did you break up with him? He's a nice guy, and you two seemed to be hitting it off."

"I don't want to date a male nurse. Plus he's got bad breath. And he's losing his hair. And he's not a great lover." She tossed her head. "Besides, Shane's always flirting with me. I think he's interested." She leaned closer, scrutinizing Lauren's face. "Did he mention me at all?"

"No, sorry to say." Lauren forced a smile. "Now, Margaret, can we get our minds back on work?" She crossed her arms and glanced at the clock. "Any minute now those doors will open and we'll be facing another life-or-death crisis."

"Doctor Reynolds." Margaret sighed and raised her eyes. "Don't try to distract me. You know how I get about these things."

"All too well."

Margaret ignored her. "I wonder if he'll ask me out. Maybe I should stop hinting around and just ask him myself. What do you think?"

"I think he'd be very lucky to have a woman like you, but he's juggling his job and his medical studies. That doesn't leave much time for a relationship."

"True. But when we're not doing the deed, I could help him study."

"Margaret...." Lauren decided to be upfront about the arrangement she and Shane had made. No point in keeping it a secret and giving Margaret false hope. "I'm sorry, but he asked me to tutor him."

"He did?" Margaret looked sucker punched. "Why would he do that?" Her voice was full of hurt. "What did you tell him?"

"I told him yes." Lauren looked at her kindly, hoping she could make her understand. "He's going to befriend Josh, and I'll tutor him. It's beneficial for both parties, you see."

"Oh, I see, all right." She sniffed, and turned away.

"Margaret...."

Lauren put out a hand to stop her favorite nurse from marching off in hurt and anger, but knew it was best to let her go. With any luck, Margaret would find another object for her affection quickly enough. The woman had a history of falling in and out of love, and Shane was simply the flavor of the month.

~

For several days, every time Shane and Rick entered the ER, she could see Margaret and the other nurses watching her, speculating whether she and Shane were having an affair. Obviously, Margaret had shared her suspicions with her coworkers.

Lauren made a point to avoid Shane as often as possible. When he and Rick brought her a patient, she talked to Rick, hoping to end the speculation about their relationship. Her professional demeanor became even more stilted than usual. She worried that soon she'd have no social skills left.

Finally, Shane cornered her. "What's up with you? Are you having second thoughts about our arrangement?"

"No, of course not. And Josh can't wait to see you." She didn't look at him as she spoke. "I'm willing to tutor you anytime you want."

"Then what is it? Everyone has gotten weird suddenly. Even Margaret." He ran a hand through his long, sandy hair. "She won't give me the time of day. Turns her back whenever I try to speak to her."

"Well, if you don't know, I guess I need to tell you."

"Tell me what?" He looked at the nurses huddled in the corner, whispering to each other.

"Margaret's got a crush on you, and I think I put the kibosh on that." She gave him an edited version of their conversation. "I'm sorry, but I think she's told everyone that we're having an affair."

He laughed. "Really?" He cocked an eyebrow. "Maybe we should do something to get their tongues wagging. Play it up."

Lauren felt her cheeks heat up. "No way."

"Come on." He leaned closer to her. "Act like I said something clever and funny, and smile and bat your eyelashes at me. Something girly."

"Why would I do that?" she asked, taking a step back.

"I saw you do it with Kevin, so I know you can."

"I did not!" She gave him a fierce look. "That's ridiculous. He's simply a good friend. I've known him and his wife for years."

"Ah. So he is married."

"Separated. But what does that matter?"

"It matters because you did get all pink and flustered. Although he's an opinionated ass, if you ask me."

"I didn't. And he's really very nice."

"So, he left his wife. For you?" Shane leaned back against the wall and crossed his arms, pretending nonchalance, but his eyes were taking her measure.

"Certainly not!" She took a step closer and hissed. "I was a friend of his wife's. She's still living in the house down the street. She's an attorney too." Lauren tilted her head to gaze up at him. "When my husband was alive, we used to socialize together, but once I was widowed, the invitations dried up. The women stopped calling."

"Why's that? Jealous housewives?"

"I can't imagine anyone thinking of me as a threat."

"On the contrary. You're attractive, intelligent. Wise women would keep their husbands away."

She laughed dismissively. "Because I'm not interested. I loved my husband very much, and I don't want to replace him. I'm perfectly content raising Josh by myself."

"Don't you ever get lonely?"

"What—with my life?" She shook her head. "When would I have the time?"

"You need to make time. A woman like you shouldn't spend her life alone." He leaned in to whisper. "Without someone to hold you, someone to love."

"I have Josh. He's all I need." She glanced around at the nurses pretending to be busy. "Why does everyone think I need a husband, when I'm perfectly content as I am?"

"Maybe they don't. Perhaps they think Josh needs a father."

"Please! Not you too. I hear that all the time, and frankly, I'm getting tired of it." She glared at him. "I wasn't a very good wife. There. I said it." Her chin tilted up. "I'm better alone. Josh is fine. We've always been fine together." Her words tumbled out as she tried to convince him. "We don't need a man in our lives."

"I'm sorry to upset you," Shane spoke gently, searching her eyes.

She blinked rapidly. "You didn't." She licked her suddenly dry lips. "I always get riled up when someone suggests that I marry so Josh can have a father."

"That wasn't quite what I meant. But I know you want Josh to have more male companionship, and since Kevin is such a close friend, I just thought..."

"You thought what? That I should date him?"

"It wouldn't surprise me." He gave her a teasing smile. "You did blush a lot around him. And I don't think you're the blushing kind of girl."

"Trust me, I'm not. And as I said, I don't do relationships well. My darling husband, if still alive, would attest to that."

"I'm sorry to hear that."

He gave her a shrewd look, and she couldn't tell if he believed her. Not that it mattered whether he did or not, she knew it was true. She'd never backed down during an argument with her husband, and she'd harp on the matter until she was blue in the face—if she believed herself right. And where did that get her? Or him?

Killed.

CHAPTER EIGHT

Shane had upset Lauren, and that hadn't been his intention at all. He preferred flirting with her instead, and watching the heat creep up her cheeks. With that in mind, he cleared his throat and darted a quick look around the room. "Look, we got off the subject. I was going to suggest feeding the gossips. They're going to talk anyway."

"What do you mean?"

"Pretend. Let them think we're having an affair." He winked at her. "At least it'll get them off your back."

Her eyes narrowed. "I can think of an easier way. I'll just tell them to mind their own business."

"No, it's better this way." Plus, he figured it would be a lot more fun. "Like this." He slipped an arm around her waist before she had time to react. "You smell good." He sniffed behind her ear. "Like disinfectant."

She snorted and pushed him away. "Now you've gone and done it."

He gave her a sexy grin. "Not yet, I haven't."

"Shane, stop that." She tried not to smile, but he could see the laughter behind her amazing blue eyes. "Behave yourself. I don't want people to think...."

"What?" he asked with just the right amount of innocence.

"That we're flirting." She glanced around to see if anyone were watching. They were.

"We're not. Only pretending." He winked. "Look, why don't I take Josh to a movie on Saturday afternoon, and then we'll grab a pizza for dinner. I'll have him back by seven."

"Only if you let me tutor you when I put him to bed," she said in a low voice.

"Sounds like a plan."

"Instead of pizza, I could cook dinner for the three of us."

"No need to do that." He was surprised by the suggestion, and touched. But he played it cool. "I think Josh needs some one-on-one time with me," he added.

"You're probably right. That's a much better idea." She gave him a warm smile. "He'd love it."

Lauren tried not to worry when Shane picked up Josh for a movie and dinner, but she remembered the first fiasco all too clearly. What if Josh acted up or was simply too much for Shane to handle? Shane seemed very evenly tempered and relaxed, but a hyper little boy who didn't even belong to him might be more than he'd bargained for. And if Shane didn't want to see her son again, Josh would be so bitterly disappointed. She hoped with all her heart that she hadn't set her son up for more hurt.

The hours of worry were quickly erased when a happy, grinning Josh burst through the door.

"Mom, it was the best. You should have been with us." He fidgeted from foot to foot, unable to stand still. "The movie was great. Do you want to see it? We could all go again."

Lauren kissed the top of his head and smiled at Shane. "No, I think once was enough for Shane, but I'm glad you had a great time."

"It was sad and scary, but it had a good ending, didn't it, Shane?"

"Yup. Your mom missed out." He gave her a lazy once-over that warmed her blood. She didn't know if he worked at it or it just came naturally, but he had a sexy way about him.

"Did Josh behave himself?" she asked. "You two didn't get into any fights, did you?"

He laughed. "No. We were very well behaved, weren't we, Josh?"

"You bet." Josh grinned his endearing gap-toothed smile. "Except I knocked over my soda. But Shane cleaned it up for me, and the waitress brought me a new one. She kept hanging around, asking Shane if he'd like anything else."

"Oh, she did, did she?" Lauren pursed her lips and gave Shane a teasing look. "That must have been very annoying. How pretty was she?"

Josh answered. "Not as pretty as you, Mom."

"Thanks, hon, but I think you might be biased."

"What's biased?" He tilted his head, wagging it back and forth.

"You have a reason to like me." She dropped a hand over his shoulder.

"Yeah, because you're my mom. And you're the best."

She squeezed him tight. "I love you, too."

Shane patted Josh on the back. "It was fun, kiddo. How about next Saturday? Want to go to the Aquarium?"

"Wow! Can I, Mom? Can I?"

"Sure. I don't see why not." She smiled at Shane. "Why don't you get settled at the kitchen table, and once I get this little monster to bed, we can go over anything you want."

When she returned, she glanced at the books lined up on the table. He'd brought biochemistry, physics, and anatomy. Taking a seat next to him, she picked up a textbook and leafed through it. "You need all three for your degree?"

"To get into a med school, yes."

"How do you find time for studying, work, and puppy training?"

"I do three eight-hour shifts." He shrugged, like it was no big deal. "It's manageable. Barely."

"You could do every second week with Josh, if that works better for you." She flipped through the books, glad her days of studying were long behind her.

"No, let's start out weekly and see how it goes." His eyes grazed her face. "I get most of my assignments done late at night. I don't sleep much."

"I guess not." She shook her head, wondering what personal demons drove him to work this hard. "This schedule would kill most people. How long do you expect to keep it up?"

"As long as it takes."

She studied him for a moment, taking in his firm jaw, the intensity in his eyes, his strong, capable-looking shoulders. "Well, you seem disciplined and highly motivated, so I'm sure you'll manage somehow."

They got down to work, and Lauren answered all his questions, which ended up being a refresher for her as much as for him.

At half past ten she tried to stifle a yawn, but Shane caught her in the act. "Sorry," she said quickly. "How about I make us some coffee? That'll help me stay awake."

"No." He gave her a shy smile. Sometimes he seemed so cocky, and at other times so endearing.

"I didn't realize it was so late." He slid his eyes away from her and packed up his books. "I'm the one who should apologize. I got so wrapped up in what we were doing, I didn't notice the time."

"Me too." She couldn't believe it, but it was true. Perhaps it was simply adult conversation or being around an attractive male. There'd been too little time for either lately. "I enjoyed it."

"Thanks. You were a great help." He gave her another sweet smile as they walked to the door. "I think I might be getting the better end of the deal in this relationship. I get to spend time with Josh, who's a really cool kid, and have the added benefit of your brilliant mind."

Their eyes met and something happened inside of her. She felt weak, empty, and overwhelmed as loneliness swept over her in a long crushing wave. Strange that she hadn't felt it for so long, and now, tonight, after spending a few hours in Shane's company, she didn't want to be alone. In bed or in life. It was all too much sometimes. She was still young, only thirty-five, and she needed—no, not needed, but *wanted*—a man to hold her and kiss her goodnight. For all her protests, she knew it to be true.

She swallowed hard, feeling extremely vulnerable. She wanted to know more about him, to delve into the mystery of this fascinating man, but held herself back, not wanting to appear needy. After all, he was here because of her son, and to be tutored, not because he had a hard-on for her. She needed to remember that and not rock the boat.

"No need to flatter me. I want to help." Taking his hand, she added, "Thanks for taking Josh today." His hand felt warm and she knew she should let go, but the personal contact felt so good that she held on a little longer than necessary. Her pulse raced and she felt flushed. "It means so much to him. And to me." She stood on tiptoe and gave him a peck on the cheek. Just a small peck, not one that would frighten him off. "Good night, Shane. Happy dreams."

CHAPTER NINE

Lauren's morning got off to a quick start. She'd just dealt with a three-car accident that had brought in four trauma patients—a mother, her two kids, and an elderly man who'd stroked and was pronounced dead on arrival. They patched up the children, but the mother's heart stopped as Lauren and the nurses worked on her. She died on the table.

Losing a patient was never pleasant, but after working the emergency room for the past three years, Lauren was practically numb to it. The children were another story. Any death involving children hit too close to home.

Now, two little children would awaken from this ordeal to find their mother gone. The father had been called, but he was on a business trip. The earliest he could get there was late that evening. She asked the nurses to let her know the minute he arrived.

For half an hour the ER was quiet; then Shane radioed in to say he had a four-year-old boy found at the bottom of a pool.

Her stomach clenched as she waited for the child, a boy younger than Josh, and she was filled with fear that he might not make it. But she couldn't think like that. Shane would keep him alive until he brought him in, and then she'd do the rest.

The moment Shane and Rick entered the ER, Lauren rushed toward the stretcher.

Shane cried out, "The kid needs an airway and a respirator, stat." As he spoke, he continued to compress the AMBU bag to ventilate his lungs.

"We're all set." She glanced at the boy's pale face as she guided the gurney into the room with the respirator and the lab. "You intubated him?"

The two men slid the boy onto the hospital bed and then stepped aside as Lauren's team gathered around the bed and the equipment.

He nodded. "Couldn't wait. He wouldn't have made it."

"Good job, Dawson." Lauren didn't glance up as she assessed the young boy. His breathing was faint, and gently she started chest compressions, listening to his breathing.

"Where are the parents?" she asked.

"They're here," Shane said. "Mother came with us, father followed in his car."

"Good. We'll get the little guy stabilized, and then I'll have a word."

She gave him an approving nod, and then her team came forward to work on the boy.

Later, during a break, she marveled at how effectively Shane had successfully intubated the boy in the field. He was always cool under pressure and had surprising dexterity with the use of his prosthetic hand. She knew him well enough now to see that he was skilled and dedicated, and took his medical studies seriously. Whatever specialty he chose, they'd be lucky to have him.

Lauren reflected on her own choices and what had prompted her to work in the ER. After Jeremy's death, she'd done a complete turnaround. She'd planned to work pediatrics, but while mourning, she couldn't bear the idea of being surrounded by happy families celebrating a new cherished life, when for her it was doubtful that she'd ever conceive again. Emergency medicine seemed a more logical choice. After all, her husband had not been saved after a collision with a drunk driver, but perhaps she could spare other families the same pain.

The following Saturday Shane spent a day with Josh. He took him to the Aquarium of the Pacific, and when he brought him home, the boy bounced into the house, excited to tell his mother everything about his day.

"We saw sharks and sea lions, dolphins, a million zillion fishes, and everything." His cheeks were a bright pink, and his blue eyes glowed. "It was so cool. You should have been there."

Shane glanced at Lauren, not sure how to read her. In the past few days whenever he ran into her, she'd been a little distant. Guarded somehow. They had a personal relationship because of Josh, but he didn't want anything beyond that. Not that he thought for a second that she did. But she had to be lonely.

The fact that she was pretty and sexy made things tricky. He didn't want to think about how she'd taste if he kissed her or how her body would feel if he held her.

"We had a great day," he said to clear his mind. "Got to see Sammy the sea turtle in 3-D. Felt like we were on the back of an octopus riding through coral reefs. As Josh said, it was pretty cool."

"Yeah," Josh said, jumping up and down in his excitement. "Like being under the ocean and having my own octopus to ride on. Next time, you gotta come, Mom."

Lauren hugged her son. "I'm so glad you had a wonderful day." She looked at Shane. "Thanks for taking him."

"I enjoyed it too. Haven't been there in probably ten years."

"Neither have I, but Josh has been with his grandparents a few times. They live in Phoenix and come out each summer to escape the heat."

"No family nearby?"

"No, his other grandparents live in Tampa, Florida, and I don't have any siblings. Jeremy, my husband, has a brother and sister, but they are busy with their own lives and rarely call except for birthdays and Christmas." She shrugged. "We do all right, don't we, kiddo?"

He nodded, not saying a word.

"Why don't you go wash up," she told him, "while I set the table?"

After he left, Lauren walked to the kitchen, gesturing for Shane to follow. "I made lasagna for dinner," she said as she took a pan out of the oven. "Figured you both might be hungry, and I can tutor you either before or after."

"Sounds good. That was real nice of you."

"It was the least I could do," she said, turning away to pull a large bowl of salad from the refrigerator. "You've been so great with Josh. He already adores you." She glanced his way. "I'm so worried that he might get too attached."

Shane's mouth dropped open. "He might, but is that a bad thing? I won't hurt him, or you, or anyone." He leaned against the kitchen sink, watching her. "You've been acting strange with me lately. Is that what's going on? You're worried about him?"

"I can't help myself. He's all I've got." She kept her back to him as she tossed the salad. "But I'm probably making a mountain out of a mole hill."

"Talk to me. Are you not okay about me seeing Josh—is that it?"

She shrugged, dishing the salad into small wooden bowls. "He gets so close to people and wants to be loved so badly, and then the men in his life leave."

"Well, I'm not about to leave."

"You will one day, and that is the right thing for you to do. Problem is, he's just a little boy, and he doesn't understand that sometimes people have to leave, even though they still love them." She scooted around him to get plates from a cupboard. "This is not your concern. It's mine. I shouldn't have shared it with you."

He rubbed his jaw, wondering what to say. He couldn't tell her that he'd never leave, because he might have to attend med school somewhere else. What did she want from him? "Hey, you initiated this deal, and if you want to call it off, fine. But I like Josh, and he seems to enjoy being with me."

"I know he does." She set the plates on a counter and finally faced him. "It's a good deal for both of us, but..." She paused, biting her lip.

"But what?"

"We will both miss you when you're gone." She rubbed her hands together and blinked rapidly. "There. I said it."

He took two steps and put his hands on her arms.

"I'm not going anywhere for the time being. At least, I have no intention of leaving this immediate area." He ran a hand through his hair. "I have obligations here. I'm looking after my friend's condo while he's in Afghanistan, for starters. I also have friends here. Guys I used to work with back in my CAL FIRE days and fellows that I've met through the Wounded Warrior Project."

"Yes. You're here for now, and that's all we can ask." She twisted her hands. "But maybe next year you'll leave. You got your college degree online, and spent the past year doing pre-med courses at UCLA. No matter how good your grades, this might not be enough to get into med school. They are highly selective, and you'll need to accept whatever offer comes your way. Very few people can pick and choose."

"True, but we will face that when the time comes. For now this is my home, and that's very important to me. Unless you've been in an Iraqi terrorist camp, you can't possibly imagine what that means."

Her eyes widened. "Of course, I don't know what you've been through. How could I?"

He gave her a sheepish smile. "I can't believe I just said that." He could feel heat flooding up from his collar, seeping into his face. "That was really pathetic, playing on your emotions like that." He chuckled at himself. "I can't guarantee what will happen in the future, but who can? Don't worry so much."

"As a mother, it's a full-time job. I have Josh to protect. Nothing matters more than his safety and his happiness. Nothing."

"Lauren, you can't close yourself, or him, off from people on the far chance that one of you'll be hurt."

"Yes, I can. I have to."

"No, you don't. You can trust me. You should trust me."

They stared at each other for a few long seconds. Without realizing it, Shane leaned closer to her, feeling as though he could stare into her blue eyes all night. They weren't ice cold any longer. They were warm and inviting, like the blue water of a lake. Or maybe like the blue of a fire, that hot blue that could burn....

"Are you guys fighting?"

Startled, Shane looked down and saw Josh staring at them with a worried look in his eyes.

Lauren straightened, cleared her throat, and pulled open the cutlery drawer. "No, we're not fighting, honey. We're having a discussion." She collected knives and forks and handed them to Josh. "Why don't you set the table?"

Josh left the room, and Shane turned back to Lauren. "I'm not going anywhere for at least a year. It'll take that long to finish up my course work."

"Thank you," she said and quickly turned away again.

They sat down to dinner, and Josh gave his mother a blow-by-blow description of their day's activities, helped on occasion by Shane. Lauren nodded and laughed at all the right moments, but Shane could see her mind was elsewhere.

Once they were done, Shane cleaned up while Lauren bathed Josh and got him into his pajamas. When she joined him at the table again, Shane didn't immediately open his books.

"Before we get started," he said, "I just want to say that I don't want to leave you and Josh or my home either. But, yes it could happen. Nothing in life comes with guarantees. All anyone has is one day at a time."

"I know that. But I don't have to like it."

"Nobody likes it, but it's just one of those nasty facts of life." He eased back in his chair, fiddling with his pen. "Since we can't do anything to change it, let's talk about something we do have control over." He glanced at her, wanting to ease her worry and hoping to coax a smile. "Like what's going on at the hospital? Does everyone still think you and I have something going on?"

"Of course." Her face didn't lighten up. "It's a little awkward, that's for sure."

"Why? It shouldn't be."

"It is. You're no longer just a guy delivering me a patient in the ER. We have a personal connection now." Her voice was flat, and she was speaking clearly and concisely, as if reporting to an ethics committee. "Because of Josh. And my tutoring you."

"It won't get in the way. We're both professionals and know what we're doing."

"Do we?" She glanced away, and when she looked back, she seemed confused. "Margaret thinks I've been distracted lately."

"That's ridiculous," he scoffed. "It's not like we're having an affair. We're just friends."

"True." She opened her mouth and then shut it again.

"What is it? Just tell me, for God's sake."

"Okay." She was silent for a few seconds, and her cheeks grew pink. Finally, her eyes met his, and she spoke. "This may sound stupid to you, but I actually look forward to you coming into the ER. I don't want to feel that way, but I do."

He closed his eyes as he tilted his head back. This was not what he wanted. The sudden rising of heat in his loins, the burning desire to hold Lauren, to take her, to have her. No. Not with this woman.

His eyes opened slowly. He took a deep breath and released it. "What if I said I hope you're on duty when I show up too?"

Her gaze was direct, her expression serious. "Then I'd say we need to address this issue and deal with it."

He crossed his arms, squashing the hunger inside of him. It had been so long. Going on two years since he'd had a woman in his arms. "So, we have a little sexual attraction going on. Who's it hurting? Neither one of us will act on it, so it's no big deal."

"It makes me uncomfortable at work." She sat up straighter in her seat. "I can't be distracted."

"You won't be." He looked at her for a long time, just studying her. Finally, he grinned. "When was the last time you were kissed?" He knew it was a mistake to bring up the subject of kissing. Knew it the moment the words escaped his lips. But he wouldn't take them back, even if he could. He wanted to hear her answer.

She straightened even more, which was darn near impossible. "That's none of your business."

"No. But I can see that you're tense. You have all that sexual energy bottled up inside. I know because I'm in the same boat." He shrugged. "Seems like we both have a problem." It wasn't him she wanted, he told himself. She simply needed a man. Probably hadn't made love since her husband died.

She tossed her head, and he watched with fascination as her soft, chestnut-colored hair moved across her cheek. "I'm not tense, and I don't have sexual energy." She wouldn't look at him. "And if you do, why aren't you dating any one of the nurses that have the hots for you?"

"Not interested. I don't have time to date, as you've already pointed out." He hesitated, and then said, "You should go out with Kevin. He's an okay guy, and definitely wants to get it on with you."

Her eyes narrowed and took on a hint of that ice. "Don't insult me—or Kevin. If he were interested in me, he wouldn't expect a quick fling. He knew my husband, and he knows how hard it was when I lost him."

"Well, someone else then."

This line of conversation was better. Safer. The last thing he wanted was to be the object of her desire. He hadn't been with a woman since he'd lost his hand; and if he wanted sex, it wouldn't be with her. It would be with...well, he didn't know who it'd be with, but Lauren deserved someone a hell of a lot better than him.

"Look, Josh really wants a father. And he and Brad are good buddies." He rubbed his jaw. "But if you're not interested in Kevin, there's probably a zillion lucky guys who'd line up to date you."

"Spare me." She rolled her eyes. "Not you, too."

"I'm just saying."

"Josh and I are a team. We don't need anyone else."

"It was hard for my mom raising me by herself, and if the opportunity comes along, you shouldn't close your mind to it. That's all I'm going to say on the matter."

"It may have been hard on you and your Mom, but we're doing fine." There was heat in her voice when she added, "Perfectly fine. Why do people think we're not?"

He threw up his hands, knowing he'd pushed too far. "My mistake. Of course you're fine. Josh is a great kid, you're a great mother, and I have two exams next week." He opened one of his textbooks.

"Yes. Sorry." She glanced at her watch, then at the door of her son's bedroom. "We got distracted."

He leafed through the book, looking for the right section. "I've been having problems with this one—"

"It's been a year."

He looked up at her. "What has?"

"Since my last kiss."

EPISODE THREE

CHAPTER TEN

Lauren waited for a reaction.

Shane dropped his pen on the floor, bent down to pick it up, and hit his head on the table's edge as he straightened. "Damn!"

He looked so embarrassed and confused, Lauren almost laughed.

"You okay?" she asked.

"Yeah." He rubbed his head. "I thought we were done with that conversation. As you said, it's none of my business."

"I changed my mind." She abruptly pushed her chair back and stood. "I'll be right back. I need to put Josh to bed."

Unusual for her, she dragged out the bedtime ritual, reading Josh an extra two pages in their current book and then letting him retell part of what he and Shane did at the Aquarium. She needed a bit of time away from Shane. This whole evening was threatening to get out of hand.

First there had been her untoward delight in having him in her home; then that long moment when they had simply stared at each other in her kitchen; and then her confession about her attraction to him. Which he had echoed.

And then she'd gone and told him it had been a year since she'd had a kiss. What was wrong with her?

Exactly that, she thought as she turned out Josh's light and left the room. It had been a year since she'd been kissed. All of these exciting sensations that went zinging inside her when she spent time with Shane were simply signs of sexual neglect. They had nothing to do with Shane himself. And she'd prove it.

"Okay," she said when she returned to the kitchen. "Where were we?"

"Someplace we didn't want to go." He tapped a pen on his open book and kept tapping.

"Oh, yes, I remember now. The kiss."

He crossed and uncrossed his legs, looking clearly uncomfortable. "I don't want to know about it."

"Sure you do. It was with Ron, the guy I told you about. We dated for two and a half months."

"And he left. The jerk."

"That's right, but before he left, he was very nice to me." Lauren gave him a direct look. "I'm not always stuffy like I am at the hospital."

"Not interested." He looked down at his textbook. "Can we study now?"

"In a minute. First things first." She sat in the chair beside his, inching it closer. "Just as an experiment, could we try something?"

"Like what?" He shifted his body farther back in his chair.

"I need to know that I'm in control. So..." She studied him. "I don't want to be thinking about kissing you when I'm at work, so let's do it once and get it out of our systems. Okay?"

"No, not okay." He shook his head. "Bad idea."

"You brought up the subject." She leaned forward, moving within range.

"Now I wish I hadn't."

She noticed he was staring at her mouth.

She eased even closer. "I'm sure it will be like kissing your sister or something. We'll satisfy our curiosity and get over it."

His eyes met hers. "This is ridiculous. It's child's play, like spinning the bottle. Besides that, curiosity can kill the cat you know." He ran a hand over his mouth. "And what if it's not like kissing my sister, which I don't have, by the way? What then?" He glanced away. "This is crazy. Playing with fire."

She grinned. "I have the fire station on speed dial."

"Your funeral." He looked up and his hazel eyes warmed and softened, as they met hers. "I'm a really good kisser."

"Stop talking and do it." She closed her eyes. "Once."

He cupped her face in his hands and guided her mouth to his. Her pulse raced, and she could barely breathe. Afraid she'd change her mind, she quickly closed the distance.

The second their lips met, she unfolded like a neglected accordion that had sat in a box too long. His lips were warm and moist, gentle but firm, and instead of pulling back, she lingered, running her tongue over his bottom lip until he opened and let her slip in. His breath was peppermint sweet from the mints he'd had after dinner. Her tongue shyly met his and lit a fire inside her, a burning need that she'd ignored but didn't want to ignore anymore.

She missed her husband, missed being held in a man's arms, being kissed, being loved. Far too long. Her hands clasped behind his neck, and she couldn't let go.

"Lauren," he murmured between kisses. "We should stop this. Now."

"Okay." She pulled him closer. "Just one more; then never again."

He softened the kiss and then broke it off altogether. Instantly, she missed his lips, the warmth of him.

She kept her eyes closed and steadied herself. Drew in a deep breath, then exhaled slowly. She knew how to be strong. Life had taught her that.

When she felt back in control, when that melting sensation had dissipated, she opened her eyes and sat back. "Thank you." She kept her voice cool, rational. "That was nice." Her heart thudded, but she didn't want him to feel her excitement or to know how much that kiss had meant. Kissing him could be highly addictive, and of course she would want a lot more than that. Foolish girl! What had she been thinking? That she could play with fire and not get burned? She'd wanted it regardless of the consequences. A memory of that kiss could warm her bed at night for a very long time.

"Nice?" His eyes narrowed. "It was better than that."

She laughed. "Okay, better than nice, but now we've done it and can put it out of our minds." She picked up his book. "So? You ready? Let's get to work."

~

The study session was a joke. Shane's entire focus was on the tantalizing woman sitting next to him. When he leaned forward to peer at the book, his nostrils picked up her scent. He couldn't identify it but loved the smell. It was her special scent, and he'd recognize it anywhere.

She licked her lips a few times, probably because he'd worn her lipstick off and kissed her mouth dry. And now, watching her, he felt his own mouth go dry.

"I need some water," he said in a voice he barely recognized. "How about you?"

"No. I'm fine."

He grabbed a bottle from the fridge, poured a glassful, and took a long slug. "You sure you want to do this tonight?"

"Do what? Oh... tutor you. Of course I do. I'm happy I can help."

He wanted to throttle her. *I'm happy I can help!* Jeez. Give a guy a fuckin' break. That kiss had been good. Damn good. It had definitely gotten a rise out of him, and she behaved like it was nothing.

Well, two could play this game. He stretched and yawned. "I can hardly keep my eyes open. Guess a day at the Aquarium with an active six-year-old can do that to a man."

"I guess so." She smiled and stood up. "Well, we'll do this another time. Just remember, I owe you one."

"I expect you to pay up, too," he said with just the right amount of nonchalance. He gathered his books. "So, I guess I'll be seeing you around."

"You know where to find me." She walked him to the door. "Good night, Shane. Thanks for everything."

"Anytime, sweetheart. You want a kiss, you've come to the right man. Yep, I'm a real kissing champ." Two could play this game. If she wanted to act casual, well so could he. Nice, my ass. That kiss had been hot, dammit. Smokin' hot.

She raised her eyebrows but said nothing, just closed the door behind him.

Shane whistled all the way to his car, then stopped the second he got in. What the hell had happened tonight? He felt like he'd just been had. One minute she was sucking the oxygen from his lungs; the next, she'd been all business. Kiss over. Had she not enjoyed it as much as he had? Maybe he was badly out of practice.

Naw. She'd gotten into it big time. The worst thing was, he'd allowed it. Big mistake. He'd allowed his little head to overrule the big one. Damn! The last thing he wanted—the very last—was to go to bed with a woman and see the disappointment in her eyes.

It had happened once, about ten months ago. He'd met a nice lady, took her out a few times. They'd gone to bed, and he hadn't been able to get it up. That had never happened to him before, but then he'd never had a prosthesis before. He'd been so damned concerned about his mechanical hand that it had taken away his sexual drive. To save them both from further embarrassment, he hadn't called her again.

He didn't need romance. Or sex. One day, maybe. But right now, he still needed to prove a few things to himself.

CHAPTER ELEVEN

Shane headed straight home, fighting the urge to stop at a bar. One year sober, and he still struggled with the demon drink. He had it well controlled, but every now and then he had the need for a sip. He knew the worst was behind him, but in truth, he could only be responsible for one day at a time.

He'd partied some in his youth, but he'd never been a heavy drinker. The fourteen months he'd spent in Iraq, including six months of captivity, had created that need in him and taken its toll. Like so many vets coming home from the recent wars, he returned broken, unfixable. The stump where his hand should be ached all the time, and the constant pain made his memories all the more real. Haunted visions filled his head when he closed his eyes. Night terrors left him screaming, soaked in his own sweat.

It wasn't an excuse, but just the God-given truth. After his rescue and back in the good ole' US of A, he'd been nurtured back to health. Surgeons had had to amputate a little of his arm and clean up the wound so he could be fitted with a prosthetic that he'd deemed unfit to wear. His mood blackened, and the medication didn't make his pain go away. Pain, both physical and emotional, went soul deep—and seeing other victims of the war only increased his anger, his hostility to the world at large, and there was no help for him.

Released from the hospital, he began to hit the bottle hard, trying to find some small measure of peace, a place in la-la land where he could dwell without hearing the screams inside his head. The more he drank, the deeper his despair.

When he unexpectedly showed up at his family home in Jupiter, Florida, he was welcomed with open arms, but after a short time his own mother threw him out. It had been his own fault, of course. He had no direction, no motivation except to get drunk enough to ease the pain.

His mood swings had been more than his dear mother could handle, and his stepfather asked him to leave. There were support groups and centers for people like him but he didn't seek them out, preferring to be left alone. Instead, he wandered around aimlessly, eating at soup kitchens and finding cover in the woods at night, until he spotted an abandoned car in a Walmart shopping mall. He'd watched it for days, and when no one came along to claim the car, he'd taken it for his.

That's when Jake, Brent's older brother, found him, and got him off the streets. If it weren't for the love and support of that family, he'd probably be dead by now.

Should be, too. After all, he'd never done a damn thing in his life to be proud of, with the exception of going to war, and even there he'd screwed up.

Well, no more. He had to be responsible now. He was going to be a doctor, help the wounded vets like himself who came back filled with anger and self-loathing, wondering why some of their comrades had to die when they'd been allowed to live.

Now he had another reason—Lauren and Josh were depending on him, too. He hadn't wanted that to happen. Hell, he had enough trouble looking after himself, keeping sober, working himself to the bone so he didn't feel the need to drink.

He never kept alcohol in the apartment, and bars were not for him. Truly, he'd never really liked the bar scene much, except in his younger years when he'd used them for picking up chicks. He'd been quite a stud in those days—young and fit, long before the war had turned him into damaged goods. Now, women still gave him the eye, but they didn't have a clue what was going on inside.

No one knew about the night he'd lost his limb. How the terrorists holding him captive had forced him to perform surgery in order to save a commanding officer's life. He'd butchered the job so badly, they'd taken a dagger and sliced off his left hand, sawing through bone. He'd passed out from the pain, and for days afterward had a high fever and fought infection. The only reason he'd survived was because they had used a tourniquet to stop the bleeding, and someone had carelessly stitched him up so he could still be of use to them. His right hand had been left intact so he could still patch up their wounded. Fucking bastards.

Why he'd had the sudden urge to stop at a bar tonight, he had no idea. Unless it was because of Lauren. She was something special and he didn't deserve a woman like her. She was probably right to be afraid. He wasn't whole, and if he continued to see her and Josh, their attraction would undoubtedly grow stronger, and where would that get them? In trouble.

His head throbbed. He wanted to do the right thing and walk away from her and Josh, but the look in her eye, the way she responded when he kissed her, how could he possibly walk away from that?

Yet, would hurting them both now be better than hurting them later? Hell, he had no idea.

Shane lay down on his bed and put his hands on his head, trying to ease the torment. A bottle of scotch would help, but he'd promised himself—never again.

The last time he'd gone to a bar, some old drunk had come up to him, razzing him about his artificial hand. When Shane told him what it was, he'd staggered over and offered to buy him a beer. "Come, have a drink on me. Least I can do for a wounded soldier."

He'd declined, wanting a quiet drink before returning to his apartment, but the old guy wouldn't leave him alone. Slurring his words, he'd said, "I'm not one of those people that think you got hosed by going over there. Hell no. So what if they didn't have any of those nuclear weapons. Makes no difference. Those damn terrorists need to be put down. I'd go myself, but the recruiters say I'm too old." He'd laughed. "Too damn old to get killed. Now does that make any sense? So how many have you killed? Bet it must have been hundreds, right?"

Shane had ignored him, but he didn't give up. He'd moved in closer and whispered, "You ever see those kids, all innocent like, just before they toss you a fuckin' grenade. I'd pop them one right between the eyes."

That had done it. Shane had popped *him* and ended up spending a night in jail. It was the night he swore to quit drinking.

~

Lauren didn't see Shane for a couple of days. When he made an excuse not to see Josh the following week, she was sure it was the kiss that had caused the problem.

She was furious with him for behaving in such a juvenile manner, but angrier at herself. Her poor son would be broken-hearted if Shane refused to see him again, and it would be all her fault. Why the hell did she kiss him anyway? To prove how strong she was, that she could control her emotions? If that had been her reasoning, it was certainly flawed.

To make it up to Josh, she decided to take him to Magic Kingdom for the day and invited Brad along. Kevin insisted on coming too, and they had a great day on the rides, followed by a wonderful seafood dinner at the White House Restaurant. Kevin ordered a delicious pinot noir, and the boys drank sodas and pretended to be walruses with their straws.

Kevin flirted with her at dinner and tried to kiss her good night, but she put a quick stop to that. One screw-up was enough.

If Shane backed out of their agreement, maybe she'd be more open to the idea of spending time with Brad and his dad. But she was perfectly happy keeping things casual for the time being.

Shane finally called and asked if she and Josh would like to go to the beach with him the following Sunday. For Josh's sake, she agreed.

"You bring a picnic lunch," he said, "and I'll bring a kite. Figured Josh might enjoy that."

"He'd love it." She paused and then added, "He was disappointed last week when you couldn't make it, so I took him to Disney's Magic Kingdom. Brad and Kevin joined us."

"Oh." There was silence for a minute, before he spoke quietly, "I see."

"You do?" she asked, wishing it didn't hurt.

"Glad to see you took my advice," Shane said smoothly, as if he didn't care. Which he probably didn't. "Kevin's available and he likes you."

"Yeah, well, that's hardly the point, is it?" She knew she sounded snappish, but she wished Shane weren't so gung-ho about pushing her into Kevin's arms. "I'm not doing this for me, but for Josh. It's his happiness that matters."

"There's no reason for you not to date. You've been widowed—what? Two, three years?"

"Three. But I'd rather spend my nights with Josh. He's my number one." Plus, she made a lousy wife. She nagged, she argued, she'd distracted her husband....

Shane made a snorting sound. "I'm sure that'll change."

"Not likely. I like my independence too much."

"I can certainly relate to that. But you're a young woman with a young child. I imagine you'll feel differently one day."

"But until I do..."

"Until you do, you still need a mentor for Josh. That's me. I'll pick you up at one."

Now that he had called, Lauren was no longer worried. Whatever had caused his disappearance the previous weekend was none of her business. He had a right to a life, one that didn't include her or her son.

Lauren was slightly nervous about being seen on a beach. She was slim, but her body was far from perfect. Wanting to look her best, she went shopping and bought a new swimsuit, a conservative black one-piece that was supposed to make her look ten pounds slimmer. Earlier in the week, she'd also stopped at a salon for a bikini wax and a pedicure.

For their picnic she filled a basket with a store-bought rotisserie chicken, a loaf of French bread, and homemade potato salad. She added some cheddar cheese and apple slices and finished packing with oatmeal raisin cookies.

She wore her swimsuit under shorts and a T-shirt, and Josh had on his knee-length swimming trunks and a purple T-shirt with a large shark in the middle. By one o'clock, they were both ready.

When Shane knocked on the door, Josh ran to let him in. "Are we really going to fly a kite?" He jumped up and down. "That's so cool!"

"We sure are." He looked at the boy's arm. "How does your elbow feel?"

"Feels good. Like I can do anything." He grinned his gap-toothed smile. "It's awesome!"

"You're awesome." Shane gave Lauren a quick glance, then turned his attention back to Josh. "Ever done it before?"

"No. Can you show me how?"

"I can and I will." He turned to Lauren. "Something smells good. Have you been slaving over a hot oven?"

She laughed. "No. Rotisserie chicken, but homemade cookies."

"Works for me." His eyes did a quick inventory of her body, and she felt a tingle of pleasure inside and out. A tingle that she quickly squelched and told herself to ignore.

CHAPTER TWELVE

Because it was still spring, the seaside town didn't have the visitors that came in droves during the summer months, and they found a parking spot a short distance from the pier.

Lauren helped unload the car, and smiled as Shane handed the kite to Josh, warning him to hold on tight.

"I stopped by earlier and got us organized," he said, pointing to a couple of chairs with an umbrella and a beach blanket.

"Excellent. You thought of everything." Lauren gave him a pleased smile. "I'll lay out the food for our picnic while you boys play."

She nearly choked when Shane stripped off his T-shirt and squirted on some protective sun lotion. She didn't know what he did for a workout routine, but whatever it was, it certainly did the job. Broad shoulders framed a nicely sculpted body with six-pack abs. He had well-shaped legs and muscular thighs with a light smattering of dusty hair that matched the thicker patch on his chest.

She licked her suddenly dry lips. Coming to the beach might have been a huge mistake. She'd never look at him again without having to wipe off the drool.

She dropped her picnic basket in the sand and sank into a chair, fanning herself before she realized what she was doing.

"You okay?" he asked with a sexy grin.

"It's warm today, don't you think?"

He checked her out, and his eyes twinkled. "It's hot all right."

"Why are you guys talking about the weather?" Josh interrupted, and Lauren had never been so glad. "Let's fly this thing." He ran around in circles, allowing the kite a few feet of freedom.

"Off you two go." She waved them away, glad she wouldn't have to stare at Shane's naked chest until she got her breathing under control. Maybe the fact that she had lived like a nun for most of the last three years had something to do with her overactive libido. Whatever the reason, she needed to get rid of it.

She managed to get the plastic plates out of the picnic basket, cut up the chicken, lay out the salad, slice the cheese and bread, but her eyes kept straying to both the man and her son. She couldn't remember seeing Josh look so happy. He was laughing and running around with the kite flying behind him, and when it dipped and fell in the water, Shane rescued it.

It was a sight that tempted to melt the frozen block around her heart. But she preferred keeping that frozen layer right where it was, protecting her, keeping her from loving again. Better safe than sorry.

Lauren watched her son and Shane for a few more minutes, then decided to use the alone time to take in some sun. She stripped out of her clothes, applied a heavy dose of sunscreen, then stretched out on the blanket and closed her eyes.

A short time later, she felt a shadow over her and glanced up. Shane stood there, grinning. "Hi," she said. "Did you boys have fun?"

"Sure did. You should have joined us. Josh wants to show you how good he is."

She sat up and looked at her son. "That's great, Josh. I'm so proud of you. I was watching, and you had the kite higher than anyone else on the beach. You guys rock."

Josh danced in place, clutching the kite. "Mom, come and watch me."

"I will, honey, right after we have something to eat." She reached for her T-shirt, feeling a little too exposed with Shane's eyes on her.

"I don't want to eat." Josh kicked the sand. "I want to fly the kite more."

Shane intervened. "We have all afternoon, kiddo. I'm starved, and the food will spoil if we leave it in the sun." He picked up a paper plate. "You want a chicken leg?"

"Yeah, I guess so." Josh didn't sound happy, but he stopped kicking sand and came to stand near Shane.

Shane put a leg and some potato salad on the plate, added a hunk of bread, and gave it to Josh. "Eat that, and then maybe your mom will let you have a cookie."

Josh sat down and did as he was told.

"Nice work," Lauren whispered to Shane. "You want me to fix you a plate?"

"I'm fine, but thanks for offering." He helped himself, then sat down next to Josh on the blanket and dived in.

Lauren took sodas from an insulated bag and handed them out. Then she filled her plate and took one of the chairs. She ate in silence, smiling as the guys polished off their food and went back for seconds.

Shane helped her put the leftover food away. Their hands accidently collided over the picnic basket, and Lauren felt a delighted thrill. Their eyes met.

His were more brown than green in the afternoon sun. Warm as melted chocolate, they made her feel all gooey inside. She tingled in long-forgotten places, and she didn't care that it was wrong to feel about Shane this way.

"You guys want to show me how to fly that kite?" She looked into Shane's eyes as she spoke.

"What do you say, Josh? Think a girl will slow us down?"

"Naw. Mom's not a girl. She's supermom."

Lauren laughed. "First time I've been called that, but I think I like it." She put on her shorts and picked up the kite. "Okay, who's going to teach me how to get this in the air?"

"Shane can show you. He's real good at it." Josh jumped around excitedly.

Shane wore a smug smile. "I think I can handle it on my own," Lauren said. "At least it'll be fun trying."

She felt her cheeks flush and didn't want either of the boys to see, so she ran off, but Shane chased her down. His arm went around her waist, and she stopped running. Slowly she turned, and felt his naked chest next to her. Her heart beat wildly, and she swallowed hard.

"This is a dangerous game we're playing," she whispered.

"I have a thing for danger," he said. His eyes darkened, and she wondered if it was desire that made them change color or simply the light. His hazel eyes could be green or brown, and she hadn't figured out what triggered the change in color.

"Uh-huh." She smiled. "I can see that."

Josh came running up to them. "Can I try now? Can I?"

She handed the kite to her son. "Go for it. I don't think I'm good at this kind of thing."

"You won't know if you don't try," Shane said with a wicked grin.

"I like to do things I can control. The wind isn't one of them. And, well, to be honest, I prefer just watching you guys."

"Oh, Mom, you're so lame."

She laughed and waved them off. Returning to the blanket, she sat down where she could keep her eye on them but not feel so vulnerable. She knew the two of them were already comfortable with each other; it was she who had a problem. Shane stirred her up, made her feel things she was better off forgetting.

By four o'clock they'd had enough of the beach and headed home. Shane took out his books and glanced through them while Lauren gave Josh a quick bath. Once her son was settled in front of the TV, she sat down at the kitchen table to give Shane her full attention.

They drank tea and were totally immersed in the studying until Josh interrupted to say he was hungry. She glanced at the clock, startled to see it was half past six.

She closed the biochemistry book and stood up. "Shane, I need to feed Josh and get him off to bed soon, but we can continue studying once he's asleep."

"Stay for dinner," Josh said, tugging on Shane's arm. "Mom's a really good cook."

"I know she is, Josh, but not today. Maybe some other time." He carried their mugs to the sink and said to Lauren, "You know, the way you explain things helps make it click. I'm retaining the information."

She smiled. "I certainly hope so."

He said good-bye to Josh, and then gathered up his books. She walked him to the door.

"I had a nice time today," he said. "I'm glad you came."

"Me too." She touched his arm. "By the way, I want to apologize for that nice kiss. I shouldn't have done it."

"No need." He shrugged. "It's already forgotten."

"Oh." Disappointment swept over her like a dash of cold water.

"But you were right," he added. "It was nice." With that, he turned and walked out.

CHAPTER THIRTEEN

Shane returned home, took Major for a walk, then sat down on the couch with the dog next to him.

"Had a great day at the beach today," he told the dog, rubbing Major's belly. "You know what she did? Last week when I didn't see Josh, she went to Magic Kingdom with Kevin and the two boys."

The dog put his legs in the air, giving Shane full access to his belly. He continued to scratch with his bionic hand.

"She needs a guy like him. Someone a lot stronger than me, that's for sure. If Kevin doesn't float her boat, hopefully soon the right guy will come along and love her the way she needs to be loved and be a good father to Josh."

If he could hang around until that special someone came into their lives, then no one would get hurt. He would have done the right thing by them and be free to leave.

He stood up and prowled around the apartment that wasn't his. He'd rented it from Brent, who'd given up fighting forest fires to fight the Taliban in Afghanistan. Same weapon—helicopters—different outcome. This one could get him killed.

Satisfied that he'd resolved his issues with Lauren, his thoughts turned to Brent. He was worried about him and had been for days. They were closer than any two brothers. Did everything together. Everything but go to war. Brent had thought Shane was out of his mind when he signed up as an army medic, eager to go to Iraq. He'd refused to do the same, saying it wasn't their fight.

As usual, he'd been right. The war dragged on for way too many years, at too high of a cost, both in lives and to the American economy. Hell, even after Hussein's regime ended, the war continued.

Brent knew this. His father was a retired general, and his older brother, Jake, had fought in Iraq too. But the damn fool had been so riled up when Shane got captured, he'd taken himself down to the recruitment center and signed up.

Now Shane got to sleep in his king-sized bed while Brent froze his ass in a foreign, hostile land.

Not that he did much sleeping. Since his return, he probably averaged three to four hours a night. He used the time he didn't spend sleeping to study, do his laundry, pay his bills, and accomplish what normal people did during the day.

He had no complaints, though. It kept his nightmares at bay. Sleeping for him was akin to torture, even now that he had a warm bed at night.

But tonight he was too wound up to sleep, even if he could. He had a bad feeling, and this kind of bad feeling usually turned out to have been justified. Picking up the phone, he called Jake in Washington.

"How's the capital city treating you?" Shane said by way of greeting. "You still working to get us homeless folks off the streets?"

"Shane, ole buddy. Nice to hear from you. What's up?"

"Not much. I'm still employed as a medic, finishing up a few pre-med courses, and studying for MCATS." He added, "Got a nice lady doctor giving me extra help at night. Not a bad deal all around."

"Sounds like you've got your hands full," Jake chuckled.

"Talk about hands full—how's that beautiful lady of yours?"

"Kari's doing great. Got that new show of hers syndicated, and it follows the evening news at 7:00 p.m." He spoke with obvious pride. "Who'd have thought her 'feel-good stories' would have made such an impact?"

"Yes, well, it's what the people want to hear. You and I both know they don't want the truth."

"Well, we're working on that," Jake agreed. "So what's really bothering you? You didn't call just to chat."

"You're right. I haven't heard from Brent in a while. How about you?"

"Jeez, I'm not sure. He normally checks in with me every month or so, but I can't say when I heard from him last." Jake didn't sound concerned. "You know that if anything happened, I'd hear about it immediately. So no news is good news, right?"

"You'd think so, but my instincts…"

"Have always been dead on. So what are they telling you?"

"Nothing concrete, just that something isn't right."

"And I think he's shacked up with some pretty army officer unlucky enough to be in that hellhole part of the world." Jake chuckled. "Trust me, he's fine. If he wasn't, we'd know about it."

"Well, if you hear from him, give him shit for me, will you?"

"You bet. Anything else bothering you?"

"No, things are good with me. I'm still working on staying sober. One day at a time."

"Glad to hear it." Jake cleared his throat. "Take care of yourself, Shane. Good luck with the doc."

"It's not like that..."

"Like hell it's not."

Shane hung up. It had been good to talk with Jake, but he couldn't shake the feeling that something was wrong. He called up a few people he knew, putting feelers out, but if anybody knew anything, they weren't talking.

~

Once Josh went to bed, Lauren turned the TV back on and poured a glass of wine, intending to unwind after her busy day. Her shoulder muscles were tight and knotted, caused solely by spending the day with Shane.

Seeing him shirtless down at the beach, she'd felt a yearning so strong, it had completely unnerved her. Kissing him had been a terrible error in judgment, because now she knew what she was missing and couldn't get it out of her head.

It wasn't the kissing or the sex she missed so terribly, but the joy of being in love, being part of a couple. Having someone besides Josh to talk to at night, to snuggle with, to share her intimate thoughts and her worries with, even the mundane details of her day. And yes, of course, she did miss sex. Being held by a man, lying beside him at night, listening to the sound of his breathing, comforted by his familiar scent and warmth.

Ron had wanted to fill that empty space, but she'd refused, partly because of Josh, partly because she hadn't been ready. He'd left when he got tired of waiting, and the hole inside of her had deepened.

She wanted a man. Not a husband, but someone to laugh with, to share good moments and bad, and to ease the loneliness once in a while. Maybe Shane was right. Maybe she should give Kevin a chance. They had sons the same age, and she knew him, trusted him. He wasn't some stranger from an Internet site. He was a rock-solid person. Perhaps the lack of chemistry could be fixed.

With that thought in mind, she went to bed, only to awaken in the middle of the night, drenched in sweat, heart pounding, and aroused. Her skin felt hot, as though it had been touched. The dreams had been real enough. She remembered hot kisses, burning flesh slapping together in the heat of passion. She'd gone to bed thinking of Kevin, but the man in her dreams had been Shane.

CHAPTER FOURTEEN

Lauren watched as Margaret strutted into the ER. She'd dyed her red hair burgundy; green eyeliner and shadow emphasized her green eyes; and her full lips were colored a dark plum. But it was her grin that gave her secret away.

"You're in love. Again," Lauren said by way of greeting.

Margaret giggled. "You bet your pretty ass I am. Guy's even cuter than Shane. His name is Anthony. Isn't that the dreamiest name?" She patted her chest. "Oh my. My heart's pounding."

"Probably because you're late and had to run from the parking lot." Lauren hid a smile.

Margaret ignored the comment. "As I was saying, I met Anthony at the dueling piano bar, and when he looked at me, I knew. He's the one. This time I'm sure of it."

"So you've known him for all of—what?" Lauren glanced at the large clock on the wall. It was one in the afternoon. "Fourteen, fifteen hours?" She spoke in mock horror. "Tell me you didn't sleep with him."

"Of course I did. How could I know if we were meant for each other if I didn't check out his equipment first?"

Trish arrived in time to hear the last part. She grinned, bobbing her head in agreement. "You got that right. Why waste your time on a guy if he doesn't do it for you in bed?"

Lauren rolled her eyes. "Really? I'm shocked at the two of you. You both know there's a great deal more to a relationship than sex." She put her hands on her hips and pursed her lips. "Whatever happened to taking it slow and getting to know each other first? It might be old-fashioned, but that system has been around for quite a while. And for a very good reason: it works."

"Not anymore it doesn't," Margaret replied. "And I don't have time to wait. I'm thirty-four years old. If I ever want to get married and have children, I need to seal the deal as quickly as possible."

"Come on, Dr. Reynolds," Trish said. "Times have changed. Men like women who know what they want and go after it."

"Sure they do," Lauren agreed. "But that doesn't mean they have to rush into anything. Slow things down. Prove you're worth the wait."

Trish shook her head. "I knew after our first date that Jared was the guy for me, so I made damn sure he knew it too. I gave him the best sex of his life, and that, my friend, is the way to a man's heart."

"Trish, you sell yourself short," Lauren replied. "You're a very smart, warm, affectionate person. That's why Jared is madly in love with you. Not because of your sexual prowess in bed."

"So you say. I'm just making sure he doesn't stray."

"Well, you girls are more up on these things than me." Lauren had heard enough girl talk for one afternoon. She turned to walk away and ran smack into Shane.

"What are you doing here?" she asked, aware that her breasts had, however briefly, made contact with his chest. The chest that she vividly remembered from her dreams.

"I came to see you." He took her arm and moved her away from the others. "I wanted to ask if you could spend extra time with me this week. I've got an exam coming up, and I sure could use your help."

"Of course. Would you like to come over tonight?" She kept her voice low, not wanting to give the nurses more fuel for gossip. "I'm off at eight."

"I work until ten. Will that be too late?"

"No." She looked into his eyes, thinking that today they reminded her of a melted Hershey bar with a caramel center. Forcing her gaze away, she reminded herself that she mustn't let her physical attraction for him get in the way. A little chemistry was bound to happen between two people. It didn't mean she really wanted to sleep with him, even if she had in her dreams. She couldn't control her subconscious, but she could control her waking thoughts.

She dragged her mind back to their conversation. "After ten will be fine. Josh will be asleep, so we won't be disturbed."

"I appreciate it. See you later then." He turned and walked away, and Lauren caught Margaret checking out his tush.

"So what was that all about?" Margaret asked.

"He wanted to know if we could have sex tonight," she said in jest, half-hoping to shock Margaret the way she always did her. "After my conversation with you, I thought, why not?"

"You're kidding me, right?"

"Right." Lauren marched off, annoyed at herself and the world at large. Why could other people just fall into bed together, call it love, and move on without guilt? Well, she knew the answer to that. They didn't have Josh. He was the one who'd get hurt, and no way would she chance that.

~

Shane quietly knocked on Lauren's door, not wanting to wake Josh. Lauren opened it right away. She was wearing navy knee-length shorts and a Victoria's Secret T-shirt. He could make out the outline of her bra underneath and quickly glanced away.

"Hi, Shane. Come on in." She led the way to the kitchen. "I made us a pot of coffee, and I baked an apple-walnut loaf."

"That was nice, but you shouldn't have bothered." Even as he spoke, his mouth watered when he spotted the loaf sitting on the counter. He couldn't remember the last time a woman had cooked for him, but Lauren didn't seem to think anything of it. "I don't want to be more of a pain in the ass than I already am."

She smiled. "You're not. Actually, it's nice to have adult conversation once in a while."

"Really, you need to get out more."

"Yes. I agree." She didn't say anything for a second and when she did, it was the last thing he wanted to hear. "Shane,

I've got to tell you something. I made the decision to go out with Kevin Saturday night."

"Wow. That was sudden." He knew he was scowling, but hell. He hadn't expected this so soon. "Got a babysitter lined up?"

"It's Kevin's weekend with Brad, so the boys are going to stay together at his apartment. He's got a regular babysitter."

Nice guy, Shane thought. Gets to see his son for the weekend but goes out on a date instead. Not that he could blame him. Lauren was one special lady, and a guy would have to be half crazy to pass that up. "I'm busy this Saturday too, but if it's okay with you, I can take Josh somewhere Sunday afternoon."

"Great. He's been really into baseball lately. Do you think you could take him to the park and show him how to hit a ball? He'd love that."

"That's easy enough." He poured a mug of coffee for himself. "So, what time's your date?"

"I'm dropping Josh off at Kevin's place at four, and then he's coming over here to pick me up at six. We don't want the boys to know we're going out together." She darted a quick look at him. "The last time I dated someone, Josh really liked the guy and was broken-hearted when it didn't work out. I don't want that to happen again."

Shane nodded, giving them both points for that sensible decision, but then she went on and spoiled it.

"Maybe Kevin and I can spend the afternoon together on Sunday too, if Saturday night works out."

"Of course." Shane's stomach tightened. He'd be taking her son out, while she would be . . . what would she be doing? Hell, he didn't want to know.

Lauren licked her lips. "Are you okay with that?"

"Sure. Why not?"

"Just checking." She tossed her head back. "I didn't want to date anyone, but everyone, including you, seems to think that I'm being unfair to Josh. You know he means the world to me. And I like Kevin. He's nice."

"I think you should date. Not for Josh's sake. For your own."

Her eyes met his, and they were honest and open, without guile. "I do get lonely sometimes. It would be nice to have someone to share my life with, I must admit. But unless I think it has a good chance of working out, it's not worth the gamble."

She played with the hem of her T-shirt, and Shane noticed the thin material stretch over her breasts. He quickly glanced away.

"If I didn't have my son to think about, it would be a different story." She sounded like she was on the defensive, and he wondered why.

"You can't always put him first. You also have to think about yourself and your needs."

"No, I don't." She straightened up and glanced away. "My needs are not all that important. Besides, it's not easy having a romantic relationship with a six-year-old around. Which is all the more reason I should try to see him both days this weekend. You have to grab your moments when you can." Her lips parted in a smile. "And the sooner I know if there's any chemistry, the better."

"I see." Shane took a sip of his coffee, which tasted too bitter. "Yeah. Now that you've explained it, it makes sense. As a matter of fact, I think it'll do you good."

"You do?" She frowned. "Why?"

"Because you need it and you deserve it." His eyes roamed over her face and settled on her mouth, thinking how sweet those lips would taste. "You're young, beautiful, and shouldn't sleep alone."

"That's nice." She cut a few slices of the loaf and set them on the table. "But I'm not planning on having an afternoon love fest," she went on as she sat down. "If it's a nice day, we could go for a drive and get to know each other better. Don't worry. I'm not going to drag him into my bed as soon as he walks in the door."

He yanked out a chair and sat as well. "I'm not worried. You can do whatever you please."

"Well, I don't please." She broke off a piece of the loaf and ate it. "I don't want to go to bed with Kevin."

"Then why are you going out with him?"

"Because I need to get out more. And Josh desperately wants a father."

He slapped his textbook onto the table. "I don't get the connection. If you don't want to have sex with him, how can you think about marrying him?"

"Jeez. I'm not! Marrying is not in the equation. Just a date. One date. Possibly two, if the first one's good." Lauren ran her fingers through her hair, mussing it. "This whole conversation is ridiculous. I like my life just the way it is."

"Then what's the problem?"

"I've tried to be both mother and father to him, and I thought that would be enough. Obviously, it isn't."

Shane put a hand over hers. "He's a good kid. You've raised him well." He lifted her chin and looked into her eyes. "Now you need to think about yourself."

"I was fine until that kiss," she muttered. "Unfortunately, it reminded me of what I'm missing. Hence, the date."

"I see." The idea of her kissing Kevin got his hackles up. "Look, I'd really love to sit around and discuss finding you a husband, but do you mind if we get to the reason I'm here? It's late and we both have to work tomorrow."

"Yes, of course."

She pulled her chair closer to his and leaned over the table, sharing the textbook. He could see the curve of her sweet, soft breasts, and his nostrils twitched from the flowery scent in her hair.

He forced his mind to concentrate, and for the next hour he managed to focus, but then she sat up straight and stretched her back. Her breasts swelled in the T-shirt, and he couldn't tear his eyes away.

His mouth dried, and he took a sip of his cold coffee. He tried not to look, but hell, when a starving man is offered a feast, he's not expected to turn away.

She noticed his expression and stood up, crossing her arms over her chest. "Are we done here?" she asked, a frown wrinkling her brow.

He stood as well and feigned a yawn. "I think so. You helped clarify a few things."

"I'm glad."

They both started to clear the dishes at the same moment, and their fingers brushed as they reached for the plate.

Lauren snatched her hand away and said, "I've got it."

Shane didn't move. She stood only inches away from him, and he wanted to pull her close, feel that sexy body against his, and taste her lips again. He wanted it so badly, it hurt.

He stuffed his hand into his pocket and his prized i-limb behind his back. Would he ever be comfortable enough with it to enjoy the charms of a woman? He wasn't ashamed of his disability, but what would he do with a mechanical hand during the physical part of making love? He'd only had it for ten months and had made great progress, finding it easy to use for most normal activity. But how would a woman feel about it when they were rolling in the sack?

"Enjoy your date," he said. He saw the disappointment in her eyes and knew exactly what she wanted. Her mouth trembled, and he had to clench his teeth together to stop from kissing it.

"Good night." Afraid to linger, he turned and walked away.

"Good luck with your exams," she called as he reached the door.

He nodded. "Good luck with Kev."

CHAPTER FIFTEEN

Kevin took several minutes to peruse the extensive wine menu and then signaled to their waiter. "We'll have the Silver Oak Cabernet," he ordered.

The waiter nodded and left, and Lauren leaned across the table toward Kevin. They were dining at Melisse, a French restaurant in Santa Monica.

"What a great choice for tonight," she said. "I hear the food is excellent." She glanced around the beautifully appointed room with curved, shuttered windows and noted the round tables covered with starched white linen, each set with elegant china. A few well-dressed couples were enjoying drinks in the cozy bar. Lauren smiled with pleasure. "I don't get out often enough, I'm afraid."

"Well, we'll have to rectify that, won't we?"

"If you say so."

Her eyes met his, and for the first time since she'd known him, she really looked at Kevin. Not as Josh's best friend's father, not as someone else's husband, but as a possible mate. He was a striking man. Just short of six feet, he was well built and tanned. A hint of silver threaded through his brown hair, and though his straight nose and strong chin hinted at sternness, his smile was wide and easy.

Any woman would think herself lucky to be in my shoes, Lauren thought, and yet, she was reluctant to encourage his interest in her. She liked him well enough but had never had any romantic inclination toward him. Maybe if she made an effort, she could change that. If Josh wanted a father, it was her job to see that he got one.

"Kevin, I have a feeling that you know how to treat a lady." She gave him what she hoped was a seductive smile. "Watch out. I might get used to it."

He laughed and clinked water glasses with her. "I hope you do."

Lauren sat back in her chair and fiddled with her cutlery. "Does this feel odd to you? I mean, how long have we known each other? Five years at least. So, why are we acting like two people on a first date?"

"Darned if I know." His eyes met hers. "Maybe because we are."

The waiter returned with the wine, and after Kevin sniffed the cork and sampled a taste, the waiter told them about the evening specials.

"We're not in any hurry," Kevin told him. "But you can bring us some caviar to start."

Lauren turned her attention to the menu and wondered if Shane had ever been here. She couldn't imagine him in such a fancy place, but she knew he'd fit in anywhere. He was that kind of guy. Easygoing, easy to like.

But what was she doing thinking about Shane when Kevin was out to show her a good time? He was being perfectly charming and witty, but there was a new awareness in his eyes. He had the look of a man who knew exactly what he wanted and planned on getting it.

Lauren wished she could feel a little more enthusiasm about being the dessert on Kevin's personal menu. What was wrong with her? She'd been tempted to sleep with Ron Hammond during their two-month relationship and had regretted not taking that step. She certainly was no prude. Sex was wonderful with the right person, and she missed it. Kevin would be more than willing to change all that.

She simply didn't want to make a mistake and screw up a solid friendship. Sex had a way of doing that.

"What's on your mind?" Kevin asked. "You look worried about something."

"No. It's nothing. I'm sorry if I seemed distracted. I'm not, I assure you." She put a hand over his. "I'm having a wonderful time."

They ordered dinner, and the rest of the evening went well. She felt relaxed with him and trusted that he only had her and Josh's best interest at heart. So when he took her home, she didn't hesitate to invite him in. They were alone, but she had no desire to go to bed with Kevin.

She made coffee and they sat in her living room to enjoy the fresh brew and each other. She was not surprised when he took the cup out of her hands and pulled her gently toward him. She leaned against his arm and turned up her face, hoping she'd feel differently about him once they'd kissed.

She wanted electricity, sparks to fly, and a heady dose of passion.

But his kiss, although nice, didn't get her pulse rate up.

It tasted like the kiss of a friend. There was no hunger. No pounding heart, no quickened breathing, no inflamed libido crying for more.

It was not like kissing Shane. Now that had been something. She'd wanted him. In her bed, inside of her, flesh pounding flesh, and hot moist kisses that went on and on and on.

But Shane couldn't afford to be strapped down with a woman and a kid. He had a goal, and it would take a lot of hard work and dedication to make it a reality.

~

The following day, Lauren's stomach did a bouncing act as she waited for Shane to come and collect her son. All morning she was nervous, but why, she had no idea. Nothing was going to happen on her date because she didn't want anything to happen. She had nothing to feel guilty about, and yet....

Just the thought of Shane, this dear man, spending time with her son while she was out with another didn't sit right with her. Even if he'd encouraged it, she knew his reasons were unselfish. He cared about her and Josh and only wanted the best for them. But what was that? Did he not fit into this picture at all? More importantly, did he not want to fit?

By noon, she was hanging around the kitchen, anxious for Shane to appear, wanting to have a word with him before seeing Kevin.

"Shane." She smiled and beckoned him in. "Josh is waiting for you, but I wanted to ask you something first."

"Sure. But first tell me, how did the date go?"

"It went fine," Lauren told him, searching his face for clues. When she didn't get any, she added, "Actually better than fine. We had a really nice time." Still not a single twitch. How did he feel, dammit? She'd wanted to test his reaction, but so far the verdict was zilch. Did he not care about her after all?

Finally Shane grunted. "*Nice.* You use that word a lot."

"I guess I do," she answered, happy to hear something in his voice, a trace of emotion. "We went to Melisse in Santa Monica for dinner. It's a beautiful French restaurant, very romantic, and the food was out of this world."

"Hmmm. That's... nice." He flexed his shoulders. "I ate at my favorite restaurant too. Pizza Hut. Had the extra-thin crust, fully loaded. Brought half of it home and ate it for breakfast. Delicious."

She made a face. "Yuck. I can't imagine eating a greasy pizza for breakfast. Do you ever cook for yourself?"

"Not unless I have an overnight guest." He grinned and raised an eyebrow. "Speaking of which. Did you get any rest last night?"

"That's none of your business, but we did make arrangements for today." She stared into his eyes, hoping to gauge his feelings, if he had any. "You don't mind, do you? Perhaps you could come back around four?"

He raised a brow and gave a hint of a smile. "Does that give you enough time?"

"Not funny," she answered, hurt by his indifference. "I have no intention of doing whatever you think I'll be doing."

"You might not, but he may have other plans." He didn't break eye contact. "So you do like him then?"

They were interrupted by Josh's reappearance. "What are you guys talking about?" He tossed a baseball in the air and didn't catch it. It rolled down the hall, and he chased after it. Running back, he said, "Come on, Shane. Let's go to the park."

"Yes, why don't you?" Lauren spoke.

"Okay, sport," Shane said to Josh. "Let's get going. Your mom has important things to do."

"I do not," she snapped. She tapped her foot, now eager to see them leave.

"Whatever. Have fun." He put a hand on Josh's shoulder and guided him out the door. "Don't do anything I wouldn't do," he said with a wink and a grin.

"Go to—" She stopped herself just in time. "Enjoy the park. 'Bye, honey."

"'Bye, Mom."

She closed the door firmly behind him and sucked back tears. She'd hoped he might show a little jealousy, but he hadn't seemed to care.

To make things worse, she wanted to spend the afternoon with him, not Kevin. He always made her laugh, made her feel good. She enjoyed his humor, his warm smile, the natural camaraderie they shared, and the way he connected with her son. But she was stuck entertaining Kevin whether she wanted to or not.

He arrived a half hour later, and as soon as he was in the door, he pulled her into his arms. "This was a great idea," he murmured against her ear. "Got both of our boys taken care of, and now I have you all to myself."

"Yes. Right." She slipped out of his arms. "There is a fabulous art auction at the Long Beach Museum that I've been dying to take in. The exhibition has been open to the public for a month, and I haven't had time to go." She grabbed her handbag. "This is my only chance. The auction's coming up on May 22nd."

"That sounds interesting, but couldn't we make better use of our time?" He glanced at his Piaget watch and frowned. "We only have a little over two hours."

"Just enough time." She linked her arm with his. "If we hurry, we can probably see the entire exhibit."

"I thought we were going to spend the day getting to know each other, not traipsing around a museum."

"We will be getting to know each other. This is one of my passions, and I hoped you might enjoy it too." She touched his face, looking into his eyes. "I want to take this slow. I don't want to have any regrets or lose you as a friend."

Kevin was quiet for the entire drive, and Lauren did her utmost to lighten his mood. She had been an active fundraiser for many years and was well known by the curators. She happily introduced Kevin to everyone she knew, but although he was courteous, he showed little interest in either the people or the magnificent works of art.

After an hour and a half they returned home, and Kevin's mood seemed to lift.

The moment they were inside, he trapped her against the wall with his arms. He bent and kissed her. "Well, now that you've had your fun, how about if we have some together?"

She slipped out from under his embrace, giving a nervous little laugh. "Behave yourself. Josh will be home soon, and it would probably be better if he didn't see you here. I don't want the children to know about us quite yet."

"What would be wrong with that? We're adults and if we like each other, why shouldn't the boys know?"

"Things are different with Josh and me. I'm all he's got, and because he's had to grow up without a dad, I've treated him like my best buddy. We don't keep secrets from each other, but this time I believe it's the prudent thing to do."

"Why? What's the big deal?"

She looked at him, not understanding why he didn't get it. "Because we don't know how things are going to work out between us. And I don't want him getting any hopes."

"What about mine?"

She smiled. "You can definitely hope." She gave him a light kiss. "I'm sorry you didn't enjoy the day, but I loved seeing the exhibits. I could easily have spent more time there."

"It was fine, but if I'd had a choice, I'd have preferred to keep you to myself."

She sighed. "Please don't rush me. When the time is right, we'll know it."

"Don't keep me at arm's length for too long, or I'll take the hint and not bother you anymore."

"Really?" She took another step back. "Fine by me. If that's how you want to play it."

"I'm sorry. I guess I'm not used to being put on hold."

"Well, I'm not used to being pressured for sex. So get used to it," she snapped back.

"I didn't mean to pressure you. That was never my intention. I just thought…well, you know, that you were attracted to me the same way I am to you."

"I like you, Kevin, but I'm not ready to hop into bed with you. Or anyone. I need to take this slow."

"Sure. Fine. I can do slow." He stayed a little longer and didn't try to kiss her again. She liked him better this way.

When he was ready to leave, she walked him to the door. "Good-bye, Kevin." She closed the door behind him and wondered whether or not she wanted to see him again.

About ten minutes later Shane returned with Josh, and Lauren's stomach did a sudden flip-flop as a wave of heat washed over her. Avoiding looking at Shane, she asked Josh if he'd had fun.

"It was great, Mom. I hit a home run."

Shane nodded. "He hit the ball out of the park. The kid's got talent." She turned aside to hug Josh. "I'm proud of you, honey. I see a baseball scholarship in your future."

He gave her a wide, happy smile, showing off his missing tooth. "You bet. Shane pitched some really hard balls too."

"Didn't want to make it too easy on you." His gaze shifted to Lauren. "You're looking a little pink. Did you get some exercise too?"

She narrowed her eyes. "Yes, I did. I went to the museum."

"Uh-huh. See anything interesting?"

He didn't believe her, which ticked her off. "Yes. I saw plenty." She picked up Josh's bat and ball, which he'd left near the door, and stuck them in the hall closet.

"Are you going to see him again?"

She shrugged. "Maybe. Maybe not."

He'd walked up behind her and was too close for her liking. She felt like she couldn't breathe, and her heartbeat had picked up a notch. Being a doctor, she knew the physical signs, and this wasn't good. She ducked around him and spoke to Josh. "Why don't you go wash up and then watch some TV? Shane needs some help with his studying."

"Don't worry about me," Shane said. "If you're too tired..."

"I'm not too tired," she said quickly. "Walking around a museum is not exactly an aerobic exercise."

He said nothing but raised an eyebrow. "You're not interested then?"

"Just because I didn't have sex after a couple of dates doesn't mean I'm not interested." She sighed. "But I am starting to think I'd prefer to keep Kevin as a friend."

"One doesn't necessarily preclude the other." He looked her dead in the eye.

"Discussion over." She stalked into the kitchen. "Let's move on to the important stuff. What did you bring today?"

While he sorted out his books, Lauren made two plates of cheese and crackers and apple slices. She gave one to Josh and set the other on the kitchen table. They hit the books for a couple of hours, and then Shane yawned and stood up.

"Great class, teacher." He touched her nose. "Thanks again." He glanced at Josh, who'd moved from the TV to his Legos. "I'll see you next Sunday," he called to the boy.

"Okay." Josh glanced up. "The park was cool. Thanks."

Lauren walked him to the door. "He really appreciates your taking the time to see him, and so do I."

He tucked a lock of her hair behind her ear. "As far as seeing Josh, I enjoy it too." His eyes met hers. "I'm also glad you got out of the house today. I didn't like thinking about you and him together."

"Shane..."

"Don't say it. I know we're friends, and that's the way we both want to keep it."

"Exactly. You're going to be a doctor, and the last thing you need is a distraction like Josh and me."

"Right. And you need a solid guy, someone who can give you both what you deserve. Not a basket case like me."

"You are no such thing," she said softly.

"Am too. Look, the reason I didn't call you for more than a week was not because we'd kissed. I was fighting old demons." His eyes slid away from hers. "I'm a recovering alcoholic, and I had the urge for a drink. It happens from time to time."

She froze. "You're an alcoholic?"

"No. I said 'recovering.' I gave up drinking a year ago." He shrugged. "When I got back, I was messed up and hit the bottle much too hard. That was a very black period for me. I was depressed and angry over the whole Iraq mess and in pain because of my stump, and I hated the old prosthesis they had me wear...." He looked down at the floor. "I was homeless for about nine months and didn't want help."

"That was before you got the i-limb then?"

He nodded. "Yes, I got this about ten months ago, and it changed my life around. I don't feel like a freak anymore, and my quality of life has improved. It's way more functional than anything else they've fitted me with."

"I have been wondering about that. How does it work? You can grasp things—even throw a baseball with my son."

He nodded. "There's an individual motor for each finger which bends at its natural joint. This particular model has 24 different grip options controlled by a Bluetooth softwear app. You can program it for a wider grip or smaller if you're working on something that needs precision. It can also be controlled by muscle signals as well." He showed her.

"I mean, this baby is stellar compared to what I've had in the past. I can type with it, tie a shoelace, open doors with a key. It also allows me to exert pressure, so I can grip heavier objects."

"Wow—that is unbelievable! What technology. Amazing. So, that's why you can do all the things you do—like be a medic."

"Yes. And this flesh-colored material covers up the robotic appearance, so it's not quite so noticeable when I'm out in public."

"I see." She bit her bottom lip. "I also get why you're so proud of it. But Shane, I know that you've sacrificed for your country and have gone through enormous difficulties, but as a parent, I need to ask: Did you drink this week?"

"No, but I wanted too." He looked down at his feet. "I controlled my urges this time, but what about the next? And the next? It won't be the last time. It never is."

She stood rooted to the spot. "My husband was killed by someone with two DUIs. I became a spokesperson for Mothers Against Drunk Drivers." Her eyes searched his face. "I have little or no tolerance for people who have no regard for themselves or others. Do you go to meetings?"

"I've been." He shifted his feet. "Didn't like it much."

"Well, you better start again. You need help, and they provide it. Would you like me to go with you?"

"No. I can control this. Getting into a good med school is too important for me to screw up."

She stepped away from the door. "I can't have you drinking and being around Josh."

"I don't intend to." His eyes roamed over her face. "But I'm not whole, and I don't know if I'll ever be."

She didn't say anything at first. "You will be if you can stay sober. And get help. It takes time, that's all."

"What about you? You lost your husband three years ago, but you haven't fully recovered from that. I see it in your eyes. I hear it in your voice when you speak of him."

She smiled, but it hurt to do so. "We both have deep wounds to heal, but we're on our way to recovery."

"Not sure about that, but we've made it out of ICU."

She bit her bottom lip. "Yes, that we have." She moved forward and touched his shoulder. "I like you, Shane Dawson. Please don't screw this up."

EPISODE FOUR

CHAPTER SIXTEEN

Shane stopped for a quick bite to eat before he returned home. The second he opened the door, he sensed someone's presence. "Brent?" He dropped his books on the floor. "Is that you?"

Major barked, and jumped all over the place. He ran back and forth from Shane to the kitchen, peeing in his excitement.

Brent strolled out of the kitchen, a huge grin on his face. "Nobody else better have a key." He hugged his friend. "See you got a dog. He's a bit crazed, isn't he?"

Shane laughed. "He's in training to be a hero dog, but he's got issues. Likes people too much."

The dog wagged his tail and tried to jump on Brent. He knocked him off, but gave him a pat on his head. "I see that." He straightened up. "So, how the hell are you? Let me see this million-dollar hand of yours."

Shane held his i-limb up for inspection. "Top of the line. Don't come much prettier than this."

Brent nodded. "Damn, that is something." He wiggled the mechanical fingers. "Do these really work?"

"Sure do. Thumb rotates too. Fingers are controlled by electrical signals from the nerves in my arm. Pretty cool technology."

"I'll say. That's fantastic. Must have taken some training to figure out how to use it, right?"

"Yeah, it was extensive, but they have a great support system and problem diagnosis if I run into problems. So far, everything's working as it should."

"That's great. You look good," Brent said. "Healthier and happier than when I left."

"I stopped drinking. Fell off the wagon once, but otherwise I've been sober for eleven months and twenty-four days."

"Glad to hear that." He lightly punched Shane in the arm, which got Major barking, and jumping around.

Brent was a big man, built like an NFL linebacker. Had to be four inches taller than Shane and outweighed him by at least thirty pounds. He could drink anyone under the table, and Shane had foolishly done his best in their mis-spent youth to keep up.

"I figured you'd died or something," Shane said, trying not to let him see how worried he'd been. "Haven't heard from you in over a month."

"You're my nursemaid now?" Brent knuckled his shoulder. "Figured I'd give you a surprise. See if you've turned my apartment into your own little love shack."

"Naw. No time for that."

"What about this doctor friend? Or Melanie? I figured you two might have reconnected. Girl was the love of your life."

"If she'd been that, I would never have left," Shane said a little too quickly. "When I came back all messed up... well, let's just say whatever feelings we'd once had were long gone."

"That's too bad. We had some good times together. Remember that rafting trip? How she fell in and came up without her bikini top?" Brent grinned. "She was some looker."

"Let's not go down memory lane. Suffice to say she didn't want to be saddled with a cripple."

"I'm surprised. I always liked her."

"Then you should have married her."

Brent laughed. "So, that leaves the doctor. Jake told me you'd met someone. Details, man."

"Nothing to tell. It's more like a business arrangement. Her husband is dead, and her six-year-old kid needs male companionship. I take him out on Sundays, and Lauren makes it up by tutoring me. Works all around."

"Yeah?" Brent's expression was skeptical. "You sure you're not using the kid to get to the hot mom?"

Shane shook his head. "It's not like that."

"Then why do you look a little worked up right now? What aren't you telling me? I bet she's real pretty, right?"

"Beautiful. And smart. But she's not interested in someone like me. Hell no. She can do a whole lot better than me." He shrugged it off. "Besides, her son is her life, and he wants a dad. That's all he talks about."

"You know how that feels. Been there, done that."

Shane nodded. "Yeah, it was rough growing up without a father around. Funny thing is, when my mom did remarry, it was too late. I was nearly twelve, turning into a snarky teenager, and I didn't want some new dad telling me what I could and couldn't do."

"Yeah, you were kind of snarky," Brent teased. "But don't dodge the subject. Have you taken the doc to bed?"

"No way. Lately, she's been seeing some attorney who's recently separated. They both have sons who are friends. Convenient, huh?"

Brent cocked an eyebrow. "So, when did that ever stop you?"

"I'm not that guy any longer," Shane said, and ran a hand through his hair. "I haven't got the time to date, and hell, if she's interested in remarrying, the hospital's loaded with doctors. She could have her pick. Why would she waste her time with me?"

"Maybe she likes lawyers better."

Shane turned away from Brent to pick up his books. "Why are we talking about her? I want to know about you." He walked across the room to the dining table, which he'd turned into his desk. "Still having fun hunting down the Taliban?"

"This conversation needs a beer. I bought a six-pack on my way here. Now that you're not drinking, will it bother you if I have one?"

"No problem. I'll take a soda, though."

Brent returned from the kitchen with a German beer and passed him a soda. Sitting on the couch, he put his feet up on the coffee table. Major sat down on the carpet under his legs.

Brent drank most of his beer before he started talking. "The Taliban have been testing our new battalion with repeated ambush attacks, so we stepped it up a notch. Believe we killed a top commander in Sangin in a drone strike."

"No shit. That's great news."

"Yeah, but we lost twenty-four Marines in one weekend, plus hundreds more who were wounded." Brent stretched his arms over his head, flexing his shoulders. "Where I am, it's constant warfare. They're out to kill us, and we're doing our best to return the favor."

"Ah, the joys of war." Shane tilted his head back and closed his eyes. "Nope. Don't miss it." He leaned forward and looked directly at his friend. "I don't like what's going on over there. Kids are getting beaten up bad. What about you flyboys? Holding your own?"

"We lose a few, but we're hanging in." He shrugged and reached for his beer. "What can I say?"

"You haven't told me how you got away. Go AWOL?"

Brent gave a short laugh. "No. Dad had a stroke a few days ago. They gave me a week's leave."

"Damn. I didn't know." He got off the chair to give Brent an awkward hug. "He was like a dad to me, too. I spoke to Jake not long ago, and he didn't say anything."

"It only happened on Thursday, and I flew home straight away. He's a tough old bird. I expect he'll pull through."

John Harrington was a retired general who'd seen many battles, raised three sons, survived the death of his first wife, and at seventy could bench press darn near twice his age.

"You bet he will," Shane said. "He still has Bambi taking good care of him, doesn't he?"

Brent made a face. "Her name's Tiffany, and yes, she's still hanging around."

A year after his wife passed away, John had taken a new wife, a woman only a few years older than his eldest son.

"Too bad," Shane muttered.

"My thinking too."

They talked for hours, catching up on the year they'd spent apart, rehashing the good old days when their troubles had been relatively simple. War had changed that for both men, and they knew they'd never view the world in quite the same way again.

"So, I guess I'm sleeping on the couch tonight," Shane said, getting up to search for sheets.

"No. I booked a room at the Hilton down the road."

Shane turned to him in surprise. "You shouldn't have done that. This is your home. You can come here anytime you like. Besides, I want you to stay. Who knows when we'll see each other again."

"I know, but I'm heading back overseas tomorrow."

"What about your Dad? You said you had a week." Shane didn't bother to hide his disappointment. They'd been friends for so long, they could be honest with one another.

"It got cut short. My CO said I'm needed. Dad's stabilized and there's nothing I can do. No point in sitting around staring at walls."

"I hate to see you go back so soon. You just got here." Shane stood there, looking at his one and only true friend, closer than any brother could be. "At least stay the night." He didn't want to say good-bye. There was too great a chance he'd never see Brent again.

Brent stood up. "You know how it is. It gets in your blood. My squad needs me, and I can't hang around here while they're getting shot up."

"You should never have enlisted. This was my war, not yours."

Brent's jaw clenched. "That's the stupidest thing I've ever heard you say."

"It might be stupid, but it's true. If I hadn't been captured, you'd never have joined the military. You did it because of me."

"Don't be an ass. You're not that important." Brent glared at him. "I have my own reasons too. I'm sick of this terrorist bullshit and what they've done to this country. Got everyone running around scared. It needs to end, and it needs to end now. Before they do something really stupid and blow us all up."

Shane looked down at the floor. He was sick of it too, and so tired of seeing other young men returning from the battlefields without legs and arms and other body parts. But the physical disabilities were the easier wounds to heal. The heart and the head were the major casualties of this war.

"Whatever you think," Shane glanced at his friend and was afraid for him, "be careful, you hear?"

CHAPTER SEVENTEEN

After Brent left, Shane roamed around the empty apartment, anxious and too wound up to sleep. He should have insisted that Brent stay the night. They hadn't seen each other in a year, and who knew when they would again. If ever.

"You fucking jerk!" he said aloud. "You, of all people, should know better than to go off to war." He punched his fist into a wall, welcoming the quick shot of pain. Bloody war was enough to make a man crazy. Talking out loud, ranting and raving like a lunatic. He was one of them now. Not mad enough to be locked up, but not right in the head either.

He flung himself onto the couch and flicked on the TV, and then stared at the screen mindlessly. He wanted to talk to someone, but the only person besides Brent that he felt comfortable talking to was Lauren. He couldn't call her, though. She'd be sound asleep, and even if she weren't, he didn't want to chance waking up Josh.

But he sure did want to hear her voice.

She always seemed to know exactly what to say. And the way she looked at him made him feel like a man again. He wanted to be a fully functional guy who could make good love to a woman and watch her face flush, her body tremble with pleasure. Damn war. It had stolen his manhood too.

Destroyed his confidence, his pride, his ability to stroke and please a woman.

He curled his one good hand into a fist and hit his thigh hard. The pain felt good. Better than feeling nothing. Then he looked at his prized i-limb. What woman would want to go to bed with a man and a stump? Hell, he didn't even know if he should keep it on or take it off. Either way, it would be a turn-off, and he didn't want to see pity or revulsion in another woman's eyes. Once was enough. The look on Melanie's face when she'd come to see him at Walter Reed had cut right through him.

Maybe he'd be lucky and his needs would simply go away. He didn't want a hooker, and the only woman he did want deserved someone worthier than he.

~

"So how did your date go the other night?" Trish asked Lauren during a lull between patients.

"We had a wonderful dinner, if that's what you mean." Lauren didn't want to discuss Kevin, or her lack of response.

"And after dinner? I hope you at least kissed the poor guy."

"Of course I did. And there's no reason to feel sorry for Kevin. Trust me, he can hold his own."

Margaret giggled. "Maybe he'd rather you hold it for him."

Lauren shook her head, but couldn't resist smiling. "You are naughty, you know that?"

She laughed. "Anthony thinks so. He likes it when I talk dirty."

"Things are going good with you two?" Lauren asked. "What's it been? A whole week?"

"Funny." Margaret tossed her head and tilted her chin in the air. "You're a very funny lady, you know that?"

Trish winked at Margaret. "Forget Anthony for a minute. I still want to hear about Lauren's kiss."

"It wasn't earth shattering, if that's what you want to know. But he also came over on Sunday and we had the house to ourselves."

"Whoa! Now we're getting somewhere," Trish said, a hopeful expression on her face. "Don't hold out on us."

"That's what he thought too—that he'd get somewhere," Lauren said. "But I took him to preview an auction at a museum that I'd been anxious to see."

"Well, you can kiss that one good-bye," Margaret said, rolling her eyes.

"*Au contraire.* He hasn't stopped calling me since. 'When are we going to get together? Can I come over? Need someone to come and tuck you in?'" Lauren made a face. "His persistence is both flattering and annoying. I'm still not sure about him yet."

"What are you waiting for?" Trish asked. "From what you've told us, he's pretty much perfect, isn't he?"

"Something is missing. I'm not feeling the passion, you know what I mean?"

"Maybe it's because you're tight with Shane." Margaret sighed, and her cheeks grew pink. "He's a hard act to follow."

"You're not still hung up on him, are you?" Lauren didn't know why it bothered her, but it did.

"No, of course not. But if he wasn't lusting after you, it might be different."

"He's not. For heaven's sake, Margaret, I told you that we made an arrangement that benefits us both. There is absolutely nothing going on." She could feel her cheeks heat up as she spoke. The last thing she wanted was for Margaret, and the rest of the hospital, to know she had a growing attraction for Shane.

"Well then, what's keeping you out of Kevin's bed?" Trish asked, hitching her butt on the side of a stretcher.

"I'm just taking my time, making sure this is what I want. When I know, he will too."

"Don't take too much time," Trish said. "Women will line up for the privilege of going out with a wealthy, handsome divorced man."

"Well, good luck to them." Lauren pretended to yawn. "We have another date this Saturday, and if it goes well, who knows?"

She'd agreed to see Kevin once more—it would be the final test. The few kisses they'd shared hadn't lit any fires, but maybe he was holding back too. They both had their kids' friendships to consider. But this was it. If the chemistry remained dormant on Saturday night, she'd let him down gently.

The ER became active again. It was the usual chaos, but the hospital staff took it in stride. A car accident brought in two; and then a seventeen-year-old kid, higher than a kite, who'd stabbed his sister and then himself. A beaten wife, brought in by her husband, and who refused to file a complaint. She insisted she'd fallen on the sidewalk outside their home. And on and on it went.

Exhausted to the point of feeling giddy, Lauren finally managed a short break. On her way to the cafeteria, she spotted Shane and Rick bringing in a stretcher.

She rushed up to them. "What have you got here?"

"Gunshot wound," Rick answered.

The young Hispanic man looked to be in his late twenties. His face was purple, and he was breathing in loud, painful gasps. His shirt was stained with blood, and Lauren could see the bullet hole between his sixth and seventh rib.

"The exit wound's under his armpit," Shane told her. "Might have nicked his lung."

Lauren's tiredness vanished. Within minutes she had a chest tube set up and a scalpel in hand. Her fingers trembled for a second, and she sucked in a deep breath, forcing herself to relax. Once the tube was in, she watched the blood pour from his chest like the red sea.

"We've got his pulse and blood pressure," she announced. "He'll live. At least for now."

"Good job, Doctor." She knew it was Shane who spoke, and she nodded in acknowledgment without looking up.

When the man was stabilized enough to be moved to a room, she pulled him aside. "I was about to grab a coffee when you walked in. Care to join me?"

He nodded and looked around for his partner. "Hey, Rick. I'm gonna grab a coffee with the doc. Call me if something comes up."

Rick nodded.

"Bad day?" Shane asked her, as they walked down the corridor.

"Yes, but probably no worse than normal. It's just that it never stops, you know?"

"Come on." He grinned and shook his head. "You thrive on the activity. I've seen you in action a zillion times. It's like you go into a zone or something."

"No way. I do not."

"Do too. It's kind of sexy."

She felt her cheeks heat up. "Saving lives isn't sexy. There is nothing even slightly romantic about it."

"I'm just saying, you look flushed, excited." He cocked an eyebrow. "It's a turn-on."

"I do not," she answered hotly. "And the idea is deplorable."

"You're cute when you're angry."

"Oh, now I'm cute, am I?" She glared at him, her hand on the cafeteria door. He was standing a little too close to her, and she could smell his day's sweat mixed with his special scent. It had its own appeal.

"Cute and sexy." He winked and held the door for her to go through.

She had to duck under his arm. "You better take that back. You know how I feel about work." Her chin went up. "I'm a professional, and that's all. I have no time or inclination to be anything but."

"More's the pity," he murmured.

She whipped her head around, and found him staring at her butt. "Find anything interesting?"

He had the decency to blush, which made him all the more adorable. "You want some dinner?" she asked. "I'm starving and I'm buying."

"Now that's an offer I can't refuse." He picked up two trays and handed her one. "Not often I can con a pretty lady into paying for dinner."

"I doubt that," she scoffed. "I bet it happens all the time."

"Not that lucky, I'm afraid."

"You could be if you wanted to be." She stepped in front of him and kept her eyes glued on the sign that listed the day's specials. Every nerve end in her body was keenly aware of his presence. As a doctor she knew the symptoms, but as a woman she guarded against them.

"Is that another offer?" His hand accidentally bumped into hers.

"In your dreams," she said over her shoulder. Her stomach fluttered and she put a hand over it, hoping to tamp it down. Being around Shane made her jumpy, feeling things she wasn't meant to feel.

"Oh, yeah. I can dream, and then some." Shane stood so close to her that she could feel his breath on the back of her neck.

She turned to face him. "What is it you want, Shane? Sometimes you flirt with me, and maybe I'm making a big deal out of nothing since you flirt with everyone, but it's annoying."

"Why does it bother you?" Shane gave her a smug smile. "As you say, I flirt with everyone. Besides, I think you like it."

"I do not. It confuses me, and I don't like to be confused." She stared straight into his eyes, not caring who could see them, or if tongues were wagging. This was important. She had to make him understand. "I don't play games and I prefer to keep everything out in the open. You say you aren't whole, that you don't want a woman in your life, yet I get vibes from you. Why?"

"Maybe I'm as confused by all this as much as you." He took her arm and moved her down the line. "What would you like to eat?" When she didn't reply, he told the girl behind the counter, "I'll have the meatloaf with all the trimmings. She will too."

Lauren looked at him. "I can order my own food."

"Then why don't you?"

"Are you always this bossy?" she retorted, wondering why she'd invited him for dinner.

"Are you always this difficult? We're just having a bite to eat."

She looked at the embarrassed serving girl, who had one plate ready and was waiting on the other.

"Meatloaf will be fine. Thank you."

Once their plates were loaded, they headed for a table near the window. "I'm sorry if I seem snarky," she said. "It's been a rough day."

"I should apologize, too. You wanted straight answers and I didn't give them to you." He reached across the table to give her hand a gentle squeeze. "Besides, I refuse to argue with a woman who buys dinner."

She laughed. "You're quite the charmer, aren't you?"

"And I think you have a problem with that."

"Not if it's genuine. Like I said, I can't tell with you." She tried to read his eyes, but they weren't telling her much.

"You asked me what I want. Truth is... I'm not sure."

"About what?"

"Us." He looked away. "I know you probably want to get married again, if for no reason than to provide a dad for Josh. And I think that's great." He leaned closer and spoke quietly. "But there's definitely some sexual attraction going on between us, and I don't want it to get in the way. You need to find someone stable."

She toyed with her food, not looking at him. "I do want to have a relationship with someone someday. But Josh is my main focus for now, and I'm not in any great rush. What we have going is fine. Josh gets to spend time with you, and I can help you get what you want."

"I know. On paper it looks good, but I don't want you to miss out on something special because I'm hanging around." He took a mouthful of food, and when he'd swallowed, spoke again. "I think I left my sex drive back there in the desert, along with my hand."

She laughed. "I doubt that very much."

"I haven't been with anyone since—since my return."

"Wow! Really?" She wasn't sure how that made her feel. Glad in some ways, but sad too. What kind of a life was that for him? She played with her mashed potatoes, no longer feeling hungry. "Maybe you should. It's not right for you to miss out on something so fundamental and important to your emotional well-being." She spoke in her doctor voice. "I know I'm a fine one to preach but you know my reasons."

He picked up a bun, broke it in half and dipped it into his food. "Don't worry about my well-being. Take care of yours first. You might feel differently about Kevin if you gave him a chance."

Lauren felt a sharp little dagger in the pit of her stomach. She understood his reluctance to go to bed with just anyone, because she shared it. But it hurt that he was so eager to push her into the arms of another man just to keep their relationship status quo.

Well, no problem. A man who cared so little was certainly not worth caring about.

CHAPTER EIGHTEEN

Lauren primped for her date with Kevin, and she was not the primping kind. But she'd stopped at the hair salon and had her hair trimmed and styled, and had treated herself to a manicure and pedicure, determined to be at her most seductive best.

She had a gnawing in her belly that wouldn't go away. She was still rankled that Shane kept trying to toss her into someone else's bed, but truth be told, he might be right. Once she made love with Kevin, her feelings could change dramatically. And if they didn't, well, who would it hurt? Kevin might be disappointed, but he'd get over it quick enough.

They were going out for dinner, and the boys were spending the night together again at Kevin's apartment. Kevin had told Josh and Brad they were going out on a date, even though Lauren had told him repeatedly that she didn't like the idea. Seeing the hope in Josh's eyes deepened her concern, but Kevin insisted the kids were fine with it.

Regardless of what their sons did or didn't know, Lauren had promised herself that this was the night. She only wished she had more enthusiasm for this particular project.

And that she wasn't thinking of it as a "project" in the first place. But never mind. She'd always enjoyed sex, and once they moved past the awkward part, she was sure it would be a pleasing experience.

She hoped.

After reapplying her pale pink lipstick, she turned away from the mirror, knowing her appearance might not stop traffic, but it was as good as it gets.

"Josh, are you ready?" she called to him. "Mr. Henderson should be here any minute, and then we'll drive you back to his place so you can stay with Brad."

Josh came out of his room, dragging his backpack. "Do I have to spend the night again?" he whined. "Last time he wanted the room dark and then told ghost stories. He said if I fell asleep, I might get my head chopped off."

"He said that?" Lauren put her hands on her son's shoulders and bent down to his height. "That wasn't very nice and I'll mention it to his father. He shouldn't be scaring you, but you know it's not real, don't you? There's no such thing as ghosts. It's all make believe."

"Yeah, I guess so. But late, late in the night, I woke up and I'm sure I felt something touch my leg. I got scared and turned on the light but nothing was there."

"Sweetheart, see? There weren't any ghosts. It was your imagination working overtime." She kissed his cheek. "I'll tell Brad no more ghost stories or you won't be able to come over again."

"Don't tell him that, Mom. He'll think I'm a wuss."

"No, he won't." She smiled, and touched his upturned nose. "You're the bravest kid I know."

"You're just saying that because you have to."

"I'm saying it because it's the truth, and I love you." They both turned when they heard the knock on the door. "Okay, Superboy, it's time to roll."

She opened the door to let Kevin in. "Hey, don't you look handsome tonight?" He was wearing a sports jacket over a pink shirt, and cream-colored dress pants. He liked nice clothes, and wore them well.

"You don't look so bad yourself," he said with a grin. Before she could move away from the door, he leaned in and kissed her cheek. "You two ready to go?"

"We are. Say hello to Mr. Henderson, Josh."

"Hello, Mr. Henderson."

"Hello, Josh. Brad is looking forward to the sleepover tonight. He's got some new movies to watch."

"Cool." Josh grabbed his backpack. "I've got popcorn and a big bag of Doritos."

"Sounds like you two kids are going to have fun." He put a hand on Lauren's back to guide her out the door. "I'm going to take your mom for a nice dinner, and we might watch a movie too."

"Mom doesn't like movies. Only the news and the history and food channel."

"Well, I'm sure we'll find something interesting to do." He gave Lauren a naughty-boy smile and let his hand linger on her back.

She scooted out of his reach and grabbed Josh's bag. "Do you have my cell phone number with you?" she asked him.

"Sure. I always have it. Otherwise, you worry."

"Good. Just checking. If you get scared, you can always call me. You know that, right?"

"Why would he get scared?" Kevin asked.

She put a hand on Josh's shoulder. "Brad was teasing him on their last sleepover. Told ghost stories, and said if he fell asleep, they'd come in and cut off his head."

"He said that?" Kevin laughed and shook his head. "What a little rascal."

"Can you ask him not to do it again?" She folded her arms, and tried not to scowl. "Josh spent half the night awake, looking for monsters."

"Okay, okay." He slid up beside her and whispered, "You might want to toughen him up a bit. You know how kids are."

She stiffened. "There is nothing wrong with how I'm raising my son."

"Of course not." Kevin smiled to soften his words. "I know you're trying to be Supermom and make up for the fact he doesn't have a dad, that's all."

"I think he's tough enough for a six-year-old."

"You're right. I apologize. I shouldn't have said that." Kevin flashed a smile.

"Kevin." She looked him in the eye. "Maybe this dinner isn't such a good idea."

"Come on, Lauren. I didn't mean to offend you." He had the car door open, and Josh was already strapped into the backseat. "I promise not to spoil the evening by saying another word. Except that you look gorgeous tonight. Pretty dress, and what did you do to your hair?"

She licked her bottom lip, giving herself time to answer. There was no point in making a scene, but if he dared to judge her son again, it would be the last time.

~

They dined at the new Queensview Steakhouse on the second floor of Parker's Lighthouse, enjoying a pleasant conversation along with the good food. Kevin was perfectly charming, and once again Lauren was put at ease. He was intelligent, knowledgeable, and attractive. She would see how the night progressed before making any decisions about him. But at the moment things were looking up.

The wine had mellowed her, and she leaned against his side as they walked back to his car. He gave her warm glances as he drove, and once or twice his hand touched her thigh.

They had so much in common, they liked and respected each other, and they both deserved some romance. If it led to love and a lifetime commitment, all the better. But she refused to think that far ahead. Tonight, if all went well, they would simply make love.

CHAPTER NINETEEN

The moment she unlocked her door and they stepped inside, Kevin tugged her into his arms. She went willingly enough, sliding her hands up the length of his muscular biceps. She knew he used the gym every chance he got, and had the body to prove it.

He walked her backward, his lips never leaving hers. When her legs met the sofa, he moved in closer. His hands were running up and down her back, getting lower with every stroke. His hips were pressed against hers, and she could feel his erection.

She broke off the kiss and tried to push him away gently, wanting nothing more than to take it slowly. "What's the rush? We have all night."

He gave her a wolfish smile. "I've been waiting a long time for this. For you."

She frowned. "What do you mean? We've been friends for years."

"Even when I was married." He ran the back of his hand down her cheek, then leaned in and whispered in her ear, "You turned me on."

"Kevin." She pushed him away. "Don't say that." She shook her head, feeling anything but turned on. "You had a good marriage, at least for a while. Didn't you?"

"It was okay for the first few years, but we drifted apart. Busy careers and all that."

"I was married when we first met. You liked Jeremy."

"True, but I liked you better." He moved closer, then seemed to think better of it and gave her a little breathing room. "Most guys think about other women sexually, even if they don't act on it. It's natural. You should know that."

"I know no such thing." Her desire had slipped away, and she turned toward the door. "This conversation is creepy, and I think you should leave."

"Not tonight, sweetheart." He moved quickly, getting between her and the door. "I let you get away with that once, but you're not going to keep this game up. I know you want me. Don't play hard to get. It's not becoming."

"I'm not playing."

He grabbed her hands and tugged on them. "Come here. I can make you feel good. You know I can."

She was about to tell him what she thought of that idea, but the phone rang, saving her the trouble. She turned to get it, but Kevin again stepped in front of her.

"Leave it," he said. "I don't want you distracted."

"I need to get it. It could be Josh. Oh, dammit." She just remembered that she had turned off the ringer to her cell phone in the restaurant and had forgotten to turn it back on. He might have called her cell and now was calling the house. "Josh has probably been calling me."

The phone kept ringing, and she attempted to get to it. Kevin again blocked her.

"He's fine," he said smoothly. "What trouble can he get into at my place?"

"I don't know, but I need to answer my phone." She glared at him. "Get out of my way."

He picked up the phone, hit end, then tossed the handset onto the counter. "Later."

"How dare you!" Bristling with indignation, she pushed her way around him, reaching for the phone.

His strong arms stopped her. "Don't be mad," he said. "You can talk to Josh later." He kissed her neck. She tried to squirm away, but his arms only tightened their hold.

"Let me go." She pushed at his arms, but he didn't release her.

"Don't be a tease. You want it, I know you do."

She stared straight into his eyes. "Kevin, I'm warning you. If you don't take your hands off me, you'll regret it."

He laughed and tugged at her blouse, the buttons popping free. His gaze fell to her breasts, and she sorely regretted the pretty black lace bra she'd bought for the occasion.

"Nice." He took hold of her breasts, squeezing them together.

"You bastard." She smacked him as hard as she could. He didn't let her go, didn't move away, so she smacked him again. Then she spun and grabbed the phone.

"Back off," she told him, ready to dial 911. "Get out of here before I do you some real damage."

He seemed unconcerned. "I've played your games long enough, Lauren, and now you're going to play mine."

Before she could react, he grabbed her wrist so hard, the phone dropped out of her hand. Tears filled her eyes.

"Get out!" she screamed.

Kevin lunged for her, but she was too fast for him. Her right knee came up and made solid contact with his groin.

He backed away, holding his hands over his private parts, cursing her and grimacing in pain. "You bitch. You're going to pay for that."

"Go to hell!" she shouted, and ran for her purse and the door. She had to get to safety and call Josh back.

She flung the door wide, and Shane stood there. "Shane. How did you get here?"

"Josh called me when he couldn't reach you. What happened? I heard you scream." His gaze dropped to her exposed breasts, and then he glanced past her and saw Kevin, moaning and holding his crotch.

He crossed the room in a few quick strides and grabbed Kevin's hair with his bionic hand, looking ready to tear the man's head off. "What did you do to her, you bastard?"

Kevin panted, "She kneed me in the balls. I only wanted to kiss her."

"When a woman screams, it means she's protesting, you fucking creep. Now get lost before I really lose my temper."

Kevin straightened up, shooting both Lauren and Shane a scathing look. "This isn't over. I'll be seeing you soon," he added to Lauren.

She ignored him and spoke to Shane. "Josh is spending the night with his son. We have to go get him."

"Of course. My car's outside. But first..." He glanced again at her breasts, and she quickly covered up.

"I'll need to change. You'll wait, won't you?"

Kevin's face had flushed an unattractive purple. "You know something. You two might deserve each other." He gave Lauren a contemptuous look. "You need a guy you can control, and what better than a one-handed freak?"

Shane took one step toward Kevin. Lauren stepped between the men, facing Shane. "He's not worth it. Let him go."

"If you insist, but personally, I think we should call the cops."

Kevin sneered. "Go ahead. I know most of them anyway. Good pals with the judges too."

Lauren ignored him, her eyes on Shane. "I'll change my top, then we'll go rescue my son."

Kevin stormed out. Shane stood guard while Lauren went into her bedroom to change and to wipe the smeared lipstick off her face.

"You okay?" he asked quietly when she returned.

"I'm okay." She walked over to him and put her arms around him, resting her forehead against his chest. "Thank you for coming to the rescue."

He kissed the top of her head. "Looks like you handled things pretty well on your own." He lifted her chin. "I'm so sorry. I encouraged you to go out with that asshole."

"Yeah, you did. But I sure didn't see that coming. He seemed like a nice enough guy. Boy, was I wrong."

"I wanted to kill him. I still do."

She put a hand over his mouth. "Don't say that. Don't even think it."

He kissed her hand and looked into her eyes. "You've had a helluva night, and I'm just glad I got here in time."

"Me too." She moved away from him, struck with a feeling of loss. She longed for his warmth and comfort, but she needed to take care of her son.

She linked her arm in his. "Come on. Let's go get Josh."

CHAPTER TWENTY

Shane was silent for most of the ride. He couldn't get rid of the image of Lauren—wild-eyed and frightened—as she'd opened that door. If Kevin had touched her, violated her in any way, Shane wasn't sure what he would have done. But it wouldn't have been pretty.

If Josh hadn't called him, or if he hadn't gotten there in time, who knows what would have happened to her.

"What are you thinking?" she asked. "You look furious. Did I do something wrong?"

"Of course not." He darted a quick glance at her. "Lauren, I was walking to your door and I heard you scream. I was about to bust that door down when it flew open and you rushed out. When I saw what he'd done, torn your blouse, I nearly went nuts." His hand shook. "I wanted to smash his face in. If you hadn't stopped me, I probably would have punched him one."

"I can't imagine you ever getting violent, and I don't want to either." She gave a little shiver, then folded her arms. "Let's not talk about tonight. Can we just drop it for now?"

"What if Josh hadn't called me?" he asked quietly.

"But he did." She tried to smile, but the effort was too great, even for a trouper like her. "We'll have to thank him later."

He could see she was struggling to hold it all together. She kept rubbing at a spot between her brows, trying to ease the tension away. But still, he couldn't let it go.

"He said he called your cell phone."

"I turned the ringer off in the restaurant, and then I forgot to turn it back on. I feel so bad. Poor Josh."

"He called the house a few times, too, then called me. He's one smart kid." He wanted to break something. Like Kevin's big nose.

"Yes, he is." This time, she did smile. "He deserves a double fudge sundae."

"How can you be making jokes? I'm still livid." He put out his good hand. "See? I'm shaking."

She laughed and squeezed his arm. "Kevin's a conceited ass, but I seriously don't think he'd have jeopardized his reputation and career by raping me."

"You'd think he was smarter than that, but I'm not convinced. He certainly was heading that direction. Forcing himself on you."

"I could handle him." She bit her lip and looked away. "I think. He did have me scared."

"Bastard," he muttered.

"I'm glad you didn't have to bust my door down."

He smiled. "Yeah. Me too."

"But I love the idea of you rescuing me." She put her head on his shoulder for a brief moment, then straightened up, regaining her damned control.

"That's what I do. Rescue people."

"I love that about you."

He took his eyes off the road to look at her. She looked so damn pretty, he couldn't turn away. Her cheeks were flushed, and she wore a special smile just for him.

The car swerved, and he almost ran off the road.

"Eyes front, mister," she teased.

"Are you always this bossy?" he said with a hint of a smile.

"And then some. If you stick around long enough, you might see for yourself."

There was an open invitation in her gorgeous blue eyes. "Is that an offer?"

"It is if you want it to be."

"I want it to be." He lifted her delicate, but very capable hand, to his lips. "I don't want you dating anyone else."

"I don't either. Not after this fiasco tonight."

He looked straight ahead. "And I don't think you should get married just so Josh has a dad."

"Trust me, I won't. I had a good marriage once, and even that took work. But I do get lonely at times, and it would be nice to have someone to share my life with. Besides Josh, I mean."

"I know. You're a smart, beautiful, sexy woman. You should have love in your life."

"I do. I have Josh." She darted him a look. "And you."

"I wish I could be more than a friend." He wanted her so bad it was killing him, but she deserved somebody so much better. "I really do."

"Why can't you be?" She bumped shoulders with him. "I have an idea. Why don't you date me?"

"I've told you, Lauren. You need someone grounded, someone whole, someone worthy. I'm none of those things."

"You are, too. And I like talking to you better than anyone else I know."

He glanced at her. "I feel the same."

"So what are we going to do about it?" She kept her eyes on him, waiting for a reply. Her face was calm now. She trusted him to do the right thing.

But what was the right thing? He knew what he wanted, but it wouldn't be fair to her or to Josh. They deserved better than a messed up guy like him.

Finally, he shrugged. "Damned if I know, but one thing's for sure. I don't want you dating guys like Kevin. You need someone who'll treat you and Josh with respect and kindness, the way you both deserve."

"I only know one guy like that." Her blue eyes never wavered from his face. They were full of trust, and hope, and warmth. He felt like a complete fraud.

"You've got a one-track mind," he finally snapped.

"Don't you want to go out with me?" she said in a soft, hurt voice.

"Of course I do. More than anything." He had no right to take this woman, to want her, to love her, but he sure didn't want anyone else with her either. He'd opened this can of worms, and it was too late to screw the cap back on. Damn his mouth. Why hadn't he left well enough alone?

"What are you thinking?" she asked.

He darted a quick look at her. "Are you sure about this? Because we both know it's not a good idea."

She nodded. "Yes, I'm sure. Although I know how terribly busy you are, and it won't be easy to fit me in."

"I think I can manage." Now that he'd agreed, he didn't want to wait. He wanted her too much. "How about tomorrow? We could take Josh to the beach, then maybe you could find a sitter and we could go out for dinner."

"I'm sure Julie can help out. She's my nanny, and she's always willing to work extra hours when she can."

"I have to warn you, though. I haven't been on a real date in a couple of years. Don't expect too much."

"Then it's time you did. And as far as my expectations go, you've already surpassed them."

"Thanks." He flashed a smile to hide his fears. Dating her might be a huge mistake. She might expect him to perform sexually, and he didn't know if he was up to the job.

A few minutes later, they pulled up in front of Kevin's apartment building. Josh was standing on the front steps, backpack in hand, the babysitter keeping him company.

Lauren ran to his side. "You okay, sweetie?"

He nodded and threw himself into her arms. "Where were you? I tried to call. You didn't pick up your phone."

"Oh, honey, I'm so sorry. My ringer was off and I didn't realize it. I'll never let that happen again."

The babysitter quickly apologized. "Sorry, Dr. Reynolds. I don't know what happened. The boys started scrapping right after dinner. They couldn't agree on a movie, then Brad called Josh some not very nice names, and I don't know who threw the first punch. I gave both boys a time-out, but Josh wanted to go home. He got very upset when he couldn't reach you." She put a hand on Josh's shoulder. "I'm so sorry. He's a good boy."

"Thank you. I know he is." Lauren bent down and took her son's face into her hands. "You did the right thing by calling Shane. We're both very glad you did."

"You got that right." Shane ruffled the boy's hair. "How're you doing, champ? You want to go get an ice cream somewhere?"

"Can we, Mom?" His eyes lit up. "I know it's past my bed-time, but I'm not tired."

"Sure, hon. You had a lousy night, and so did I. We all need a little ice cream to make things better."

"Cool." Josh slipped his hand into Shane's bionic one. He seemed to prefer it. "What kind are you gonna have? I like Reese's peanut butter cup. How about you, Shane?"

"I don't know. Let's go to Baskin Robbins and see their flavors."

"I'll have Jamoca almond fudge," Lauren said, slipping her hand into Shane's. She preferred flesh and blood to plastic. "A double."

~

The following day they went to the beach, and Shane offered to give Lauren and Josh bodysurfing lessons. Before hitting the water, Shane turned aside to pull off his prosthetic, attempting to hide behind the board.

Lauren didn't give a crap about seeing a stump, but she glanced at Josh, wondering how he'd react. It took Josh a second or two, but when he spotted the i-limb on the beach towel, he ran toward it.

"Holy cow!" he shouted with glee. "It comes off. Super cool." He picked it up and tried to put it on his own hand, looking frustrated when it wouldn't fit.

Lauren and Shane glanced at each other and then burst into laughter. "Looks like you're going to have to learn to share," she told Shane, who picked the bionic hand up and chased Josh down the beach with it.

Later, the three of them waded into the water with the surfboard, and Shane showed them how it was done. He paddled out to catch a wave, then got up on his knees, and rode the wave in. He demonstrated time and again in a tireless effort to teach them. Neither she nor Josh could get the hang of it, but they had fun trying. Lauren especially enjoyed the hands-on lesson, knowing it was all foreplay.

He was getting to her, and she hoped that she could handle whatever the future held. She trusted Shane, and knew that he'd never intentionally hurt her or Josh, but what if he started drinking again? He'd warned her often enough that he wasn't whole, but she'd never seen that side of him. She only saw the side he cared to show.

Like Kevin. Not that she thought Shane had a dark and dangerous side, but she had to be careful. And yet, every time his eyes met hers, she felt a burst of joy bubbling inside. This worried her most of all.

"You had enough of this for one day?" he asked finally. He flicked the strap of her bikini top. "You're getting pink. Probably time to go in."

"No!" Josh cried. "We aren't tired yet, are we, Mom?"

"Well, honey, truth is, I'm just about done in here. If you boys want to stay longer, okay, but I'm going to head back to the beach and pack things up."

Shane gave her a wink. "Ten minutes, tops. Josh and I will try to catch another wave or two."

"Be careful," she warned. "The wind's picking up."

Shane held the board, and after a few attempts Josh managed to get to his knees. Lauren watched from the shore, so proud of Josh. He was trying hard not to fall off, wanting desperately to please Shane. He loved being with him, but she knew he was like that with every man he met. What would happen if their potential romance ruined a perfectly good friendship? Josh is the one who'd wind up getting hurt.

Maybe she was being selfish, wanting him for herself.

~

When Shane dropped them off, he told her he'd be back at seven and to wear something nice.

"You're coming back?" Josh asked, his face lighting up.

"I am, buddy. I'm going to take your mom out for dinner."

"Can I come?" he asked with a hopeful expression.

"Not this time. We'll be out past your bedtime, and we kept you up late last night."

"Yeah, I know, but I can always skip school tomorrow." He made a face. "I don't want to see that creep, Brad."

"Now, Josh, you know you can't skip school," Lauren said smoothly. "And you can still be friends with Brad, just not best friends. Why don't you invite someone over for a play date this week? Make some new pals."

"I don't know. Some of the kids don't like me. They make fun of me behind my back."

Lauren glanced at Shane, sharing a worried look. "Why is that, sweetheart? What could they not like about you?"

"Sometimes the teacher asks me questions when I haven't been listening, and I hear the kids laughing."

"That's unkind of the children and I would be very disappointed if you did that. But, sweetheart, could you maybe listen a little more"—Lauren spoke gently—"so that the next time it happens you'll know the answer?"

"I try, but sometimes I forget."

"Okay, hon, but try real hard, won't you?"

"Uh-huh."

Shane gave him a hug. "Your mom's right. I didn't do real well in school, but I tried hard. What about sports? You could play T-ball. You're great at it."

"Yeah." A shy smile lit up his face. "I hit a home run. Maybe I can do it again."

"You sure did, slugger." Shane grinned at Lauren. "See you in a couple of hours."

She blew him a kiss. "Thanks for today. It was fun."

Once Shane left, she bathed Josh and fed him dinner. When Julie arrived, she took her shower and got dressed for the evening. She wondered where Shane would take her for their first date. They could grab fast food for all she cared. Being with him was what mattered.

She liked him more than she should. For all his warnings, and all her misgivings, she wanted him.

EPISODE FIVE

CHAPTER TWENTY-ONE

He showed up in a navy blue suit, white shirt, and flashy tie, and looked so darn handsome, Lauren's knees went weak. To keep herself from melting into a puddle at his feet, she backed up, holding onto the back of the couch for support.

"What's the matter?" he asked, looking worried. "Are you okay?"

"I felt faint all of a sudden. Must be low blood sugar. I'm probably hungry after all that exercise today."

He grinned. "Good, because I'm taking you someplace special tonight."

"Can I ask where?"

"No, you can't. But trust me, you're dressed perfect."

She had selected a soft yellow silk dress that gave a hint of cleavage, had a fitted waist, and flared below the hip. It was one of the few designer dresses she owned. Lauren rarely bought dressy clothes because she had no use for them, but she'd needed something for a friend's wedding. The moment she'd seen the dress, she'd known she had to buy it.

Now she was glad she had.

After a quick good night to Julie and Josh, she followed Shane to his car. He drove a late model Toyota hybrid, which she was coming to learn was typical of him. He didn't just want to save lives; he wanted to save the world.

They chatted during the drive along the Pacific coastline, until he pulled up in front of the historic Breakers at the Long Beach Hotel.

"The Sky Room?" she asked in surprise. The Sky Room was considered the most romantic dining room in Southern California.

Two valets appeared and opened both the driver's and the passenger's doors. She stepped out and Shane took her hand.

"Do you approve?" he asked, grinning.

"Most definitely." She hugged his arm. "But I would be just as happy at McDonald's with you."

He laughed. "Next time, I'll remember that."

She gave him a warm smile. "I was here once, a few years ago. It was a twenty-fifth anniversary party for one of the doctors I work with."

"Nice place to celebrate." He linked her hand in the crook of his arm. "Since I've never been through the doors, you can lead the way."

They rode the elevator to the top floor. It was eight o'clock on a Sunday night, and they had no trouble being seated. When Shane slipped something into the maître d's hand, they were given a window table that overlooked the Pacific Ocean and the city skyline.

A wonderful quintet played easy listening music and pop tunes, and between the salad and their main course, she led him onto the dance floor. He guided her into his arms, and she fell into step, moving against him as if they'd been dance partners most of their lives.

They lingered over their dinner, enjoying their conversation and the view. Once they'd finished eating and the waiters had cleared they plates, they danced some more.

He whispered in her ear, "I thought I might take you somewhere else for dessert, unless you'd rather stay here."

"I'm open for suggestions." She tilted her head back and gazed into his eyes. "What did you have in mind?"

"Key lime pie at my place."

"There's an offer I can't refuse."

He gave her a serious look. "You can if you want to."

"I don't want to."

He tugged her tight against him, and she felt his heart hammering along with her own.

"I hope I don't disappoint you," he murmured.

"You can't. No matter what happens, I won't be disappointed."

"You say that, but what if?"

She could see the fear in his eyes, the tight set of his jaw, and hastened to reassure him. "I don't care about what if." She nuzzled his neck. "I just want to be alone with you."

They retrieved his car and drove back to his apartment, with hardly a word spoken between them. Lauren knew a lot was at stake. If this turned into a disaster, their comfortable relationship would suffer, and he might not want to see Josh anymore.

She should put a stop to it, but it was already too late. Besides, every inch of her hungered for his touch, and she was pretty sure he felt the same. He needed her as much as she needed him.

Lauren understood his fear of being a failure in the bedroom, but she'd make sure he wasn't. And if it didn't happen, that was fine too. But he needed to get back on the horse, so to speak, and she was more than happy to accompany him.

She giggled and looked out the window.

"What are you laughing at?" he asked.

"I had a funny thought, not worth sharing." She turned to him and stroked his cheek. "I had a wonderful time tonight, and I'm glad you invited me back to your place. I'd like to see where you live."

"Well, it's not really mine. I'm just minding it for a friend." He told her about Brent, and how he had agreed to take over the rent until Brent returned from Afghanistan.

He seemed relaxed talking about his friend, so she asked questions and learned more in the next ten minutes than she had in the past two months. She heard in vivid detail about his months of being homeless, how he'd bottomed out in a bottle, and that Brent's brother Jake had found him sleeping in a car and had turned his life around.

"I'd like to meet your friends one day."

"I hope you can."

He parked in the underground lot, and then they rode the elevator. Lauren fought back the butterflies in her stomach the whole way.

It would all work out. It had to.

She walked into the apartment, noticing that everything looked new and nice, as well as spotlessly clean, as though no one lived there. The furniture consisted of a black leather couch and recliner, set around a large square coffee table, facing an enormous plasma TV hanging on a wall. Bookshelves lined one wall, and some potted silk plants filled up the corners.

A wicker table with four chairs separated the living room from the kitchen, along with a granite counter with two bar stools.

It was a very nice bachelor pad, but lacked a woman's touch—no carpets or window treatments or pictures to brighten the walls.

She walked around, nodding with approval. "Very nice," she said, and then opened the balcony doors to step outside. A lovely sea breeze was blowing. She stood at the railing, enjoying the partial ocean view, trying to calm her nerves.

He touched her arm, and she turned to face him. "It's such a beautiful night," she said. "I've had a wonderful time."

"It's not over yet."

She laughed. "Oh, I know that, but I wanted you to know how much I appreciated the dinner and dancing and...well, you being you."

He put his hands against her back, and only a scant space separated their bodies. "I don't want your appreciation." He bent his head and kissed her lips. "I'm not sure what I want, but it's a lot more than that."

"I know it's complicated between us, but does it matter?" She ran a finger over his mouth. "I do want you, Shane. Even for just the night. Let's leave it at that."

"That's not enough for a woman like you."

"We're only getting to know each other. Two months isn't long, and we have the rest of our lives to make decisions. Besides, I don't want either of us to make promises we can't keep."

His eyes glowed darkly, and the intensity behind his gaze made her knees weak.

"Kiss me," she whispered. "Really kiss me."

He didn't need any more encouragement than that. He cupped her face and captured her mouth in a searing kiss that left no doubt that he wanted her too.

She slid against him, her entire body seeking his warmth. Her hands were behind his head, holding him so she could drink her fill. Too much time had gone by without someone to kiss, someone to love, and every part of her hungered for that connection.

Her pulse raced, and she squirmed with impatience. It had never been one of her strong suits. As an ER doctor, she lived life in the fast lane, making quick decisions, rushing from one catastrophe to another. She had learned to talk fast, walk fast, eat fast, and now wanted to love fast.

She broke away from his mouth long enough to ask, "Bedroom or living room?"

"For what?" His mouth found her neck and stayed to graze, then moved on to her earlobes.

She shivered. "You know. Making love."

"I thought we were." His hand cupped her breast, and she moaned in pleasure.

"Oh yes, that feels good." She moved her hips against his.

He didn't take the hint. His hand moved away, and his mouth regained possession of hers. Deep, soulful kisses, while his tongue swept in and plundered her mouth.

Her muscles relaxed, and she felt weightless, as though she were floating in deep water. "Your kisses are intoxicating," she murmured. "I want more."

"You can have as many as you want." He held her up or she would have slid down the rail. "Do you want to go inside?"

She nodded and took his hand. “I thought you’d never ask.”

He guided her to the couch, where she fell back against the armrest, her entire body limp and waiting for him.

Finding a narrow space next to her, he resumed the passionate kissing until the yearning inside overwhelmed her. She pushed his chest, making him sit up. “Do you, by any chance, have a bed?”

He laughed. “I knew you were bossy, but who’s running this show?”

“I am.” She pulled his tie free and started unbuttoning his shirt. “I want to see you, and feel you. Take your clothes off.”

“Not until you do.” He sat there, grinning at her, not doing anything to help.

Her fingers stopped their downward path, then resumed. “Don’t think for a moment that that’s going to stop me.”

She had his shirt open and his chest exposed. She sucked in a breath. “You are so beautiful.” She ran her hands up and down his chest, marveling at the feel of his soft skin and hard muscles, the strength and core of him. She kissed his chest, his stomach, noticing a few scars where obviously he’d been beaten. She kissed them tenderly, running her finger over them lightly.

She didn’t want to talk about his time in the desert. Not tonight. Another time, she’d ask him all that she needed to know.

Her hands inched lower to his crotch, and she found him hard and waiting. He groaned, and she smiled.

“Lauren, stop doing that or this will be a wasted night.”

She gave a wicked laugh. "No staying power, huh?"

"Give it a break. Hasn't seen action in years."

"Poor thing." She quickly unzipped his fly. "He needs to come out to play."

"Lauren." His voice was strangled, his expression a mix of anxiety and desire. "Dammit. You know this isn't easy for me."

"Relax. Let me do all the work. Just sit back and enjoy." She pushed him back down on the cushions and got off the couch to remove his shoes. She pulled his pants down his legs and folded them on the coffee table.

"Only one thing left to go," she said with a playful smile.

"You need to get out of that dress." His eyes were like hot coals as they raked over her. "I can't be the only one naked around here."

"Oh. All right." She turned around so he could unzip her, then stood and let the dress fall.

"My God, Lauren. You look even better out of your clothes then you do in them."

She laughed. "I could say the same for you."

His gaze roamed over her slowly, and the heat in her body soared to a scorching temperature. Surprisingly enough, she was not embarrassed standing half-undressed in front of him. She was aroused, confident, enjoying her moment of power.

"Glad you like what you see." She straddled him and began kissing him again. Her lace panties rubbed against his boxers, and underneath the silk she could feel him pulse, every hard male inch of him.

"I want you now." She took hold of his cock and got rid of his boxers. Her mouth got him wet and ready, then she handed him a condom. "Look what I found in your pocket."

He used his teeth to open it, and while he was busy with that she removed her panties, tossed off her bra, and slid on top.

"Just go with it," she whispered.

And he did.

CHAPTER TWENTY-TWO

Shane had never met a lady like Lauren. He didn't even mind her being so bossy. Not when she was torturing him so sweetly with her mouth, sliding her tongue along his shaft, teasing, tasting, coaxing him to the edge of ecstasy, then backing off in the nick of time.

He wondered where she learned such tricks.

When she tossed off her bra and panties, he'd expected her to move things to the bedroom, but she'd planted herself on top of him, as natural as if she'd been there before.

He'd slid inside of her, his erection as strong as it had ever been. He'd filled all her empty places, and she'd moaned with pleasure. That little moan, the shudder that ran through her body was almost more than he could bear. Burying his head in her gorgeous, full breasts, he'd ached with desire, want, need. Like a feast for a starving man, he couldn't get enough. His mouth captured a nipple while his one good hand played with the other.

He still wore his prosthetic, and he was sure that Lauren had planned it that way. His stump didn't mean a damn thing to her, but she didn't want the night to be ruined with his thinking about it.

She arched her back, giving him better access to her breasts, and he took his time pleasing her, while she rocked gently over him, a soft smile on her pretty face.

Finally, he'd had enough and flipped her over, wanting to taste the core of her. She'd cried out his name but he didn't let go. He let his tongue run over her sweet spot until she bucked and yelped, and then did it again. When she began to squirm he slid back inside, then gently slid out, giving her a little more with every thrust.

His heart raced, and both of them were gasping for air. Finally, with one last thrust he felt her shudder, and gave in to his own release, a release so strong it rolled over him in wave upon wave, and nothing had ever felt quite so sweet.

She lay panting beneath him. "You okay?" he asked, tucking a lock of hair behind her ear.

She smiled. "Uh-huh. And you?"

"Couldn't be better." He grinned too, feeling young, happy, and more than content. Having made love successfully made his heart swell with relief.

She shifted onto her side and stroked his cheek. "That was great, Shane. You are such an amazing man in so many ways."

He kissed the tip of her nose. "I still need a lot of practice. We may have to do it again, and again."

Her eyes twinkled. "What? Tonight? I don't think so. I'm going to be sore all over tomorrow."

"Was I too rough?" He kissed her shoulders, and her breasts. "I hope I didn't hurt you."

"No, but you did give me a nice razor burn." She grinned. "In certain places."

His hand stroked her inner thigh. "Here?"

"Uh-huh. Thighs, breasts, I feel like a chicken that just got pummeled."

He laughed. "You have no romance in your soul."

"I do too. But I want you to kiss them better."

"Happy to." He dropped gentle kisses between her thighs, along her tummy, and up to her breasts. "Is that better?"

"Yes." She closed her eyes, and sighed with pleasure. "Much better."

He kept kissing. Then he had an idea. "Hey, you want to go to bed?"

"I'd love to, but I really should get home and let Julie leave. If I'm not there in the morning, Josh will be upset."

"I'll be upset if you're not here in the morning too." He kissed her brow. "But maybe another time."

She stood up, unashamed of her nudity. "I'd like that, Shane. But we need to take this slow, and not let Josh know how we feel."

"Agreed." He stood up too. "I'll take a quick shower, then I'll drive you home."

Later, when he returned from dropping her home, he couldn't wipe the grin off his face, knowing he'd performed better than expected. He'd been good, perhaps even great if her moans of pleasure and release meant anything. He'd have enjoyed a second go-round just to be sure, but he understood her need to get home.

The high he was on was slipping fast, and the memory of their love making now made him feel more alone than ever. He knew he wouldn't be able to sleep, so he got out his books, intending to study. His concentration was shot, his brain fuzzy. Emotions ran rampant, both elated and frustrated, and he wanted things he couldn't have.

~

Lauren took a bath before she went to bed, her body more relaxed than it had been for years. The sex was good, bordering on spectacular, and even now, lying alone in her bed, parts of her hummed with awareness.

A girl could get used to this. It would be easy to fall into a routine of slipping over to Shane's for a few hours of R&R, keeping their relationship where it most likely should stay—a sexual one, not one of the heart. And yet, wasn't it already? She cared about him deeply, and if it wasn't love, it was heading in that direction.

She flipped over to her side, burying her face in the pillow. Though she was tired, her mind was too active to sleep.

He was an amazing man, sensitive, caring, and so humble. It would be all too easy to fall for him. Big time. She never did anything halfway—she was an all-or-nothing kind of girl. Her husband had been the second man she'd slept with, and the only one she'd deeply loved.

They'd met the second year of college, long before either of them entered med school. It was funny how they met—Jeremy had been dating her roommate for a few months, and she'd been hanging out with a guy who considered himself a poet. They all went to the local sports bar one night, grabbed some dinner and a few drinks, and Jeremy had been unable to take his eyes off her.

She'd made an attempt to ignore Jeremy and talk to her boyfriend, but had stolen looks at him too. It felt like a big magnet drawing them together, and they'd been unable to resist the force. Finally, her roomie seemed to notice and stormed out. The poet, Timothy, ran off after her, and Lauren had been alone with Jeremy.

They were inseparable after that. They moved into an apartment together their senior year, and had entered med school a year later. Three years after that they married, and Josh came along shortly after. It had been a love that was meant to be, and she'd never regretted it.

If only she'd waited until he got home instead of having that conversation in the car, maybe he'd be asleep beside her right now.

She could forgive herself most things, but not this. It was not just a drunk driver who had killed her husband, it was her damn mouth. She'd been rightly concerned about Josh, but she couldn't let it go. Not for one day, or the hour-long ride home. She'd contributed to his death, and deprived Josh of his father, the only man she'd ever loved. She didn't deserve happiness. She deserved what she got. A lifetime of loneliness.

CHAPTER TWENTY-THREE

Shane and Rick raced into the ER. They'd been in radio contact, and Lauren was prepared for their arrival. A woman who'd had chest pains during the night, waited until morning to call 911, and was now in extreme distress.

She'd flatlined on the way in.

"We got her back," Rick called. "She's all yours, doc."

Lauren and her team jumped in, got a heartbeat for a few seconds, and then lost it again. After a few harrowing minutes, the woman began to respond. Her sinus rhythm settled down to a nice normal eighty, and she opened her eyes.

Lauren wiped away the sweat on her brow and breathed a deep sigh of relief. The woman would live to see another day.

She nodded to Rick, avoiding eye contact with Shane. "Good work, guys."

"You too, doc."

Shane waited until the patient was rolled away before speaking to her. He kept his voice low. "You all right? Not regretting anything, are you?"

"I only have one regret, and trust me, it isn't you." Her eyes met his briefly. "I had a good time."

"Glad to hear that." He ran a hand over his jaw, which hadn't been shaved this morning. "Didn't want things to get awkward between us."

"No, we certainly don't want that." She kept her own voice neutral, not wanting to throw out any signals. He didn't respond, so she politely asked, "How did your exams go? Get the results back yet?"

"Sure did. Got a couple of A's, and an A–. Thanks to you."

"Good job." She gave him a warm smile. "And it was my pleasure."

"You don't mind if I take Josh to a ballgame this Sunday, do you?"

"Not at all." She tried to read his eyes, not understanding the need for the question. "He'd love that."

"Good. I'll pick him up at noon."

She watched him leave, wondering why he hadn't asked if she'd like to come along. Was he taking a step back? And if so, why did it have to hurt so damn much?

~

When Shane arrived to pick Josh up on Sunday, she cornered him, needing answers to the questions that had plagued her all week. "What's going on? I must admit that I'm feeling a little bit hurt that you didn't invite me."

His eyes shot to hers. "You are? I'm sorry. That was never my intention."

"Well, what was?" She folded her arms, not looking away from him. She wanted to keep everything out in the open between them.

Whatever it was, she could handle it.

"I can't get you out of my mind," he said. "I'm getting even less sleep than I did before, and my concentration is shot. How can I study if I can't think straight?"

The heavy weight around her heart disappeared. She wanted to kiss him, but Josh was nearby, getting ready to leave. She gave him a loving smile instead. "Oh, so that's it. I thought maybe you hadn't enjoyed yourself."

"Are you crazy?" He ran a hand through his sandy hair, looking frustrated and utterly adorable. "You can do that to me anytime. As a matter of fact, that's all I think about."

"Well, I'm sure we could arrange something." She glanced at Josh. "You ready, honey?"

"Yeah. How come you're not coming?"

"Oh, I have too much to do. You boys have a good time by yourself. I'll cook the three of us a nice dinner tonight, so go easy on the hot dogs."

"You don't have to do that," Shane said. "Why don't you see if you can get a babysitter tonight, and I'll take you out for a bite, then we can study back at my place?"

Her eyes met his, and she shook her head. "I wish I could, but Julie needs more advance warning than that. Sorry. Maybe next time."

"You mean in a week?" His face showed his disappointment.

"Or sooner. I could probably tutor you one night this week." She gave him a meaningful smile.

"At my place?" he asked hopefully.

"Sure. Why not?"

He grinned. "Okay. Don't knock yourself out over the dinner. Save your energy."

She laughed. "Have fun, boys."

She walked them to the door and watched them leave. It felt so right, almost as if the three of them were a family. But of course they weren't. Shane was on a different path. He had to prove to himself and the rest of the world that, disabled or not, he could be anything he wanted to be.

She didn't expect him to stick around forever, but she'd enjoy him for the time she had. And when it was time for him to leave, she'd buck up and let him go. Maybe then she'd seriously look for the right man to share her life with.

Lauren did all the chores that, as a single working mother, she never had enough time to do. Paid bills, did laundry, went grocery shopping, and spent time in her garden weeding and nurturing her plants.

While she gardened, she decided to make a bouillabaisse, and ran in to shower before going to the market for fish fillets, clams, mussels, and shrimp. Not that she was trying to impress anyone, but she rarely had a chance to cook anything remotely exotic.

Once back at the house, she poured some olive oil into a large pot, tossed in chopped onion and shallots, and crushed garlic and a sweet red pepper. She let it sauté, then added tomato, celery, and fennel. After cutting the fish into small pieces, she put it in the pot with water, clam juice, lemon, and white wine, and left it to simmer.

While dinner cooked, she changed into a tight pair of white jeans and a boat-necked top that drooped off one shoulder. She glanced in the mirror and decided to leave it that way. It was sexy. And she was only thirty-six. She could flaunt it once in a while.

She fluffed up her hair, added lipstick, sprayed on some perfume, then went back into the kitchen to complete the dinner. She tossed in the shrimps, clams, and mussels, added saffron, salt, and pepper, and another dash of wine. She sliced up a sweet potato for fries, and put them in the oven with some chicken fingers for Josh.

Nodding with approval, she poured herself a glass of wine and sat down at the kitchen table to wait for her son and lover to arrive.

Lover. It gave her tingles thinking about it.

She didn't wait long before they burst through the door.

"Hi, Mom." Josh gave her a big hug. "We had the best day ever. The Dodgers killed them. They only got three runs." He lifted his fingers. "Three."

Lauren glanced over his head at Shane. "Sounds like a great day."

"Sure was. The Cardinals didn't know what hit them." He sniffed the air. "Something sure smells awfully good around here." He took a step closer to her and pretended to sniff her neck. "Is it you?"

"You think I smell fishy?" She teased him with a smile.

"You smell delicious enough to eat," he whispered in her ear.

She bumped hips with him, knowing that the island in the kitchen partially hid them from Josh's view. "I made bouillabaisse. And chicken fingers for Josh." She stood still, every nerve in her body aware of him, and eager to keep it that way.

"What's bullybase?" Josh asked. "It sure is stinky."

Shane laughed. "Maybe for you, but it smells finger-lickin' good to me." He leaned closer to her. "Did you go to this trouble for me?"

"No. Well, maybe. I thought it would be different. I don't get to show off my culinary talents too often."

"I saw some talent the other night," he said with a sexy smile.

"What are you guys whispering about?" Josh wanted to know.

"Nothing, honey. Just grown-up things."

"What kind of grown-up things?" Josh tossed a ball against the wall, hitting a picture, nearly sending it crashing to the floor.

"Don't do that," she said automatically. "You know you're not to throw balls in the house."

"Why won't you tell me what you were talking about?"

Shane glanced at her, and started to answer, but she put a hand up to stop him. "You have private conversations with Shane, and once in a while, I can too."

"I don't like it." Josh glared at her.

"That's too bad," she said, giving his shoulder a squeeze. "Come on. Take a seat, boys. Dinner is almost ready."

"I'm not hungry." Josh said.

"That's because you ate a hot dog and a whole bag of popcorn." Shane spoke up. "Told you to leave some for me."

"What would you boys like to drink?" She turned around to take the chicken fingers and sweet potato fries out of the oven, and Shane was right behind her.

"Here. Let me do that." He put his arms around her, took the oven mitt, and pulled the tray out of the oven. Her body was encased in his. Sweet torture.

The back of her head was against his chest, and she turned to see him. He dropped a quick kiss on her lips and then spun her around. "Josh, your dinner is looking awfully tasty."

Shane opened up the fridge and pulled out two bottles of water, handing one to Josh. "Here ya go, pal."

Lauren watched him making himself at home. Not intrusive, but comfortable, the way he was with her son.

She poured herself a little more wine, cut up some French bread for dipping, then ladled out the fish stew in two big serving bowls. The three of them enjoyed every bite of their meal, and then it was bath time and bed for Josh.

"Do you have to leave right away?" she asked Shane, who'd insisted on doing the dishes.

"No, get Josh ready for bed, and then I'll be in to read him a bedtime story."

"You will?" Josh cried, smiling ear to ear. "My favorite's Dr. Seuss."

"Mine too."

"Which one? I like *The Cat in the Hat.*"

"Me too. Now, no more questions. Have your bath and I'll be in once I get this load of dishes done." He sighed. "A woman's work is never done."

Josh giggled. "You're not a woman."

"Oh." He glanced down at himself. "I forgot."

Once the bath and bedtime routine was over, they both kissed Josh good night, closed his door behind them, and returned to the family room. Lauren turned on the TV, and Shane sat next to her on the sofa.

"Thanks for reading him a story. It meant the world to him."

"You don't have to thank me." He slipped an arm around her, and pulled her close. "I'm about to make out with his mother."

She smiled. "You are?"

"Unless she objects." He nibbled on her ear.

Lauren snuggled into him. "No objection from me."

He lifted her chin and kissed her lips. The gentle kiss was sweet, tender, and enough to melt the hardest heart. She would have to be very careful around this man. He was so easy to love, and if she didn't guard against that, she'd be a goner, so hooked on him she'd never be free.

"What are you thinking?" he asked quietly.

"That you're a really good kisser. But I guess you hear that all the time."

He grinned. "Yeah, all the women in my life tell me that. It gets old."

"For me too. All the men, I mean."

"There better not be any other men." He kissed her deeply, his tongue plunging in and capturing her own. He nibbled on her lip, and murmured, "I want you all to myself."

A thrill rushed over her. This making out business was intoxicating.

"I'm rather fond of you too." She pulled his face down to hers, wanting to taste his lips some more. Kissing was all they could do with her son in the house, but she intended to make the most of the moment and refill the empty well inside her. She'd gone far too long without being loved, or being held, and now she had a lot of making up to do.

His mouth took hers again, hot moist kisses, their tongues circling each other then mating. It made her hungry for more. She grabbed hold of his hair, holding him so she could take his tongue deep in her throat, wanting every inch that she could get. She moaned with pleasure and whispered his name.

His busy hands were everywhere, on her neck, in her hair, down her back, pulling her shirt out of her jeans. Their bodies fought to get close. They were feeding off each other, two people who'd been alone too long and were hungering for someone's touch. But of course it was more than that. She could try to simplify it, but she knew they respected and liked each other, and at the moment, they were both very turned on.

After a long while, he pulled away. "I better go while I can still walk. But I want you so bad it hurts."

"Me too. It's a nice pain, though, isn't it?"

He gazed into her eyes, and she saw the simmering passion that lingered there. "Oh, yeah. But I look forward to your coming back to my place and…tutoring me. You can teach me anything you want."

She laughed, but it didn't sound like herself. It was a husky, sexy laugh, one she'd never heard before. Whoever this woman was inside her, she should stick around some more.

CHAPTER TWENTY-FOUR

The next day started with a drug addict who'd overdosed, moved on to a heart attack victim, followed by a motorcycle accident in which the young man sustained head injuries. After each, the nurses squeezed in a few patients who didn't have life-threatening injuries but still needed treatment in the ER.

It was all in a day's work, but by the time Lauren finished her shift, she was wound up tighter than a drum.

What she needed was a stiff drink, and a stiff…

Shane. Sex with Shane, kisses with Shane, and to spend some mellow time in the magic of his arms. But it was not meant to be. Julie's schedule didn't allow her to work overtime all that week, and Lauren's second sitter had jobs lined up too.

She returned home to Josh, who was having a bad week as well.

"I don't like Brad anymore. He called me a sissy and told everyone that I'm a crybaby who's scared of the dark." Josh kicked a soccer ball around the narrow confines of the family room.

Lauren didn't normally allow him to play with the ball inside, but she held her tongue. "You're a very brave boy, and he shouldn't be saying bad things about you. But kids sometimes trash each other and nobody thinks anything of it, right? I'm sure the other kids make fun of him, too."

"No. He's got lots of friends, but now nobody will sit with me at lunch."

"Oh, Josh, I'm sorry. That's awful." She tugged him onto her lap, kissed the top of his head, and held him tight. She felt his pain as sharply as if it were her own, perhaps more so. She sucked back tears so he wouldn't see her cry.

"Would you like me to talk to your teachers about this?"

"No. They can't do anything." He sniffled and wiped his eyes. "Can't force the other kids to like me."

"There must be something I can do to help." She tilted his face up and wiped away the tears with her thumb. "I'll think on this and find a solution. I promise."

"Why don't they like me?" he asked in a small, pitiful voice.

"I have no idea. You're a great kid. It's impossible not to like you."

"There's a father/son day coming up soon. Do you think I could take Shane?" His face became animated. "He could tell us war stories and show off his bionic hand. That would be so cool. Maybe then people would like me."

"Well, I could certainly ask him." She kissed his forehead. "I don't think he'd object."

"Could I tell people that he's going to be my new dad?"

"No, hon. No." She drew in a sharp breath. Had she somehow given Josh this impression? Could he see that Shane and she were growing close? Or was it simply that he wanted it so much, he'd leapt to that conclusion?

She felt a sharp pain, wishing things could be different. "That wouldn't be true. But you could tell them that he's a family friend, and that he takes you to ballgames and teaches you to surf. Stuff like that."

"Okay. I guess that would be all right."

"What would you like to do this Sunday? Maybe all three of us could do something special."

"Yeah." He jumped up, excitement written all over his face. "Could we go surfing again? Please, please, please?"

"I don't see why not."

"Ask him, Mom. I like the three of us doing things together."

"So do I." Lauren spoke calmly, hiding her concern. Josh was getting very close to Shane, and he had high hopes that they'd become the family he so desperately wanted. She should warn him not to care so deeply or want so much, because his little heart could so easily be broken, but he couldn't face another disappointment tonight.

Shane's shift had just ended when Lauren called later that night. She quickly told him about the boys at school and how Josh sat alone at lunch, without so much as a friend.

"There's a father/son day coming up, and he wanted to know if he could take you." Lauren hurried on, "I know it's an imposition and puts you on the spot, so we could easily say that you're busy working or whatever."

"No, don't be silly. I wouldn't do that to Josh. Tell him I'll be there, even if I have to miss a class to do it." Shane knew from experience how cruel kids could be, and he didn't want Josh to suffer the same fate he had. When he'd been in grade school some of the bullies had decided that he was an easy target. He was a skinny kid without a father, and they'd enjoyed tormenting him on the back of the bus.

They'd flick things at his head, kick the back of his seat, and call him insulting names. He didn't say anything to the driver or to his mom, because if he did, the bullying would only get worse.

"You're such a kind man, Shane. How did we get so lucky?"

He didn't bother to answer, since he considered himself the lucky one. If they knew what he was capable of, the way he had caved under pressure simply to save his own skin, they wouldn't think so damn highly of him.

But he could pretend to be a hero for just a little longer.

"You know how I feel about Josh. He's my buddy, and I'd like to horsewhip the kids at school who make fun of him."

She sighed. "Why do they do that?"

"I don't know, sweetheart. But nationwide, bullying is getting out of control—between twittering, Facebook, and text messages, the unpopular kids don't stand a chance."

"I had a patient come into the ER recently. He'd been doused with gasoline and set on fire. By his classmates."

"Jesus." He winced. "Were you able to save him?"

"Yes, but he has burns over fifty percent of his body, and he'll never be the same. Why do kids torture each other like this? Why don't they accept that people are different and embrace that? Not everyone can be the same, and how boring it would be if they were."

"You're asking me this? You should see how it was before I got this prosthetic. I had a plastic hand that didn't look too bad but was pretty much useless. Tried the hook because it was easier to use, and then I refused to wear it because of the way people looked at me. I was in pain, both physical and mental, and that's when I started drinking hard, left here and went back to Florida. I was bitter and depressed, and just sunk lower and lower into my own private hell."

"How long were you homeless?"

"Eight, nine months."

"Why didn't you seek help?"

"I didn't want any. I was in such a bad mental state that all I wanted was to be left alone." He was ashamed at the memory, but wanted Lauren to understand him better. "Part of the reason I didn't want you and me to get close was because I still have nightmares. Wake up screaming, flashbacks. On nights like that, I still feel the need for a drink." He hated telling her this, but if he slipped again, he wanted her prepared.

"After my escape from that terrorist camp, you'd think I'd be grateful to be home, but instead I didn't want to live. Not like this, without a hand. With only pain and memories of torture. Choosing a life on the streets was probably my way of trying to kill myself. Lived in the woods, drinking cheap shit. Hoped I wouldn't wake up."

"Oh, Shane." Her voice conveyed sympathy. "How awful."

"Brent's brother found me, got me cleaned up. Even went into therapy with me."

"Why?" she asked with concern. "Was he messed up too?"

"Most of us coming home from these recent wars have some kind of issues. Jake's no different. He fought in Iraq and was in a two-truck convoy when the first one hit a land mine and blew up. He had severe burns, but others in his truck didn't make it out alive. So when he got back, he had depression and nightmares, and other problems, too."

"You've never told me, how did you come to lose your hand? Was it an accident like Jake's or did the terrorists do this to you?"

"Terrorists. We were ambushed in a busy marketplace, and they found me in the back of a Humvee. When they discovered I was a medic they took me to a guerrilla training camp. I was forced to work for the Iraqis, made to patch up their wounded. When I didn't comply, they chopped off my left hand, leaving my right until I agreed to do what they asked." The last part was a little white lie, but he didn't see any need to tell her the entire ugly truth.

She let out a shaky breath. "Oh, my God. You were lucky they didn't leave you to bleed to death."

"I wouldn't have been any use to them if I had."

"Thank God, you were rescued," she whispered. "How did that happen?"

"A team of SEALS crept into the enemy camp and carried me out. Had to be a couple of weeks after I lost my hand, but those first few days I was floating in and out of consciousness a lot. Lost track of time. I remember hearing gunfire, men shouting, a lot of commotion. Found out later that a couple of members of their team got hit. Took a bullet for me."

"Die they die in the rescue mission?"

"No. But they could have."

"I can't believe how much you've gone through. And yet, you're so positive now, and seem at ease with your new hand."

"I'm lucky," he said lightly. "When I was treated at Walter Reed a team of surgeons amputated a portion of my arm so that a prosthesis could be fitted. But the first couple didn't work out so well, then this new technology was developed. Once I got back here and found the Wounded Warrior program, things started to look up. Guess I happened to be in the right place at the right time."

"They amputated?"

"Had to clean up the stump. My terrorist friends weren't very particular when they sawed off my hand."

"You're lucky to be alive."

"I know it now, but I didn't know it then." He lifted his hand to admire it. "This changed my life. That's why when kids stare, I try to amuse them, then come up and talk to them. I think it helps to educate kids early on that being different isn't something to be sneered at."

"That's nice, Shane. Very admirable of you."

"Has to be done. In the next few years more and more disabled vets will be coming home. They've suffered enough, and it's time that the general population show them some respect, no matter how they personally feel about the war."

"I agree."

"Sometimes I worry that even if I ace all the exams and do everything right, I'll never make it as an intern. People see my disability first and make their own assumptions from that."

"I'm sure the professors don't look at you that way."

"I hope you're right, but lately, I've had a foreboding that something bad is going to happen. And with my history of screwing up, perhaps I'm just waiting for that to happen."

"Why do you keep insisting that you screw up? I haven't seen any evidence of that."

"Not lately. Hopefully I've learned a few lessons." He swallowed and continued, "But I didn't take school seriously, and was a bit of a hell-raiser when I was a kid. Got into trouble a lot, gave my parents grief. Then I talked Brent into coming to California with me, when he was supposed to go to Notre Dame on a football scholarship. Don't think his father ever forgave me for that."

"How did you two end up working for CAL FIRE?"

He laughed. "We couldn't make it into the movies, and declined the offer to be porn stars. We were pretty much broke when CAL FIRE accepted our applications. Mr. Harrington didn't want his son to be a firefighter, so he paid for his helicopter training."

"And how did that make you feel?"

"I was okay with it. Brent's dad is a retired general with high expectations and standards that he expects his sons to live up too." Shane added, "He's all right."

Lauren cleared her throat. "Shane, let's get this straight. You're not a screw-up, and I have high expectations for you too. You'll get into a good med school, I promise."

"Thanks for your vote of confidence. Now to more important details. When am I going to see you again?" He needed her. It had been nearly a week since they'd been together, and he was desperate to touch her, hold her, see the special look in her eyes. With Lauren, he felt whole again.

"What, now? You want to come over?"

"Sure. Is Josh asleep?"

"Uh-huh." He could hear the smile in her voice. She whispered, "I miss your kisses, and you holding me."

"Anything else?"

"That too." She spoke so quietly, he strained to hear her. "I want to make love to you. I think about it all the time."

"Me too. You were incredible, and you were so tight around me. I'm not just saying that because it's been a long time. You're an amazing woman. Both in and out of bed."

She cleared her throat. "I promise I'll get a sitter this week, even if I have to ask one of the nurses."

"Good, but if you want, I can be at your place in about twenty minutes." He held his breath, hoping for the invitation.

"If I didn't have Josh, I'd say yes. But if he wakes up and you're here, it would send him mixed signals. I don't want that."

"I understand. And you're right. I'm just being selfish." He paused for a second, not wanting to hang up. With only Major for conversation it got a little dull around the place.

"I'll make it up to you. I promise."

"I'm sure you will." He hid his disappointment. "It's getting late, and you have a full day ahead. Sleep well and dream of me."

CHAPTER TWENTY-FIVE

A school bus on a field trip had collided with an SUV at the intersection of 710 and West Pacific Coast Highway, and Shane and Rick were among the convoy of ambulances bringing in the children. By the middle of the afternoon, all the gurneys were full and beds had been shuffled around to make room for the new arrivals.

Although he'd been unable to speak to her, Shane had seen Lauren fighting to save some kid's life, and had known the moment she lost him for good. In a trembling voice she announced the time of death, then she tore her gloves off and stormed out of the ER, leaving a scene of chaos behind her.

He followed her out and found her leaning against a wall, her eyes closed, hands shielding her face. He called her name, and she opened her eyes. They were brimming with tears.

"You okay?" he whispered, putting his hands on her shoulders.

"No." She leaned against him and sucked in a deep breath. "No, I'm not okay."

"Lauren, you can't blame yourself. That poor child was barely hanging on when we brought him in. He was lucky to have made it to the hospital."

"Lucky? You call him lucky? He was nine years old." She stuffed her hands in her pockets. "He'll never be a teenager, never have a first date, never graduate from high school, never grow up. It isn't fair." She rocked back and forth on her feet, clearly stressed.

"I know how you feel. I saw so many young kids blown up. And for what? But this is different. He didn't have any choice but to be where he was." Shane sighed. "But you couldn't save him. Nobody could."

"I should have." Her eyes flew open, and she beat her fists against his chest. "It's not right for children to die. It's my job to save them."

He captured her fists. "Get it together, Lauren. You have other patients who need you right now. Ones that you can save."

She straightened and ran a hand through her hair. "Yes, I know. You don't have to tell me how to do my job. I just needed a moment. I didn't ask for your comfort."

"And I didn't give it. You're stronger than that."

She glanced away from him, blinking back tears. "You're right about that." She sniffed and sucked in some air. After a few seconds, she hooked her arm through his. "Let's go save some lives, shall we?"

They never got another chance to speak. But he could see in the lines of her face the toll it took on her.

They saved most of the children, and minimized the severity of the wounds of the less injured, but the good they did was overshadowed by their loss.

~

Lauren didn't get home until close to midnight. It had been a grueling day. Of the twenty-eight children on the bus, nine had sustained serious injuries. Of those, three were in critical care—and two were in the morgue.

She poured a stiff drink and took it with her to Josh's room. She sat in a chair facing the bed and watched her son sleep. Tears slipped down her cheeks as she listened to his steady breathing, watched the soft rise and fall of his chest. Her son was alive tonight, while two other families were facing the unbearable heartache of knowing their child would never come home.

She put the cool glass against her forehead and closed her eyes. She was a doctor. It was her job to save them. Losing a patient always hurt, but when it was a child, it was unacceptable. Why couldn't they save them all? In what world was it okay to let a child die?

She lifted a hand and caressed her son's cheek, smoothing his hair off his face, then straightening his bed covers. He was the most precious thing in the world, and she loved him more than life itself.

Sniffing, she blinked back tears, thinking of the mothers who'd lost their babies tonight. She couldn't imagine living without Josh. It had been unbearable enough losing her husband, but a child was a part of you, more than an eye or a limb. A child was your heart and your soul, and all your happiness wrapped into one. She lived for his smile, his tiny embrace, the way his eyes could light up, his rosy cheeks glowing with happiness.

~

A busy week passed, and Shane never did get his "date" with the beautiful doctor. But on Tuesday of the next week he took a personal day so he could be with Josh for bring-your-father-to-school day.

Wearing a pair of khakis and a short-sleeved shirt, Shane picked Josh up at seven-thirty. He hadn't been sure what to wear, but didn't want to overdo it either.

Josh beamed the moment he saw him. Lauren looked pleased too. Brownie points never hurt. It might make their lovemaking even sweeter—if they could ever find the time for it.

Lauren walked them to the car, kissed Josh good-bye, and asked him if he'd remembered his book for reading time. He hadn't and ran back into the house for it, and Lauren whispered to Shane that she'd found a babysitter for that evening.

It was going to be his lucky day after all.

When they arrived at school, they were invited to join a continental breakfast in the auditorium. Shane was amazed to see the number of fathers who had shown up to support their kids. Must be close to a hundred, he figured.

"What's going to happen today?" he asked Josh while he put a second doughnut on his plate.

"You shouldn't eat that. Mom tells me it's full of sugar, and to eat a bagel instead."

"Your mom is right, but she's not here, and I'm not telling."

"You mean I can have one?"

"Sure can. If I were you, I'd go for the chocolate."

Josh dumped the bagel into a bin and grabbed a big, gooey chocolate cream doughnut, a guilty smile on his face.

"It's okay to be bad once in a while. My mom tells me that when she eats things she shouldn't."

"Your mother is a very clever woman."

"I know. She's a doctor."

"Is that what you're going to be when you get older?"

"No. I want to be a firefighter, or an astronaut."

"Well, they've shut down the space program for the time being, so you better set your sights on being a firefighter."

"Or a policeman. I could catch the bad guys."

"That you could. But police officers get shot at sometimes." He pretended to shiver in fright. "It can get scary."

"Well, I could work in an ambulance like you. You get to go through red lights, and have a siren on, and everything."

"Yes, but that's not all we do."

"But that's the fun part, isn't it?"

"You got me there." Shane drank his chocolate milk through a straw. "This is pretty good."

"Mom lets me have it, but she prefers white milk."

"Natch. I wouldn't expect less from her."

Josh wiped his mouth with his sleeve. "After you're finished, we can go to my classroom and you can meet the teacher and the other kids." He stood up. "Are you ready yet? This is so cool. Extra, extra cool. Can you stay all day?"

"Sure. I'm all yours today."

Shane followed Josh down the hall to his classroom and sat in a small chair next to him. Nearly all the fathers were there, and only a few children sat alone. He was glad Josh wasn't one of them. Not today.

The fathers joined in during the regular classroom activities, and even got to go out for recess. When they returned, the teacher invited the fathers to speak about their careers. A few of them got up, and Shane did too.

"My name is Shane Dawson, and I'm here with Josh because I'm a close family friend. Some of you may know that his mother is a doctor in the emergency room at the hospital, and I'm an EMT. That's short for Emergency Medical Technician, or paramedic. When someone calls 911, we show up. Our job is to keep the patient alive and get them to the hospital where they can be properly treated."

One hand shot up. "Have you ever seen anyone die?"

"Yes, all too often." He glanced around to see the other hands. He pointed to a child in the back row.

"What happens when they die?" the skinny kid asked. "Do they go to heaven?"

"Well, I can't say for sure. All we can do is hope."

Shane tried to sit down and let the other fathers have the floor, but the children didn't want to know about ordinary professions, they wanted to hear about the life and death world of the paramedic.

After fifteen minutes, the teacher stepped in to save him.

"That's enough questions, children. It's been a fascinating discussion, but I'm sure we'd like to hear from some other fathers too." The young, attractive teacher smiled at him, and Shane smiled back.

"She likes you," Josh whispered. "Don't smile at her. Mom won't like it."

"Naw. She's just being friendly." He ruffled Josh's strawberry blond hair. "Your mom wouldn't care."

"Yes, she would. And you're wrong. Miss Marshall keeps looking at you." He hung his head. "I wish you were really my dad and not just a family friend."

"We have to start somewhere."

"Yeah, I know." His face brightened. "Mom really likes you."

"The feeling's mutual. I like her too."

"Then why don't you marry her? Then we could be a real family." He hugged Shane's arm. "I want you for my daddy."

Shane wasn't sure how this conversation got started, but he certainly knew it was headed down the wrong path. He needed to nip it in the bud before Josh got too carried away. But how? What could he say that wouldn't completely dash this boy's hopes?

He figured honesty worked. "I have a few problems that I still need to sort out. Coming back from the war, I got a little messed up, and I wouldn't want you or your mom to have to deal with it. Like I can't sleep, and when I do I have terrible nightmares. Sometimes I scream and thrash around in the middle of the night." He grinned. "Now who would want to marry a guy like that?"

"Mom would. You should ask her."

"Josh, I know how much you want this, but it's better if the three of us remain friends. At least for now."

CHAPTER TWENTY-SIX

Lauren had found a babysitter for the night, and was eager to spend the evening in Shane's arms. When he brought Josh home from school, her son made a beeline for the kitchen and his after-school snack, and she told Shane what she'd planned.

"Instead of wasting time going out for dinner, I'll drive over to your place and we can order Thai food. You like Thai, don't you?"

"Sure, love it, but you don't have to do that. I'm happy to pick you up and take you someplace nice. We don't get a chance to go out very often." His eyes locked on hers. "Let's make it a romantic night."

"Forget it. Our time is too limited, and I don't want to spend it dining." She lowered her voice, just in case Josh had big ears. "We see each other all the time, but I don't get to make love to you very often."

He grinned. "You are impatient, aren't you? Whatever happened to foreplay?"

"When I come over we can have as much as we want." She leaned in close and nuzzled his cheek. "Although I could do you right now and be happy."

He linked his fingers with hers. "I had a great time with Josh today. I'm glad I was there. Nearly all the kids had their fathers, and the kids that didn't looked completely miserable. I felt for them."

"You're such a good person, and I can't wait to show you my appreciation."

"Neither can I." He raised his eyebrows suggestively. "Will it take long?"

"A good portion of the night."

"What are you guys talking about?" Josh walked into the room, glancing from one face to the other.

Lauren moved away from Shane. "We're making plans. I'm going to tutor him at his place tonight and Mandy is going to babysit you."

"I don't want a babysitter." He plopped down on the floor and put his face in his hands.

"You like Mandy. She helps you with your homework and then plays games with you."

"Will she play Wii with me?"

"Sure she will. It'll be fun." She put a hand on his shoulder. "What do you have to say to Shane? Did you enjoy having him with you today?"

He looked up. "I did. It was the best. But I think Miss Marshall has a crush on him."

"Why do you say that?" Lauren glanced at Shane and noticed his heightened color. A pang of jealousy shot right through her. Caroline Marshall was in her early twenties, tall and slim, with naturally wavy long blonde hair. She had a small upturned nose, perky boobs, and a perky smile. Just too damned perky. "Well, is it true?"

"Heck if I know," he said. "I didn't talk to her, if that's what you mean."

"I don't mean anything. Just curious." She looked him up and down. "After all, I know what the nurses think of you."

"I don't care what anyone else thinks of me."

She felt warm relief and gave him a big smile. "That's nice." She turned back to her son. "So what else did you want to say, Josh?"

"Thanks, Uncle Shane."

"You're welcome, son."

Josh had started calling him uncle without anyone suggesting it, but it seemed natural and right. Still, she felt a flutter of panic hearing him call Josh son. That sent another message entirely.

Shane was not theirs to keep, no matter how much she was starting to wish things could be different.

~

When Lauren showed up at Shane's apartment, she was delighted to see that he'd set up the small table on the balcony with a white tablecloth and a large candle. There was a soft breeze, but it was a beautiful night to dine outdoors.

"Knowing how impatient you are," he said, "I ordered the food already. It should be here any minute." He took her in his arms and kissed her neck and bare shoulder.

"Did I ever tell you that I love your shoulders?" He dropped kisses along the length of one. "Strong, decisive, just like you."

When she was young, she'd been embarrassed by her large, square shoulders, but now she carried them with pride. "I'm glad, because they're here to stay."

He smiled. "And I adore your perfect little nose and your sweet pointy chin." He gave it a little squeeze. "But most of all, I love that sexy mouth." His lips found hers, and he kissed her softly. Lauren deepened the kiss, tasting him, hungering for him, tongue matching thrust for thrust.

Out of breath, she pushed back for a second. She ran her fingers through his hair and her tongue along his neck. She peeked up at him and whispered, "I love your smile, your touch, the way you kiss me and say the sweetest things."

"It's easy to say things when you mean them." His eyes were so earnest, she felt a pang of longing deep inside.

"When's that food going to arrive?"

He took her hand and led her to the couch. "Shouldn't be long, but why waste time? Why don't you kick your shoes off and make yourself comfortable?"

She did as she was told, and then pulled him down on top of her. "I like your weight on me. You feel just right."

He shifted enough so that he could slip his good hand between them and cup her breasts. "Perfection. Did they come from a catalogue, or were you just born lucky?"

She grimaced. "They're too big."

He nuzzled them with his nose and mouth. "They're just right."

"Can we—"

"There's the door." He jumped up and grabbed his wallet from the kitchen counter. "Back in a minute. Hold that thought."

"It's about time," she grumbled teasingly.

She helped him unpack the cartons and carry them to the balcony table. The sun had set, and a few stars glimmered on the horizon. They could see the ocean in the dim light, but they caught a whiff of the sea breeze before it was lost in the scent of the candle and the delicious aroma of food.

They wolfed down the spicy pad thai and the shrimp Penang, and nibbled on skewers of tasty chicken with a refreshing cucumber dressing. When their appetites were satisfied, they returned the food to the kitchen, snuffed out the candle, and walked hand in hand to his bedroom.

Lauren moved into his arms, kissing him with all the hunger in her soul. She pulled at his shirt, wanting to feel his naked flesh, hating the cloth that separated them. As she quickly unbuttoned the shirt, her mouth followed her fingers, kissing his chest as each inch became exposed.

When the last button was undone, she pushed his shirt off and got rid of her own top, needing to feel him chest to chest.

Only her lacy bra kept her from her goal. "Undo me," she commanded. Then she softened her voice. "Please?"

He laughed and happily obliged. Pulling her up against him, he ran his good hand up and down her side.

She squirmed against him. "This isn't enough. I want more."

Without another word, he used his legs to topple her onto the bed, and fell next to her. His hands were at her zipper, but his i-limb got in the way. She helped him with her zipper, then he tugged her Capris and panties past her hips.

"Help undress me," he said in a husky voice. "I know exactly what you want, and I'm going to give it to you."

His words sent a delicious tremor through her body, and in moments she had his pants undone and his cock in her hands.

He kicked his pants off, and she wrapped her legs around him, lifting her hips to him. In one solid stroke he entered her, and she gasped with surprise and delight.

"Has anything ever felt so good?" she asked.

"Not as long as I can remember," he murmured, driving deeper and deeper, until he could go no farther. "Are you ready?"

"Oh, yes. Give it to me." She arched under him. "Don't make me ask twice."

He slid halfway out, then slammed back in again. "Like this?"

She licked her lips. "Uh-huh. I want more."

Their movements became frantic as both tried to please the other, until they found a natural rhythm and slowed down. Shane brought her to a fevered pitch, then eased back, prolonging the inevitable; teasing, tasting, giving her everything she needed, taking more time than she wanted.

And it was just the way she liked it.

Later, they got up and showered, then sat on the balcony watching the stars. It was such a perfect night, and Lauren wanted to stretch it out as long as she could.

She tilted her head back and closed her eyes. "I'm at such peace. Surely I died and went to heaven."

"I hope not." He reached over and tickled her side. She squealed. "Nope. You're still alive."

She laughed. "I dare you to do that again."

"You're asking for it, aren't you?" He smirked, looking pleased with himself. "Wasn't once enough?"

"With you? Never."

"I could get used to this." He folded his arms behind his head, flexing his muscles.

"*This* being what?" She stared at him, unsure of how she wanted him to answer. Of course, she wanted him to say that he loved her and Josh, and they'd live happily ever after, but that wasn't realistic, not part of their game plan. She knew that, but it didn't stop her heart from hoping.

"This," he said. "You and me. Spending our nights together. Think we can swing it a little more often?"

She swallowed the tiny lump of hurt inside. Whatever their relationship was, it was good for the present. She knew not to plan a future with him. Unless he wanted it, of course.

"I'm going to try." She smiled at him, refusing to let her emotions get in the way and spoil this wonderful evening. Being with him right now was enough.

"Maybe we could set something up a couple of days a week," he went on. "Have a babysitter booked for those nights, and I'll make sure I don't have a shift."

"We could do that, I suppose. I work three nights a week, but Josh is in bed by eight. He won't miss me if I come home late."

He was silent for a moment, then he cleared his throat and leaned forward to take her hand. "Am I being fair to you and Josh? Wouldn't you be better off with a marrying man?"

"We've been through that." She gave him a meaningful glance, wishing he'd just drop the subject. "I like things the way they are. I don't need to remarry. I have Josh and my work, and for now that's all I can handle."

"Okay. If you're sure." He ran his hand up her arm, sending tingles everywhere. "I think I've got the better end of the deal. You're a beautiful, passionate woman, and the smartest person I know."

She leaned over to kiss him. "Thank you. That's the nicest thing anyone has ever said to me."

"Well, get used to it then. I plan on paying you a lot of compliments. Starting with your mouth." He kissed it tenderly. "It drives me crazy."

"I'll show you crazy." She stood up and slid onto his lap. "I want some more foreplay. Or afterplay. Whatever we want to call it. Something that'll tide us over until the next tutoring session." She planted little kisses all over his face and down his neck. "I sure hope you can keep up your good grades, because we're not going to get a lot of studying done."

"This is worth failing for."

"You say that now." She kissed him softly. "But I'd never forgive myself."

His hand slid under her top. "Want to bet? I can make you feel so good, you'd forgive anything."

Just to prove it, he did.

EPISODE SIX

CHAPTER TWENTY-SEVEN

After Lauren left a little past midnight, Shane couldn't settle down. His mind was filled with thoughts of her, the scent, the taste, the heart of the woman. She was the most amazing person he'd ever met, and he loved everything about her. The touch of her hands, the hot kisses she showered him with, the strength and feel of her legs wrapped around him, her beautiful breasts as she arched above him. But all that would mean nothing if she didn't have that kind, loving heart or the bright, inquiring mind, or her selfless attitude when it came to her son. She'd do anything to protect him, even if it meant bringing harm to herself. His happiness and safety came first, above her own.

Shane normally worked better at night. This was his quiet time when he could study and work on his assignments. But tonight his mind was wandering, and he had to force himself to sit upright in a chair and work through his studies. That worked for the better part of an hour, until he grew restless again.

Lauren was like a drug to him now. He wanted her there, lying next to him. Wanted to smell her special scent, gaze at her beautiful face, feel the warmth of her body pressed against his.

He should have known this would happen, that he'd get in too deep. He'd tried to warn her; he'd tried to hold back. But Kevin's attack on her had changed everything. He didn't trust other men around her. Or, more to the point, he didn't want other men hanging around her, touching her, kissing her, giving her the love she needed.

She was his. At least for now. Until she could see past his charming grin and look inside, and discover the coward lurking there. No one, especially someone as wise and as brave as Lauren, would respect him once she knew.

Lauren woke up late. She didn't bother with an alarm because her inner clock never failed her. But this morning it had. She dashed out of bed, not bothering to make it. She only had an hour to get herself and Josh showered, dressed, and ready to go.

If her body hadn't been so completely sexually sated, she'd never have slept this long. She hummed in the shower, and didn't even try to wipe the smile off her face.

Once dressed, she woke up Josh. "Rise and shine, sweet pea. We're running late today."

"What time is it?"

"Seven-fifteen. Go use the bathroom." She gave him a gentle nudge in that direction. "I'll lay out your clothes and then get your breakfast ready."

He rubbed his sleepy eyes. "What time did you get in? I waited up, hoping you'd come in and kiss me good night."

"You were sleeping soundly when I got home. It must have been late, after ten for sure."

"Can I have pancakes for breakfast?"

"Sorry. Not this morning. You're having an egg on an English muffin. It only takes a minute to make."

"Okay. With cheese?"

"Sure. Be quick, hon. We don't want to be late."

"I don't care. I hate school, anyway."

"I know it's hard right now, but you just need to make some different friends. Isn't there a new boy in your class? What's his name? Is he nice?"

"Yeah. Thomas. He's okay. Kinda dorky, though."

She smiled. "Dorky's good. He'll probably own an Internet company by the time he graduates."

"You're weird," Josh said with a puzzled look, then left to get washed up.

When she let Josh off at the school drop-off area, his teacher waved and strolled over to the car. "Hello, Dr. Reynolds. Hi, Josh." She put a hand on Josh's shoulder. "We enjoyed meeting Mr. Dawson yesterday. He's an interesting guy, that's for sure."

Lauren gritted her teeth, and managed not to roll her eyes. "Yes, I'm sure he had plenty of stories to tell."

"The kids were certainly entertained. They would have happily kept him answering questions all day."

"I'm sure they would." She glanced at the pretty, young teacher, wondering what Shane had thought of her. "Sorry to be rude, but I'm running errands this morning."

"Not a problem. Just wanted to say hello."

"Miss Marshall? Now that you are here, I do want to ask you something. I'm concerned about Josh. He seems to have so few friends and says no one will sit with him at lunch."

She nodded. "Would you like to set up a meeting?"

"I would indeed."

"What time suits you?" Miss Marshall asked.

"I could come early. I work a few afternoon shifts, but tomorrow I start at nine."

"How about tomorrow at seven-thirty? Will that fit your schedule?"

"Yes, it's fine. I'll see you then."

Lauren had to drop off her dry cleaning, buy groceries, and do a quick housecleaning. All that time, she couldn't chase the worry away about Josh, and carried it right to the hospital.

The one good thing about working the ER was that the moment you entered, your own problems got lost amid the unfolding chaos.

Today was no different.

She started off with a good-looking high school student. His knee was propped on a pillow, and he was in a great deal of pain. He'd been playing basketball when his knee had gone out. Lauren gave him something for the pain, ordered an X-ray, then popped the knee back in.

Next came a twenty-eight-year-old man, a car accident victim with head and facial trauma. Unconscious on arrival, he'd lost over a pint of blood, and it was still pouring from the wounds on his face. The doctors and nurses worked quickly to obtain an airway and stop the blood flow, but even as they fought to stabilize him, they sensed it was a losing battle.

The CT scan confirmed their worst fears, but he was moved to the ICU just the same and became someone else's responsibility. With a sad heart and a guilty sigh, Lauren knew she was off the hook. Someone else would be informing the family that their son was brain dead.

The usual bumps and scrapes and non–life-threatening injuries took up the rest of the afternoon. By the time Lauren's shift ended, she was eager to flee this life-and-death world for her peaceful home with her son.

It wasn't until she sat with her glass of wine, watching her son sleep, that she remembered the appointment with the teacher in the morning.

CHAPTER TWENTY-EIGHT

Caroline Marshall ushered Lauren into a small room and asked if she minded if the school counselor sat in.

"No, of course not." She shook hands with Lisa Simpson, having met her on several occasions.

The three women sat at a small conference table, and Lisa started the conversation. "You mentioned to Miss Marshall that Josh has few friends and eats alone most days. This concerns us as well. How does he get along with others at home?"

"He doesn't bring many kids home," Lauren admitted. "There's really only his nanny and me. But he says the other children don't like him and won't play with him at recess or lunch." Her heart ached for her son, and she felt so helpless. It was her job to protect him, to ensure his happiness, but how could you force other boys to like him? Were they to blame? Or had she failed him somehow?

"I'm deeply concerned by this," she added. "I want my son to be happy and enjoy school." Lauren stared down the two women. "So what can the school do to make sure he's not isolated?"

The teacher and counselor looked at each other. "I think it all started due to the bullying."

Lauren clenched her fists under the table. "Who's responsible?"

"I can't say," Caroline Marshall replied. "But there is a certain group of boys that has made it their business to ridicule him every chance they get."

"Why can't you stop them? Call in their parents and address this issue with them?"

"It's not so easy." Lisa met her gaze. "They haven't actually broken any school rules, or done anything to your son except make fun of him behind his back. But what it has done is it's made Josh a social outcast. No one wants to befriend him because they don't want to be the next kid under attack."

"That's horrible and unfair. What do we do to stop this?"

"Well, we plan to have an assembly and address the issue of bullying, and also reinforce the rules of the school," Caroline Marshall said. "That might help. We are also considering asking one of the other students, a boy a year older, to be a playground buddy, if he agrees, of course."

"I'm glad to hear that, but what if he doesn't?"

The two women looked at each other. Lisa spoke, "Then I'm not sure what our next plan will be, but I do think we should set up another appointment in a month or so to revisit this situation."

"Agreed. But please keep me informed and let me know if it gets worse." The women started to gather their belongings when she stopped them. "I have something else to discuss while I'm here." She was silent for a moment, knowing what a difficult decision she had to make. "I wanted to ask about his performance at school. Does he seem to be having trouble concentrating or staying on task?"

"He has his moments, but we know it's difficult for him."

Lauren nodded. "He's usually okay at home. We have a reward system to reinforce his good behavior. I use a chart, and he gets a sticker every time he completes his homework, makes his bed, cleans his room, and does what's asked."

Caroline nodded. "We do that with Josh and all the children. It's common practice to reward them for good behavior."

"I guess what I also want to know is whether you think his ADHD is impacting his social life at school. I mean if it is..."

Her voice trailed off as tears threatened her composure. She sucked them back and straightened her shoulders. Had her decision to not medicate her son somehow contributed to his being a social outcast? If so, she'd correct it at once.

"Do you think he should be put on meds? Might that help?"

"That's between you and your pediatrician, but we have another little boy who's on Dexedrine, and it has improved his hyperactivity and increased his attention span."

Lauren didn't answer right away. Like most parents she had hoped her child could be helped through proper diet and discipline, and keeping to a rigid schedule, but in Josh's case, it might not be enough.

Her son needed friends, and he needed every chance to be as normal as everyone else. "I'll speak to the pediatrician right away."

~

The following night Lauren and Shane had dinner out, and then went back to his place. After they'd made love, they remained in bed, holding hands and talking.

"Do you think I'm a good mom?"

"The best," he replied, walking his fingers up her arm. He kissed her shoulder.

"I've tried to be both mom and dad to Josh. I've tried to make it up to him for losing his father."

"You've done a great job. Why are you doubting yourself now?"

"I'm not sure why I'm bringing this up, but I've been carrying a load of guilt around, and I've never told a soul."

Shane sat up on one elbow. He gazed at her face. "What in the world do you have to be guilty about?"

She felt tears sting her eyes. Embarrassed, she wiped them away. "When Josh was a toddler, maybe two or three, I could tell he was different from other kids his age. I discussed it with my husband, but he disagreed. Told me that I was imagining it, that it was too early to diagnose, and that I was worrying about nothing. We'd had this conversation plenty of times, but what I can't get over is that I brought it up the day he died."

"Oh, Lauren. I'm sorry." He pulled her head down to his shoulder and kissed her forehead. "But everyone has disagreements. You shouldn't focus on that. I'm sure he didn't."

She shifted her pillow and sat up. "After the accident, I was devastated, and sure that my actions contributed to his death. I was sick with grief and guilt. Anyway, because of all that, I pushed my worries about Josh aside, wanting to believe that Jeremy was right and I was just being an overprotective mother." She sighed, pushing a lock of hair out of her eyes. "I finally had him tested last year, in kindergarten." She told him about the subsequent meeting at school after the diagnosis of ADHD, and how they'd suggested he be put on medication. "How is he with you?" she asked.

"He's a pretty happy-go lucky kid. Doesn't sit still much or stop talking, but that's all right. I like his energy."

Lauren bent down to kiss him. "Thank you. Still, I'm having a meeting with his pediatrician tomorrow."

"Well, he can advise you better than anyone."

"I know. I hate the idea of having him on medication at such an early age, but if it'll help him at school—socially and academically—I've got to consider it." She slipped back down into the bed and laid her head on his chest. "It breaks my heart to think of other kids bullying Josh, of him sitting alone at lunch and recess, without any friends."

"If a low-dosage drug can improve his symptoms, then he'll blend in and make friends easier. I'm all for it."

She smiled. "Why do you always say exactly the right thing to make me feel better?"

"I know you." He touched her left breast. "In here."

After a few minutes of kissing, he began gentle stroking. He kissed her softly, and massaged her shoulders and back, her legs, and between them too. Her tensions melted away, and for once she lay back and allowed him to be in charge.

CHAPTER TWENTY-NINE

Days later, Shane got a call in the middle of the night. Even though he hadn't been sleeping, the sound of the phone at 4 a.m. startled him.

Fearing the worst, he reached for the phone, his hand shaking and his heart hammering. "Shane here."

"It's me, Jake. Sorry to be calling you at this hour, but we got some bad news." He cleared his throat. "It's Brent. His helo has gone down."

"Fuck no." Shane sank into a chair and rubbed his eyes. "Give it to me straight. Is he dead?"

"All we know is that his helicopter was brought down by small arms fire." Jake swore. "Six men were on board, and Brent and the men are still out there."

"What do you mean?" He was wide awake now, and pacing the room.

"Look, Dad just got the call minutes ago from a senior official in Washington. He said at the crash site the insurgents were firing weapons at the helicopter in an attempt to blow it up, but the QRF forces were on them. The Afghans are wiry little bastards, I'm telling you. Can climb those steep terrains like a pack of invisible mountain goats."

The Quick Reaction Force were the first to be called in a crisis and had been on the Taliban in a matter of minutes, but couldn't get near. Since John Harrington was a retired general, it was not surprising that he'd been given this information.

"Shit." Shane sucked in a painful breath. "I told Brent not to go, but the stubborn jerk wouldn't listen." He continued to stalk the room, his adrenaline fueling his anger.

"I know, Shane. We all did."

"Fucking bastards. Wish we could obliterate every damn one." Shane gritted his teeth and snarled, "You know that the Taliban brag about it, don't you? They like to take credit for every kill. Even when it's friendly fire."

"Yeah, yeah, I know all about it. But look, Shane, there's no sense in getting all worked up right now." Jake sounded like the voice of reason, which ticked Shane off. "We don't know anything for sure," he added.

"Good God. He's your brother," Shane cried. "You know he's either dead or injured. Isn't that enough?"

"You're right." Jake made a choking sound, then in a husky voice he spoke again. "This isn't easy for any of us, but I'm trying to think positively, and you should do the same. As soon as I hear anything, I'll keep you informed."

"Look, Jake, I'm sorry if I sounded harsh. I know how much you love Brent, and how your family look out for each other."

"That's all right. I know how you feel." Jake had done two tours in Iraq; he knew the dangers for his brother better than anyone. "I want to get my hands on the bastards too."

"Dammit. I feel so helpless!" Shane made a fist with his hand and thumped the table. He closed his eyes and took a steadying breath. "I can't believe that our own forces can't get to him. Some of these outposts are in really bad positions. They're like sitting ducks out there."

"I hear you." Jake added, "But we have to trust our government that they know what they're doing. They wouldn't put our boys in harm's way."

"Do you believe that?"

"I have to. The commanders make difficult choices, but they know what they're doing, and back their men. To think otherwise, well, let's say it would shake my very core."

"I know, Jake." Shane remembered Brent's last visit. "Hey, your father's all right? Last I heard he'd had a stroke and was on life support."

"You know you can't keep a good man down," Jake said smoothly. "Not only did he pull through, but he's getting better every day. Still has partial paralysis on his left side, but things are looking up. He's in rehab, but he can speak and feed himself, and his cognitive skills weren't affected."

"That's great, Jake. Really great." Shane's thoughts returned to Brent. "Where did the helo go down?"

"Happened in the Alasay district of Kapisa Province, in East Afghanistan. It was a search and rescue mission, and obviously the Taliban were just waiting for them."

"Thanks, Jake, for calling me right away, and keep me posted."

"I will. Dad's already on it. He'll get the information before anybody."

"Give him my best, will you?"

"Sure thing."

After they said their good-byes, Shane couldn't sit still. His stomach churned, and he felt as though he'd burst out of his skin. He began to prowl the apartment, as antsy as he'd been the first week without a drink.

Just the thought of booze made his throat dry and his hands shake. He wasn't going to drink. No way. No how. He'd made a promise to himself, and Lauren deserved better from him.

Lauren. He needed to talk to her. She always understood everything, and just hearing her voice would act like a tonic. He knew Josh would be in bed, but she'd be certain to answer her cell. Maybe she would even allow him to come over.

He dialed her number and it was busy. Called again, and no answer. He called her home number and left a message. Where the heck was she? He needed her more than ever.

Maybe he'd jump in his car and drive over. Her welcoming smile, the warmth of her embrace, oh God, please let that be enough. He didn't want to slide down this sinkhole again. This blackness of despair would eat him up. Every minute that he sat there, his shaking grew worse, and his thoughts turned to the bottle.

He got up and tossed his cell phone to the floor. No use. Tonight nothing could keep him away from drowning his fears. Not even Lauren.

There had to be some booze hidden in the house somewhere. Surely, Brent hadn't gotten rid of every ounce of alcohol before letting him move in? If he'd been so opposed, he'd never have brought over that six-pack. Come on, come on, it had to be here. Brent was a social drinker but he always had Scotch in the house. And he used to have a collection of fine wine. Where would he stash it?

Shane looked under the beds, in the back of the cupboards, closets, storage area in the small guest room. Like a tunnel rat, he darted one way and another, head swimming, his mind focused on only one thing. Booze. He needed it now and plenty of it. Damn near trashed the place looking, and when he came up empty, he stormed out of the apartment in search of an all-night liquor shop. He found a convenience store, bought a bottle of Scotch, and didn't wait until he got home to taste it.

He cracked it open in the parking lot, and without thinking, he closed his eyes and took a swallow. It burned his throat on the way down, and tears sprang into his eyes.

He wiped the tears away and poured some more down his throat. After several slugs, he wedged the bottle under his arm and walked the short distance home. He stumbled over to the elevator, pushed the button, and collapsed against the elevator wall for the ride to his floor, still sucking on the bottle.

By the time he reached the apartment door, he was having trouble focusing. He had to stab at the lock several times before the key slid in, and he fell through the open doorway. The bottle slid through his hands, but he managed to catch it with his knees before it hit the floor.

He slipped down, leaning against the door, and took another long slug of Scotch. Tears slid down his face, and he almost gagged, but he didn't stop. He kept drinking, needing to punish himself, to hurt until he could stop hurting, to drink until he felt nothing, remembered nothing, and cared about nothing.

~

Lauren had been called in to work as there had been a twelve-car pile-up on the freeway, and ER needed an extra set of hands. When she returned home at 4 a.m. Julie told her that Shane had called and left a message.

She thanked Julie, told her to take the day off, and crept into bed. She slept until seven-thirty when little hands woke her up.

"Mom? Wake up. I'm going to be late for school."

She blinked, stared at the clock, trying to figure out if it was morning or night. She glanced at her son. School? Holy crap.

"Mom. Mom. I'm already dressed. Hurry up."

"Just a second, honey. I'm not quite awake."

"Today, we're going to the science museum, remember? It's a bus trip. You signed permission. Remember?"

The fog in her brain cleared. "Yes, yes, that's right." She yawned, and sat up. "Can you have some cereal while I hurry and get dressed? I'll get you to school on time, don't worry."

"Okay, 'cuz I don't want to miss it."

Lauren's head hurt, as she swept her legs out of bed and stood up. She was so exhausted she felt like she could sleep on her feet. Of all days for the museum trip, it would have to be today.

She stumbled into the bathroom, splashed water on her face, then turned on the shower. She stood under the warm water for a few minutes, then stepped out, not feeling any better than she had a minute before. She squirted some drops into her bloodshot eyes, brushed her teeth and hair, and put on a pair of shorts and a tee.

Josh was standing at the door, school bag in hand.

"Hurry up, Mom. I don't want to be late."

Lauren grabbed her car keys, slipped her feet into flip-flops, and then turned to her son. "You haven't brushed your hair or teeth. Do that, and I'll get the car running."

He grumbled but did as he was told. A minute later they were in the car, driving the five blocks to his school. She dropped him off with a kiss and a wave, then returned home to fall asleep for another three hours.

Feeling a little more human, she made a pot of coffee and checked her phone messages. There was a call from Shane on the house line and two missed calls on her cell. She called back and got no answer, then wandered around her place, cleaning up, making beds, figuring out what they'd have for dinner.

It was only eleven and she had several free hours before picking up Josh from school. She called Shane again, not sure if he was at class or working today, but was unable to reach him. She couldn't sit around with nothing to do, so Lauren decided to go to the hospital and check on a few of the patients she'd patched up last night. Several were on the critical list, and might not have made it through the night. She knew it wasn't her job to care, but as a human being with a heart, she had no choice.

After she made her round and learned that everyone was still stable, she called Shane's cell again, but he never picked up. She pushed him to the back of her mind and hurried over to the school, wanting to be outside when the school bus returned.

Josh was one of the last kids off the bus, and he grinned and waved when he saw her. He ran up, jumping up and down. "Hey, Mom. We had a super-duper time. Some of the mothers went with us. Too bad you didn't come. Next time, I want you to come. Okay?"

She kissed the top of his head. "Sure, Champ. If I can."

"Yeah. I know. You always have to work."

She felt a nudge of guilt at the disappointed look on her child's face. "Next time, if I have enough notice, I'll make sure I ask for the day off. Okay? Unless there's an emergency, I'll be there, I promise."

He didn't say anything, then his face brightened. "Maybe I could ask Shane. He'd come, I know he would."

"He would want to, that's for sure." When they got home she tried calling Shane once again, but still no answer.

Josh went to his bedroom to play with his Legos, while Lauren made spaghetti for dinner. He came out a half hour later and turned on TV. She heard the familiar lyrics of *SpongeBob*, her son's favorite show, and watched him for a few minutes as he sat there engrossed with the characters he knew and loved.

He looked up. "Spaghetti for dinner? Yum. I had a hot dog for lunch and some chips, yogurt, and a sippy drink."

"I'm glad you had a good day. Who did you sit with on the bus?"

"A new guy at school. He's nice."

"That's good, honey. I'm glad you made a new friend."

He nodded and went back to his TV show. She called Shane once more and left him a detailed message but he never returned her call. Her feelings were hurt, and she was tired from having worked all night, and was not in the mood to chase him down.

After dinner, she bathed Josh and turned in early, but thoughts of Shane interrupted her sleep. She had a niggling worry that something was wrong. Why would he not call?

The following day she didn't hear from him either, and by nighttime she was quite convinced that her fears were valid. Shane would not go this long without calling her. Something had happened and she had to know what.

She called Julie to say something had come up and could she work a few extra hours?

"Of course, Dr. Reynolds. You know I'm always happy to stay whenever you need me."

"I know, and that's one of the things I love about you."

Julie laughed. "And why you pay me the big bucks too."

"You're worth every cent. I don't know what I'd do without you."

"I'll remember that." Julie added, "I can always sleep on the couch if you're very late."

"Thank you, but I'll try to make it before midnight."

When Lauren left work, she drove straight to Shane's apartment and pounded on his door. When he didn't answer, she shouted through the door, "Shane, it's me, Lauren. Are you all right?"

No answer. She pounded harder. Finally, she heard a noise on the other side of the door. Major barked, and made scratching noises.

"Go away," a husky voice answered.

"Shane? Open up. I'm worried about you."

"Said go away." He slurred the words, which made Lauren even more anxious. Had he been drinking?

"Can you open this door? Do you need help?" She fought back panic. "Please speak to me." She tried the door handle, but it didn't budge. "I need to see you."

Someone in another apartment peeked out. "Is everything okay?" a middle-aged Hispanic man asked.

"I don't know. Have you seen the young man that lives here?"

"Not in a few days." He eyed her with curiosity. "You a friend?"

"Yes, and I'm worried about him."

"There's an office downstairs. Always have a manager on duty."

"Thanks. I'll get him if I need to." She knocked again, more quietly this time. "Shane, if you don't open up in the next minute, I'm getting the manager and coming in. I have to know you're okay."

The curious neighbor stood there watching her. "I'm a doctor," she told him. "He's in good hands."

"You want me to go downstairs and get help?"

"No. Not yet." She heard a bumping noise, some cursing, and then Shane fumbling with the lock.

"He's coming now," she told the neighbor. The door slid open, and she walked into the dark.

She didn't see him at first, but then her eyes adjusted to the dim light. He was disheveled, unshaven, and reeking of stale booze.

When she realized that he hadn't suffered a stroke, her worry turned to anger. "What happened?" she asked, trying to hold back her emotions. She didn't know if she wanted to scream at him or cry.

"Had a little party." He waved an empty Scotch bottle at her. "I'd offer you a drink, but as you can see, I'm all out."

"You think this is funny?" She trembled with rage. "You dare laugh at this?" Her gaze swept around the room, and she could see the carnage he'd done. He'd been sober for a year. What had driven him to this?

"Shane." Her voice cracked. "How could you do this?"

He threw the bottle against the far wall. Major whimpered and ran off to a corner. Lauren backed away in fear as shattered glass littered the floor. This was not the Shane she knew. This wild-eyed creature was frightening her to death. She swallowed hard, tasting the acid bile that rose in her throat.

"Why'd you come?" he asked. "Go home. Go back to Josh." He smashed his fist into the wall, breaking through the plaster and wounding his one good hand.

"What are you doing?" In a second she was by his side, inspecting his hand. Already it was swelling, the skin turning red. "Look what you've done. What's happened? Please talk to me, Shane."

He stumbled into her, and she smelled the booze on his breath. She recoiled. "Why are you crying?" he asked.

"I'm not. You're just scaring me, that's all." She folded her arms around her chest, holding the hurt, the anger deep inside. If she let it out, she'd say things that could never be unsaid.

And no matter how devastated she felt, he must somehow feel worse.

"Come sit down and tell me what's happened," she said in a gentle voice. "I want to understand."

"Nothing to tell." He hung his head, staring at the ground. "I'm a useless shit. Now you know."

"Oh, Shane. You are not. Don't even think that about yourself. I love you, but I can't believe you did this." She bit her lip, and a tear dribbled out of her eye. She could never allow an alcoholic in her life. Not after losing her husband to a drunk driver—a man who had just been released from rehab and stopped in a bar to celebrate.

"Your hand," she said softly. "You could have broken it." She felt her heart splitting in two when she asked, "Why? Why would you do that?" She put her hands in the air. "And this?"

"I needed to smash something."

His voice sent a chill running through her. "What's happened? Help me understand."

He crossed his arms, hiding the stump on his left arm under his armpit. His precious i-limb was nowhere in sight. "You know my buddy, Brent? Well, his helo went down and he's probably dead right now. No one knows, because our forces can't get to the crash site. The Taliban have dug in and are fighting them off."

"Oh, Shane." She bit her lip and sucked back a sob. "I'm so sorry. I know what a good friend he is to you." She reached out a hand to him, but he pushed it away.

"Yeah, well, I threw a little pity party. So now you know. I'm a stinkin' drunk. Not worth shit."

"Don't say that. It's not true." She grimaced, for she knew the truth. An alcoholic would always be an alcoholic, and could only stay sober one day at a time. "I'll help you through this, Shane."

"You can't help me. Nobody can." He stormed away from her and smashed his fist against the wall, again and again.

Major began to howl.

"Get out of here, Lauren," he said between blows. "Get out. You don't want a guy like me in your life." He turned bloodshot eyes to her. "Not with a kid."

Lauren stood still as a stone, while her world crashed around her, destroying her dreams of Shane.

"Shane. You need help right now. Let me take you to the hospital and get your hand looked at."

"I'm not going to the hospital. I'm fine. Don't need you. Don't need anybody."

"You are far from fine." She bit her lip. "You probably need your hand set, and to detox."

"Don't bother me. Okay? Just leave."

"I'm not going to leave you. I'm a doctor, remember? And you clearly need help."

"What I don't need is your pity, and I can take care of myself. Been doing that most of my life."

"Doing a fine job too," she snapped, getting angry. So much for pity. She wanted to shake him hard. Let him see exactly what he'd done, and how difficult it was going to be to fix it.

"Yeah, right on, sister." He gave her a contemptuous look. "Now you can see the kind of man I am. You need to take your boy far, far away from me."

"I'm not afraid of you. And Josh adores you." Even as she said the words, she knew his relationship with her son was over. It had to be. There was no other choice. Josh's security and stability came first.

Shane's face changed, as if something had finally gotten through to him. "I'm not worth your tears," he said, and stepped close. "Don't cry, Lauren."

She met his gaze. "I'm crying because I can't bear to see you like this."

"I'm sorry about that. But you see, I'm not the man you wanted me to be."

"Maybe." She didn't flinch. "But I can't leave you like this. I'm calling Rick. You need help."

"Don't." He shook his head. "Don't do that. I need my job. Besides I'm okay. Physician, heal thyself," he muttered and laughed.

"You need treatment on your hand, and rehab."

"I certainly don't need rehab and I can fix myself."

"That doesn't seem to be working at the moment." She glanced around the room, not hiding her dismay. "You can't stay here alone."

"I can and I will. Told you I'm fine."

"Sure. Until a crisis comes along. Well, I've got news for you, buddy. Our lives are chock full of crises, and if you're going to be a medic, or a doctor, or anything worthwhile, you're going to need a support group to keep you on track."

"I don't need shit."

"Give me Rick's number or I'll call the EMT dispatcher for it."

"He can't help me. Nobody can."

"You're wrong. That's what partners are for. They've got each other's back." She watched him closely, afraid to take her eyes off him. He was in a self-destructive mood and she didn't know what he might do.

"Who's got yours, Lauren? Did you ever ask yourself that?"

CHAPTER THIRTY

After she'd called Rick and assured herself that he could take care of Shane, Lauren headed home. She thought about Shane's taunting question on the long drive back.

It was true that no one had her back, but she had Josh's and that was all that mattered. Once again, they were on their own.

What could she possibly tell Josh that wouldn't break his heart? And what would she do now without Shane? She didn't love him any less because of what had happened, but she couldn't let him near her child. No matter how much it hurt, she had to curtail their friendship, and put an end to her love affair with Shane.

The violence he'd displayed had shocked her, and maybe he'd done it for that purpose—to push her away. He wanted her to see the worst in him, and that glimpse had not been pretty. But it didn't stop her from loving him. She couldn't turn her feelings on and off like that.

But this wasn't about her. Or Shane. Josh would be inconsolable, and he would require even closer supervision. She hoped the new medication that his doctor prescribed would help him cope better with his pain.

When she walked in, Julie was immersed in a late-night movie. She unfolded herself off the couch, pulled her pink T-shirt down over her generous hips, and clicked the TV off. She was a pretty, forty-something woman from Costa Rica, and had no family here, but supported a grown daughter and her mother back home.

Seeing Lauren's face, she asked in alarm, "You okay, Dr. Reynolds?"

Lauren nodded. "Yes. It's just been a really bad day. That's all."

"Well, is there anything I can do? Would you like me to stay over?"

"No, no. You've been here long enough, and I appreciate your staying late for me." She walked Julie to the door. "I have to tell Josh something in the morning, and he's going to be upset. I'll need you to take extra special care of him right now. He might act out for a while."

"There is nothing that boy can do that I can't handle. You just go to work like always, and leave him to me."

"You're a gem, Julie. I'll let his teacher know that he's had an upset, and we'll all just have to do what we can to help him handle his grief."

"Can I ask what's happened?"

"It's his friend, Shane. He won't be able to see him anymore."

"Oh, dear. That will break the poor boy's heart."

"Yes. I'm sure it will, but nothing can be done about it."

"I'm terribly sorry. He's a good man, but I know you have your reasons." She gave Lauren a quick hug. "I'll see you tomorrow."

After Julie left, Lauren poured herself a glass of wine and sat down on the sofa. She knew her mind was too troubled to allow her to sleep.

The following morning she decided to hold off telling Josh until he returned from school. Still, as if it would help, she made him blueberry pancakes for breakfast, adding slices of banana on top in the shape of a happy face.

"Mom, is it my birthday or something?" Josh attacked his pancakes, dipping each piece in a pool of maple syrup.

"No, honey. It doesn't have to be a special day for you to enjoy your favorite breakfast. I've also decided to take the day off and pick you up after school."

"Wow." His eyes grew big as saucers. "Is it your birthday?"

She laughed to hide her true feelings. She was uneasy, sick at heart, and exhausted from worry. She'd had a sleepless night, and had cried for much of it. "No, dear. I've been working a lot lately, and I've decided we should have a night to ourselves."

"Can Shane come?"

Her heart squeezed painfully. "No, not tonight, honey. It's just you and me."

"I want Shane." He stabbed his pancake over and over. "I want Shane."

"I know you do, but he can't make it. Besides, we've always had fun together. Remember all the cool things we used to do by ourselves? How about bowling? We could go after school and eat hot dogs for dinner."

He stopped attacking the pancake, and looked up. "Can I bring a friend?"

"Sure. If you want to. But I thought it might be more fun if it was just you and me."

"If I ask Brad, maybe he'll like me again."

"What about that new boy? Thomas? Isn't that his name?"

"Yeah, but like I said. He's a dork."

"Come on, give him a break. He doesn't know many people here yet, and I'm sure he'd like to make new friends."

Josh gulped down his milk. "I'll ask."

"That would be nice, dear. And if not today, perhaps he could come over this weekend."

She put the dishes away while he ran off to brush his teeth, and then she drove him to school. She watched him walk inside, a lonely figure, with no buddies around to greet him. Her heart ached for him, for her, for all the good things that should have been.

~

When Josh was out of sight she called the hospital to say a personal issue had come up and she wouldn't be in, then drove over to check on Shane.

He opened the door at her first knock and stepped back. Although his eyes were red-rimmed and blurry, he'd shaved and cleaned himself up. His hand was bandaged, she noticed, and the furniture was back in place. The books and paraphernalia that had littered the floor had been picked up. Only a broken lamp stood as a reminder of the violent storm that had erupted during the harrowing night.

"Well, you're looking better," she said in way of greeting. Major danced around her feet, begging to be petted. She dropped her hand and let him lick it.

"Look, I'm sorry, Lauren. I screwed up. It won't happen again." His shoulders were hunched over, and he had a sheepish look on his face. But his eyes wouldn't meet hers.

She swallowed hard, and she couldn't look at him either. "Yes, you did."

"Rick came by after you left, and he promised not to tell anyone at work as long as I join AA and go to all the meetings."

"That was kind of him." She kept her voice neutral, not giving him any hint of her feelings. He had to know that he'd disappointed her, and that he'd broken her heart. He would have to live with that guilt too.

"Is that all you've got to say?"

"No." She folded her arms, holding on tight, keeping herself together. "I have a lot more." Major slinked away, no longer fighting for her attention.

"Then let it out. Don't hold back." He cocked his chin defiantly. "I deserve it and more."

She knew he still didn't get the severity of what he'd done, and how it would affect their relationship and devastate her son.

She spoke gently, like she would to a sick patient. That's what he was. Sick. He was not a bad person. He was ill and needed help. "It hurts me to say this, but I have to." She straightened her shoulders and took a deep breath. "You can no longer see Josh, and our agreement is off. I'm sorry."

He staggered back as if she'd punched him. "What do you mean?"

"I have strong feelings for you, Shane." She shook her head. "No, strong is too mild a term. I do love you, and Josh is mad about you." She looked into his face, hoping he'd see she had no choice. "But you have a drinking problem and other issues, and I can't bring that into my household."

The blood seemed to drain from his face, and he sank into a chair. "You don't mean that. It was a mistake." He pleaded, "It won't happen again. I'm going to start AA. I'm going to do it right this time. I promise."

"It's too late for promises, Shane. I trusted you." Her voice broke. "I believed in you, and I can't risk this happening again."

"No." He shook his head and held out his bandaged hand in a plea for understanding. "You know what happened. My best buddy in the entire world had his chopper shot down."

"I know." She bit her lip. "I understand." She wanted to touch him, to hold him, but she couldn't allow that weakness. This was the time to be strong. "I'm so sorry."

"No, you don't understand. You can't possibly or you wouldn't be saying these things." His voice rose in panic. "Let me explain."

"Nothing you say will change my mind."

"It has to. Please? Here me out." He paced the room, clearly agitated. "I called his brother Jake this morning, and our forces still have been unable to break through and rescue the men. It's a terrible situation over there. You have no idea."

"I'm deeply sorry, Shane. I really am."

He gave her a pleading look. "He's lying on the side of some fucking mountain with a bloodbath going on around him. He's either dead or wounded, and I can't get to him. Nobody can."

"I understand completely. I do." She ground her fingernails into the palms of her hands. "I understand your need to have a drink, possibly to drown your sorrows, but you don't have that luxury anymore. You're a recovering alcoholic. That means alcohol is poison to you."

"I will never touch another drop as long as I live. I swear it."

"I can't take that chance." She sucked back tears, refusing to let them fall. "I would never know if something else might set you off. I have to protect my son."

"I'd never hurt Josh. You know that." She could clearly see the agony on his face, but it didn't matter how he felt. How she felt. Nothing could change what she had to do, and even if it killed her she couldn't back down.

He continued in desperation, "I love that kid. And one night of getting shit-faced doesn't amount to a hill of beans." He took a step toward her and Major barked. "I'm disgusted by myself, too, but you have to believe me, Lauren. It won't happen again."

"I wish I could believe you, but I can't take any chances with my son's welfare. He's all I've got, and it's my duty as a parent to keep him safe." She put a hand up, to ward him off. "I wish you all the very best, Shane, and I will always care about you. This isn't easy for me either." Tears blurred her vision as she turned to walk away.

He stepped in front of her. "Please, Lauren. Don't go. Don't leave me like this."

She looked at him for a long moment, not saying a word. He'd broken her heart, and her son's too. There was nothing left to say.

She opened the door and escaped.

CHAPTER THIRTY-ONE

Lauren had a sick feeling in her stomach all day, and by the time she picked Josh up from school, she had a massive headache too. She regretted telling Josh that he could invite a friend to come with him, and for once, felt relieved to see him alone.

Today was not a good day for him to make new friends. He had to be told the truth, and the sooner the better. Still, she wanted to give him an hour or two to laugh and play before she ripped his world apart. She did ask him if he'd invited Thomas. He said he had, but the boy had T-ball practice after school.

"But maybe he can come over this weekend. Would that be okay, Mom?"

"Yes, I'm sure that can be arranged. And I'm glad it's just going to be you and me today. We haven't had alone time for ages."

He got into the backseat of the car, fastened his seat belt, and talked nonstop all the way to the bowling alley.

Once they had their shoes on and found their lane, they selected their favorite ball to use.

"You go first," she told her son.

He gave her a little wave and a gap-toothed smile, then tossed the ball. It bounced a couple of times and then rolled into the gutter. He jumped up and down, before turning to his mother with an excited grin. "Is it your turn, Mommy?"

"Not yet. You get one more try." She showed him how to throw, and once again, the ball bounced into the gutter.

"Okay. Let's see if I can knock one of those pins down. Can't be too hard, right, buddy?" she asked.

"Yeah. Knock 'em down, Mommy." He clapped his hands. "Knock 'em dead."

Lauren put her fingers into the holes and lined up the shot. She took a couple of fancy steps and was about to let it rip, when the ball slipped from her fingers and landed inches from her toes.

Josh laughed, but much to her horror, she burst into tears.

"What's wrong, Mommy?" He came up beside her and hugged her legs. "Why are you crying?"

"Nothing, dear. I don't know what's wrong with me. I don't usually cry." She scrambled for her handbag, found some tissues, and mopped her face.

Josh watched her for a long minute. "Is something wrong? You've been acting weird all day."

"I'm just emotional that's all. Ignore me and let's play."

Josh got up. "Okay. I'm going to do it this time. You don't need to help me." He picked up a ball and tossed it. It weaved slowly down the lane, and took out two pins. He shouted with joy and raised his hands in the air. "I did it. I did it!"

She clapped and grinned. "You sure did. Nice going." She nodded. "You get another try. Knock the rest down."

He sent the next ball careening into the gutter. Lauren stepped up. "Okay, I'm ready to give it a shot."

She took a big arc, and released the ball which traveled straight and narrow down the gleaming wood lane. It knocked the middle pin down and took out three others, leaving only one pin standing. She then sent a curve ball flying down the lane and scored a direct hit. Turning to Josh, she slapped his hand in a high five. "Got a spare."

"I want to get a strike." Josh jumped up and down. "How can I, Mom?"

"Here, let me help you." She fitted the ball to his fingers and showed him again how to line up for the shot. He practiced the arm swing and at her encouragement, let it rip.

The first ball seemed to stagger and sway but it eventually made its way down the long lane, taking out the two middle two pins. His second knocked out the rest. Josh yelped. "Strike. That's a strike, Mom."

"It sure is, hon." Close enough, she decided, figuring they had enough for one day. "Let's go get our hot dogs. I'm starved. Aren't you?"

She grabbed his hand and marched him off to the refreshment stand. After wolfing down hot dogs, French fries, and an apple juice for him, a diet soda for her, they returned their shoes and headed back to the car.

Lauren waited until they reached home, knowing she couldn't stall any longer. Josh had to be told, and postponing it would not make the situation go away. She sat him down in the family room, and told him they had to have a talk.

Josh sat on the sofa, looking uneasy. He shuffled his feet, and his eyes darted around the room, as if he was searching for a place to hide.

Lauren sat next to him and patted his knee. "You know that I would do anything for you, don't you?"

"Yeah, I know."

"I just want you to know how much I care, and that I would do anything, anything in the world to avoid hurting you."

"Okay." He looked up hopefully. "Can I go now?"

"No, sweetheart. I have something important to tell you."

He nodded, but looked down in his lap.

"We can't see Shane anymore." She rushed on, "I know we love him, but he's got problems that he needs to sort out."

Josh looked up. "What kind of problems? You mean, his hand?" His face brightened. "I can help him with that."

"No, no, that's the least of his worries." She brushed Josh's fair hair back from his eyes. "Something bad happened to him when he went to war. Something worse than losing a hand. It injured him here." She touched her heart. "And in here." She pointed to her head. "He's got to work some things out, honey, and until he does, we can't see him."

"Why not?" His face took on an angry look. "I want to see Shane. I don't care about any old problems."

"You can't, sweetie. Shane has to do this by himself. We can't help him. I wish it was that simple and that we could."

"Why not? He's my friend."

"It's not an easy fix, hon. When he was at war, terrible things happened to him and he gets very sad sometimes."

"That's okay for him to be sad. At least he doesn't yell like Brad's father. He yells all the time."

"I didn't know that." She frowned. "Why didn't you say anything before?"

"You never asked." Josh began scratching his arms, clearly agitated.

"Well, I am now. He never raised his hand to you, did he?"

"No, not me. He tried to smack Brad once, but Brad ducked and his dad missed."

"I see." She couldn't believe how duped she'd been by Kevin. All the years she'd known him and his wife, he'd never displayed any temper. He'd always been charming and amusing—until that last evening when she'd thrown him out of her house.

"Shane's nice," Josh said. "He's not like Brad's dad." He glared at his mom. "I want Shane."

"I know, honey, but he has a sickness inside him. It's not his fault, and he's trying his very best to control this sickness, but there is no easy cure. It's not like the measles or mumps that come for a week or two then go away."

"Will he die?"

"No, he won't die. And he may get better, but it could take years." She smiled at her son. "We can pray for him. Every night when we say our prayers, we can say one for him."

That seemed to pacify him a little. He stopped scratching and smiled. "Good. Can we say one now? I want him better soon, so I can see him again."

"Me too, Josh." She kissed the top of his head. "But it will take a very long time before he will be completely well."

"What about my medicine? Maybe it'll help him too."

"He needs a different kind of medicine, dear."

"Okay. Why don't you go to the drugstore and buy him some, so he can get well? Please, Mom. Please?"

Lauren blinked rapidly, fighting back tears. "It's not that kind of medicine, Josh. I know you'll miss—"

"I don't want to miss him!" Josh shouted. "You always take everybody away from me."

"That's not true. We had to stop seeing Gary, I know, but that was because he quit the Brothers organization."

"What about Dad? You sent him away too."

A piercing pain shot through her chest. "I loved your dad with my whole heart." She struggled to maintain control of her emotions.

"Then why did he go to heaven?"

She bit her lip to stop it from trembling. "God had a special job for him up there, and he had to go. But you know that he's always looking down and watching over us. He loves us very, very much."

"Well, I don't want him. I want Shane." Josh jumped off the couch and began kicking the wall. "I want Shane. I want Shane."

"Come, sweetheart." She tried to calm him, but he became increasingly distressed.

"Get away from me." He cried hysterically. "I hate you. I hate you."

CHAPTER THIRTY-TWO

Lauren knew it would be tough seeing Shane at work, but her relief turned to alarm when he didn't show up after a week. She cornered Rick after he'd brought in a patient another doctor worked on. Finding a relatively quiet spot, she asked about Shane.

"He can't work until his hand heals." Rick shook his head. "What a crazy ass thing to do."

"Is he still drinking?"

Rick shrugged. "I don't live with the guy, so I can't say for sure, but he joined AA, said he'd go to the meetings, and swears he hasn't had a drop since."

"Do you believe him?"

He nodded. "Yeah, I do. He told me what happened, and his excuse for taking a drink was a damn good one. Would take a saint not to, if you ask me."

"An alcoholic doesn't have excuses. And he did a little more than 'take a drink.'" She ran a hand through her hair in frustration and despair. "No one said it was easy, but he needs to be stronger than that."

"He needs you, Dr. Reynolds. You shouldn't turn your back on him."

Her face flushed. "Did he tell you about us?"

"Didn't have to. It was obvious by the way you two looked at each other. Not to mention that you're the one who called me and told me to get over there."

She couldn't meet Rick's eyes. "If it were just me, I would stick by him. It's not like I don't care. I do, very much, but I can't allow him around my son. Josh already loves him, and if things became worse and he returned to drinking, it would make leaving him harder than it already is. I have no choice."

"We always have choices."

She could see the accusation in his eyes, and resented it. He had no idea of what she was going through. How much she had come to love Shane and dream about a future together. He had let her and Josh down, not the other way around.

She met his eyes with her head held high. "Shane had a choice too. And he chose drink over a future with me."

"He didn't see it like that."

"I know he didn't, but he should have. I'd give anything to change what happened and to make this all go away." She batted back tears. "He tried calling me that night, and I was called in to work. Twelve-car pile-up that night on the freeway. Maybe if he'd reached me, maybe none of this would have happened."

"I think you should give him another chance," Rick said stubbornly, as if all her words had fallen on deaf ears.

"I wish I could, but I can't."

Rick turned to walk away, and she put a hand out to stop him. "I wish him well, and I believe that he can lick this thing. He'll make a fantastic doctor one day. Tell him for me never to give up on that dream. One day at a time. He can do this."

"Why don't you tell him yourself?" Rick was looking over her shoulder, and she turned to see what had captured his attention. Shane had just walked in.

Lauren caught her breath as her heart pounded with elation simply at the sight of him.

Rick grinned. "I'll leave you two alone."

Shane slapped Rick on the shoulder. "How you doing, buddy?"

"Good. But the rookie they put me with can't hold a candle to you. How much longer before you're cleared to work?"

"Another week or so." His eyes were on Lauren as he spoke. "Which is fine by me. Gives me more time for my studies."

Lauren cleared her throat. "I'm glad to hear you didn't drop out of school."

"No, I wouldn't do that. Although I wish I hadn't been crazy enough to put my fist through a wall. Typing my assignments with two fingers is a challenge, that's for sure."

"I hope you aren't asking for my help," she answered briskly. "Even if I could, there's Josh..."

"No way. I'm just saying that it was pretty damn stupid. It's not like I had another good hand to use."

She didn't smile. "Is everything a joke to you?"

"No, but I don't have to make things harder than they are." His eyes never left her face. "How is Josh? I miss him."

"He asks about you all the time."

Shane looked down at the floor. "Couldn't you let me see him for a few hours each Sunday? You know I'd never go near a drink."

"I know you wouldn't. It's not that. It's...it's just everything. You, me..."

"I wish you could forgive me."

She bit her bottom lip. "It's not about forgiveness. It's about trust." She took a step back, away from his magnetic force, although every inch of her hungered to get closer.

Rick looked from one to the other, concern written all over his face. Finally, he made a move. "Gotta get going. I'll see you soon, Shane. Be good."

Shane waved off his partner and focused on Lauren. "Can we talk? If not today, sometime?"

"There isn't much to say." She crossed her arms in front of her, going into protective mode.

"Let me buy you a coffee," he asked. "Or dinner. I owe you one."

"That's not a good idea."

"I think it's a great idea." He gave her his cheeky grin, which should have annoyed her, but didn't. Instead, her knees went weak.

"Don't," she said. The feelings he stirred in her could melt away her resolve, and she couldn't let that happen. She had to protect herself and Josh. Stay strong.

"Don't what? Flirt with you?" He stepped closer. "Why, Lauren? You still have feelings for me?"

"Yes, and you know it!" She glared at him. "And so does Josh. He loves you too. That's what makes this so difficult."

His face changed, and his eyes grew moist. "I know, but I can't walk away from you, Lauren. There is only one thing in this world that I'm afraid of. Losing you." He dared another step in her direction.

"Shane." She put up a hand to stop him. "That's not fair. You're playing on my emotions, and it's just not right.

I can't trust you not to drink again, and unless I do we have no future."

"I know I have a problem but I'm getting help," he said, all cockiness gone. "I'm doing everything I can to stay sober and will continue for every day of my life. Please, Lauren. Give me another chance."

She shook her head. "I can't."

"Okay. I'll beg." He lowered his voice and gave her the sweetest, most loving smile. "Please, sweetheart? One chance. That's all I'm asking."

"It's not that easy." She was backed up to a wall, with no place to run.

"It's not that hard."

"You know I don't have any choice. This isn't easy for me. You know that."

"You have to forgive me sometime. I don't intend to let you go."

"No, Shane." Her entire body was stiff as a rod, but she had to retain control.

"I'm sorry." He took one step closer. "But I can't give you up. I will prove myself to you, even if it takes a lifetime."

"That's how long it'll take." Her chin went up and she met his gaze. "So have you had any news on your friend, Brent?"

"Yes, his brother Jake called a couple of nights ago. Told me he's in critical condition and has been flown to Landstuhl Regional Medical Center in Germany. He'll stay there until he's patched up enough to fly back home."

"That's great news." Her guard dropped a notch. "I'm glad, Shane."

"Thank you. Tell Josh I miss him and that I'm sorry I screwed up. Okay?"

"I told him you're sick, and that if and when you get better he could see you again." She shook her head. "That could take years and by that time, you'll have moved on."

"Never. I'm not going anywhere." He dropped his eyes and his face was etched with sadness. "I didn't mean for any of this to happen. I would go back and change it if I could."

"I know." Her shoulders slumped, and she released a long sigh.

"How can we make things right?" His voice was full of anguish, which made her loss harder to bear.

"We can't," she said simply.

"Please?" He stared at her, his eyes filled with longing and hope. He looked like a puppy that had been kicked too often, and her heart went out to him.

"Let's take it one day at a time," she said.

"You know me, Lauren." He spoke with some heat. "If you don't trust me, then just walk away."

She felt her will weakening. How could she leave him when he needed her so badly? "Why do you have to be so damn nice?"

Before he had a chance to answer, Margaret came flouncing down the hall. "Well, lookie here. Shane's back." She marched up to him and laid a big kiss on his cheek. "I've missed you, darling."

He grinned. "Missed you too."

She put a hand on her hip and gave him a come-hither look. "What are we waiting for? Why don't we find ourselves an empty bed? Or a linen closet," she added with a naughty twinkle in her eye.

He laughed. "And spoil the anticipation? Not a chance."

"Oh, phooey." She winked at Lauren. "Do you still have the hots for this gorgeous doctor lady?"

Shane looked from one to the other. "Yeah, but it's not getting me anywhere."

"Well, if you ever change your mind," Margaret said, "you know I'll be waiting."

"On that note," Lauren said, "I think I'll go back to work." She walked away before either of them could give her a reason to stay.

~

Shane watched her leave, and his spirits sank. He didn't deserve a second chance. The best thing he could do was leave her the hell alone.

"Don't look so sad," Margaret said softly. "You're going to get me bawling."

"I'm sorry. It's pathetic, I know."

"Come here." She wrapped her arms around him. "What you need is a good old-fashioned hug." She nearly squeezed the stuffing out of him, but it did feel good to be fussed over.

"You're a good woman, my friend. I should have fallen in love with you."

"It's never too late." She grinned and patted his cheek. "But I think we should put our heads together and figure out a way for you to win her back."

"It's not going to happen. There are things in my past that you don't know."

"You want to hear about mine?" She gave him a devilish smile. "I'll tell you sometime."

"This is different. After I got back from Iraq, I went into a dark hole. Lived out of a car for a year and drowned my sorrows in a bottle. I swore I'd never drink again."

"So? Why did you?"

"Last week I got some bad news. Bad enough to make me head straight for a liquor store and drink myself into a stupor."

"That's not good."

"Then I busted my fist by hitting it into a wall." He gave a sheepish smile. "Not my finest moment. Anyway, bottom line is, Lauren doesn't want me around her son. I can't blame her. She's afraid I'll do it again."

"And will you?"

"How the hell do I know? I thought I could handle this on my own, but clearly I can't. I joined AA and have attended a couple of meetings." He looked down at the floor. "Still sitting in the back of the room. Haven't gone up and laid my soul bare."

"You want a friend to go with you?"

He glanced at her. "You'd do that?"

"You bet I would. You need help, and I'm happy to give it."

"You're a sweetheart. Did anybody ever tell you that?"

"Not often enough." She put a hand on her hip. "So, when and where?"

"The Vets Hall on Pacific Avenue. There's a meeting on Monday morning. Figured I'd go before my shift. Does that work for you?"

"Sure. Why not?" She grinned. "I can't wait to tell Dr. Reynolds that I have a date with you. A little jealousy will go a long way."

"I don't think that's a good idea."

"You want to make a bet? I know women, and if they think someone is interested in their man, they'll fight to keep him."

"I don't think Lauren is that type."

"Trust me. All women are that type."

CHAPTER THIRTY-THREE

It wasn't easy for a man like Shane to open up and confess his sins in front of strangers, but if it helped him stay on the straight and narrow, he'd do it. Even if he did feel self-conscious.

Margaret being there helped. It was reassuring to know he wasn't alone. Someone cared, even if it wasn't that special someone.

"Do we have any new members here today?" the tall, ponytailed man on the podium asked.

Shane glanced around and found a few people glancing at him. This was it, he told himself. His big moment. Awkwardly, he got to his feet. "I'm Shane, and I'm an alcoholic."

"Welcome, Shane."

He didn't know what was expected of him, so he helped clarify his reason for coming. "When I got back from Iraq, I hit the bottle pretty hard. Hit rock bottom before someone came along and rescued me." He glanced around, saw a few nods, and continued. "I sobered up, but when I got some bad news recently, I drank myself into a stupor. I'm here because I need help."

"Glad you found your way here," Ponytail guy said. Other people murmured and nodded, and Shane knew that whatever he'd done in the past, he wouldn't be judged.

Margaret put a hand on his knee and gave it a squeeze when he sat back down. "Congratulations. You've taken the first step."

He smiled back, feeling prouder of himself than he had in a long time. "You're right. And I'm glad you're here."

They stood around after the meeting, chatting with fellow members. Before he left, they assigned him a mentor, someone he could call anytime, day or night. He hoped he didn't need a lifeline, but it was reassuring to know it was there if he did.

~

In the weeks following the breakup Josh began acting out in class more than ever, and Lauren was called in to discuss his behavior.

Lisa Simpson, the counselor, sat her down, and gave her the disturbing news. "The other day he tripped a boy, and he's been purposefully bumping into kids in the hallways."

Lauren's stomach clenched, and she felt a heavy weight on her shoulders. "That is so unlike him. He's not a mean boy." She glanced at Lisa. "I can't bear for him to be so unhappy."

"You did tell me that there has been a recent separation in his life. That could cause a boy like Josh to act out."

Lauren sighed. "Yes. I know. He misses Shane dearly, now that he's no longer a part of our lives. But he can't be. He just can't."

"I'm sorry to hear that, but do you have anyone else who can fill that role? An uncle, grandfather, friend of a friend?"

She shook her head. "We don't have family here. No support system."

"Studies indicate that having a male role model is very beneficial. Other students have been helped by the organization Brothers for Life." Lisa crossed her legs and leaned back in her chair, never taking her eyes off Lauren. "I'm sure they could find you someone suitable. Would you like me to give you a number to call?"

Lauren quickly explained the Gary situation. "This is the reason I found Shane. I see him every day at work, and he's always kind to everyone. Everyone loves him."

"Could you possibly supervise the time they spend together?"

She didn't want to discuss her own relationship with Shane, or the fact that she was in love with him, so she shook her head. "When he drank that night, he showed a side to his nature that I'd never seen before. I can't chance that it will happen again."

"I see." Lisa leaned back in her chair and tapped a pen on her desk, looking pensive. "Well, I must say, I don't have any answers either. How's he doing on the new medication?"

"It seemed to help his concentration, but now with this latest development, I don't know anymore. He throws tantrums, and when I talk to him, all he does is cry. If I mention Shane's name, he becomes sullen and withdrawn."

"Well, we'll both keep an eye on him, and if you ever have any concerns, please don't hesitate to give me a call."

Lauren stood up, they shook hands, and she left the school more dejected than ever.

~

Shane thought living with only one good hand had been difficult, but now he didn't even have that. His own fault, of course. What had possessed him to beat his good hand to a pulp, and frighten the daylights out of Lauren in the process?

He did some soul searching and came up with an answer. After a full day of drinking, his demons had come out to play. As on so many occasions, the horrors of war had resurfaced, but because he was drinking, they'd been magnified. He remembered the long day, how he'd shivered and sobbed, beating his head against a wall to stop the memories from flooding his brain.

Like a kaleidoscope inside his head, flashes of his capture had resurfaced. He'd been riding in the back of a Humvee in a busy marketplace, when they'd been surrounded. An explosion went off, and still stunned by the blast, he'd been barely aware of men grabbing him, tying his hands, and blindfolding him. They dragged him off to a guerrilla training camp in some remote part of the desert. When they arrived, he had flailed wildly at his bearded, turbaned captors, and they'd retaliated by kicking him senseless.

They'd stripped him naked, pissed on him, and taken pictures of him bloodied, beaten, in handcuffs. At any moment he'd expected to die.

He survived by playing doctor in a primitive hut with no real medical supplies, only his instinct, a cool head, an element of skill, and, yes, luck. The luck ran out when a commanding officer was hit by a grenade. When he arrived, his guts were spilling out all over the place, and Shane was expected to put him back together.

He wasn't a fucking doctor. He didn't have the know-how to do what was expected of him. The officer died in that hut, and the bloodthirsty insurgents tortured him for days. Finally, tiring of that game, one guerrilla had taken his dagger and sliced off Shane's hand, leaving the other so he could still be useful.

That was all in his past, and no excuse for his recent behavior. But it explained the poison inside him, and why someone like Lauren should stay clear. He needed to prove to himself and to her that a drunken episode like that would never happen again. Only then could he ask for her to take a chance on him.

That might take a miracle, though, and he was fresh out of them.

EPISODE SEVEN

CHAPTER THIRTY-FOUR

The following weeks were mostly uneventful. Shane's hand healed and he returned to work. He attended AA meetings three times a week, and he maintained a B average in his medical studies. He was back on track, but Lauren barely spoke to him in the ER; and outside of it, she wouldn't give him the time of day.

Margaret accompanied him to most of the meetings, and people there thought they were a couple. Shane got an uncomfortable feeling that maybe she did too.

One evening, she linked her arm in his as they sat and listened to one of the speakers discussing the Big Book twelve-step study. They both had the night off and were there for a six o'clock meeting, and then planned on catching dinner afterwards.

During a lull in the lecture, she leaned in and whispered, "Hey, did you hear the news? Dr. Reynolds has been seen with Dr. Knowles. They have dinner together in the cafeteria nearly every night, and once I saw them getting into the same car in the parking lot." Her voice rose in excitement. "It was a silver Bentley. The latest model, I think. Very classy."

"No, I didn't hear," he answered grumpily. "But thanks for sharing."

"You're welcome. I don't want you harboring any false hope. She refuses to talk about you. Lord knows I've tried, but she won't let me utter a word in your defense."

He didn't respond, so Margaret added, "George Knowles is a very nice man. He's been widowed for eight years, and I think they make a sweet couple. Don't you?" She looked at his face. "No, of course you don't."

"I never liked the guy."

"Why not? He's not a condescending ass like a lot of the others. He's very handsome and nice to everyone, actually quite pleasant. His wife had an aneurism when she was only thirty-two. Imagine. They didn't have any children. So sad." Margaret sucked in a breath. "Too bad he isn't any taller. But it isn't true, is it, that short men have short…" She clamped a hand over her mouth. "Oh, never mind."

"I'm not worried about his equipment, or lack of it," Shane answered sharply. "Fact is, he's got no personality. When was the last time you saw him crack a smile, tell a joke, or do anything particularly interesting? He's nice enough, I suppose, but about as exciting as marmalade."

She laughed. "I hate marmalade."

"My point exactly."

"Well, thing is, she's moved on, and so should you."

"I'm not counting on getting back with her, if that's what you mean. I need to get my head on straight before I'll be good for any woman."

"Your head looks pretty good to me." She gave him a flirtatious smile. "Why don't you come over to my house later and I'll help you study? I know Lauren used to do that."

He swallowed hard. He couldn't bear the thought of anyone other than Lauren being his study partner. The scent of her hair, the taste of her lips, the way she wrapped herself around him....

"What are you thinking?"

He shut down the memory. "Nothing. I just don't think it'll work. Okay?"

"No, it's not okay, but you're my buddy, and I'm not going to turn my back on you, like someone else we both know."

"Please don't. This isn't Lauren's fault. I'm the one who screwed up." He couldn't look at her. "I still have feelings for her even if she won't give me the time of day."

Margaret's mouth dropped open, and color rose on her plump cheeks. "Fine. I get it. I don't like it, but I get it."

"I'm sorry." Shane took her hand and gave it a squeeze. "You're a great friend, Maggie-pie, but if you ever get tired of hanging with me, just say so."

She slid out of her seat. "Would you mind if I didn't stay?" She blinked rapidly, as if fighting back tears.

"No problem. I'll give you a ride."

"No need to do that. You stay here, I'll grab a cab."

"I don't want you running off this way." He stood up, knowing his words had hurt her. He was sorry, and wanted to do what was right.

She shook her head. "Stay. I'm outta here."

He knew it was useless to argue. "Be good, you hear?"

She laughed, and he knew that being good was not on her mind. Most likely, she'd hit the bars and find someone to take home.

A little acid indigestion roiled his stomach. He should stop her. That's what a good friend would do.

"I'm going straight home. Don't worry."

He nodded, hoping she spoke the truth. Maggie was a good woman and deserved better than she got. Why couldn't she find a nice man to fall in love with and marry? Not a guy who hung around bars looking for one-night stands. Someone safe, maybe even boring. Like George Knowles.

He ground his teeth. How could Lauren be dating somebody else so quickly? They'd been sleeping together only a couple of weeks ago, and now she was climbing into George's Bentley with him?

What the hell had she been doing in that car anyway? In full view of the hospital? He hoped to God she hadn't been making out.

One thing was for sure. He damn well intended to find out.

~

He drove straight over to the hospital, hoping to catch Lauren, George Knowles, or both. He needed to see for himself if Margaret was telling the truth.

Walking down the main corridor, he spotted his first person of interest. Knowles.

"Dr. Knowles. May I have a word with you?"

The doctor turned slowly and peered at him as if trying to remember his name. "You're a medic here, right?"

At Shane's nod, Knowles smiled pleasantly. "What can I do for you?"

Shane stuck out his hand. Might as well be cordial even though he'd prefer to pop the guy. "Name's Shane Dawson." He wasn't sure what else to say. He couldn't tell this fellow not to see Lauren anymore, not if he hoped she'd ever talk to him again.

"What do you wish to see me about?"

"Need to ask you something. Are you seeing Dr. Reynolds? Off-duty, I mean."

"I don't see that that is any business of yours."

"I'm making it mine." Shane said curtly. "It only requires a single response. Yes or no?"

The doctor looked him dead in the eye. "I have seen Lauren socially once or twice. What's it to you?"

Shane's gut clenched. He breathed in deeply, and sighed. "Take care of her, won't you?" He felt a twitch in his jaw, but didn't break eye contact. "Make her happy or step aside."

"Lauren can be the judge of that." Doctor Knowles marched past Shane, dismissing him as though he had no more importance than a fly.

Knowles had been born with a silver spoon in his mouth and had an Ivy League degree. He was solid, mature, and emotionally stable. The only real problem Shane had with him was the fact that he was probably a perfect match for Lauren.

CHAPTER THIRTY-FIVE

Shane entered the ER and saw Lauren immediately. She shot him an angry look, then came over to his side. "Did you confront, Dr. Knowles?"

"I spoke with him," Shane answered.

"He said you asked some questions about the two of us." She glanced at him. "Why would you do that?"

"Is there a two of you?" His eyes held hers.

"That's none of your business." She folded her arms and looked away.

"Seems to be the standard reply. Knowles said the same thing. Now, if someone asked me if I was dating you, I'd be more up front. Would be happy for people to know."

"What do you want, Shane?"

"I want you to forgive me. I'm doing well, going to AA. I have not even looked at a drink, nor do I want to." His stomach churned and he felt a sharp pain in the region of his heart. How could he ever make it right with her? What could he say to make her trust him again?

She shrugged. "I'm glad to hear that, but whether I see Dr. Knowles or not is clearly not your affair. Please don't interfere."

He didn't say anything for a moment, then blurted, "He's probably exactly what you need, and if you care about him, then I'll stand aside. But if there's the slightest chance, just the slightest, then I'm going to fight for you."

"I don't want you fighting for me, or standing around waiting. I need to move on and so do you. What we had together was special, but I can't risk it again." She had a guilty expression on her face when she said it, but looked him square in the eye.

He had no intention of giving up easily and letting her run off with George. He'd already thrown her into one man's arms, and look how that had turned out. "Remember I told you about that bike race at Monmouth, for the Wounded Warriors? It's in three weeks, and I'd really love you and Josh to come along and support me."

She touched his arm. "I'm glad you have something else to focus on besides me. It's an amazing organization, and I'm pleased that you've stayed involved."

"It's my goal to work for them some day."

Her expression softened, and she gave him a brief smile. "That's wonderful, Shane. Make me proud."

He intended to.

~

Lauren returned to the ER, and the everyday chaos helped put Shane out of her head. But when she returned home, Josh reminded her soon enough.

"Mom? Did Shane come into the ER? I called him when I got home from school and he said he spoke to you today. Did he, Mom? Did he?"

"Well, yes, but why did you call him, dear?" She felt chilled inside. "I asked you not to."

"We didn't talk about much. I just like talking to him." Josh became agitated, scratching his arms, eyes darting everywhere.

"I know you do, honey, but please don't call him again. He needs to focus on getting well. It's best if we leave him alone for now. Understood?"

"I guess so." Josh jumped up. "I have an idea. Why don't we go bowling this weekend and ask Shane to come too? Bowling won't make his sickness worse, will it?"

She smiled. "No. It won't make it worse, but he needs to be alone right now to figure things out."

"What kind of things?"

"Oh, the kind of things that are important to him." She turned away, "But what are we talking about him for? You haven't told me about your day. What happened at school? Anything new or fun?"

"No. Thomas wouldn't play with me, and the other kids weren't very nice. I hate school. Do I have to go tomorrow?"

"Oh, hon. You're the best kid I know. I don't understand why anyone is mean to you. Have you been nice to them?"

"Yeah. Mostly. But if they say bad things, I don't like it. I took Bobby's lunch and threw it into the garbage and then I had detention. It wasn't fair! It wasn't my fault." He started to cry. "Why are they so mean?"

She had no answer for that. "Why don't we do something special this weekend? You want to go to a water park or go down to the boardwalk and play at the arcade? Won't that be fun?"

"Yeah, okay. Wish Shane could be with us, though."

Me too, she thought, but if he wanted to be a part of their lives again, he had some hard work and a lot of making up to do.

The following Saturday, Lauren and Josh went to the boardwalk and spent hours trying to win big prizes at the arcade. They had fish and chips and rented a single surrey and rode up and down, waving at everyone they passed. They ate ice cream cones, and took a paddleboat out too. The only thing marring the afternoon was Lauren's realization that something was missing. Without Shane, neither one of them was happy.

She hadn't cared deeply about anyone since her husband died, and even though she'd told herself a thousand times Shane was not hers for the keeping, she hadn't truly believed it. A part of her had hoped that, given time, it would all work out.

It wasn't in her nature to love someone a little. She'd always been an all-or-nothing kind of girl. And although Shane had never spoken words of love, he hadn't needed to. She'd known his feelings ran deep. Just as she knew he was a good, kind man, a man of principle, someone worthy of love. He'd risked life and limb for his country and had paid a heavy price.

When would his torment end, when would he find peace? It seemed so unfair.

"Mom?" Josh said. "Can we go home now? I'm tired."

"Me too." She took his hand, and they walked toward the exit. "I'm sorry we didn't win one of those panda bears, but we sure had fun trying."

"Can't we call Shane? I bet he'd win one of those bears. And other prizes too. We don't have to see him all the time.

Just once in a while." He gave her a pleading look. "Please, please, please?"

The look on his face, the words, deepened her pain. She desperately wanted to give in and make her son happy—make herself happy too—but she knew it would be the wrong thing to do. Shane still had a lot of healing to do.

"I wish we could, honey, but it doesn't work that way."

"Why not?" Josh yanked his hand away, and pouted.

"Because if we become friendly again, we'll want to see him all the time." Truer words had never been said. She'd want more and more of him, a part-time Shane wouldn't be enough. Not near enough.

"What's wrong with that?" Josh wanted to know. He began kicking at the ground, scuffing his shoes.

"He has nightmares because of the war, honey. Bad dreams that upset him and make him act…strange."

Josh looked baffled, and she couldn't blame him. But there was only so much she could tell him.

"He's not a bad person," she added. "He just needs to figure a few things out, and when he does, maybe then we can be friends again."

"I hope he hurries, because I don't want you to date anyone else."

She gave him a curious look. "What makes you think I'd do that?"

"Because I heard Julie on the phone and she said you were out on a date last week." He pouted and gave her a fixed glare. "You told me you had to work late."

"Maybe I did. You might have misunderstood what Julie said. Besides, if I wanted to go out with someone, that's my decision as an adult and a parent. Right?"

"I guess."

"Okay, son. Let's go home and I'll help you with your homework. You do have some, don't you?"

"No." He stopped his skipping, and returned to scuffing his shoes.

"You sure?" She narrowed her eyes at him. "You always have schoolwork on weekends. Anything I can help you with?"

"Uh, let me see." He thought for a moment. "I have my reader, and some numbers to do. I'm lousy at both."

"No, you're not, but we can do them together. I'll be happy to help." There was a line of taxis waiting, and she opened the rear door of the first one. "Your carriage awaits," she said, and made a flourishing movement with her arm.

"You talk funny." He slid in, made room for her, and immediately yawned. "I'm too tired for homework. How about if I go to bed and you do it?"

"Good try, o sleepy one." She kissed his head. "Take a nap on the way home."

Within seconds, Josh's head lolled back, and he was fast asleep. She was exhausted too. Every night she tossed and turned, tortured with indecision and helpless longing.

But for Josh's sake, she had to be strong.

CHAPTER THIRTY-SIX

That Monday, Lauren went to the hospital cafeteria early, hoping to see George Knowles and have a word with him. Instead, Shane walked in.

She hoped he wouldn't see her, but lady luck wasn't on her side. He glanced around, spotted her immediately and marched over. "Lauren . . . can I join you?"

"I'm here to meet someone," she replied. "What are you doing here, Shane?"

"I came to see you. You won't let me get near, so I have to hang around places you frequent." His eyes roamed over her face and she felt her cheeks heat up. "Pathetic, I know."

"Please give up, Shane." She crossed her arms.

"Never." His eyes held hers. "Not until you find a man worthy of you. And I don't mean Dr. Knowles."

"Why? What's wrong with him, dare I ask?"

Shane frowned. "George isn't the man for you." He moved in closer and her breath hitched. "He's okay if you like handsome, successful doctors, but I can tell you one thing. He doesn't love you the way I do."

She stepped back. "I thought I found the man who was right for me, but I made a mistake." Her eyes held his. "We both did."

The moment the words were out of Lauren's mouth, she regretted them. Shane's eyes darkened, and he looked as though he might kiss her. Right there in the cafeteria, before God and all the gossipy staff.

She actually licked her lips in anticipation, but then he seemed to think better of it and moved back. She hated the disappointment that surged through her, chilling her blood. Wanting this man was an addiction. Nearly as bad as his addiction to alcohol.

Clearly, she couldn't be around him. He was the most intoxicating man she'd ever met.

"What are you thinking?" he asked.

"You don't want to know," she answered, and swiftly turned away. She practically ran from the room, forgetting dinner, the reason she'd come.

In his presence she couldn't think straight. She became weak when she needed to be strong.

She dived back into work, and fortunately had enough emergencies to distract her from her thoughts. First came a motorcycle accident. The passenger didn't have her helmet properly fastened and now faced head trauma. A child came in next. The parents swore she'd fallen down the stairs, but Lauren noticed old wounds and feared the worst. An alcoholic, reeking of booze and vomit, came in with a wound on his head, probably from falling, and blood pouring from his nose.

At last her shift was over, and she gratefully walked out the door. As soon as she did, she stood rock still. Shane sat in an idling car, waiting for her.

"Get in," he called. "We have to talk."

She reached for the door handle, not sure if she wanted to open it. But curiosity got the better of her.

"Come on," he said. "I don't bite." He grinned. "Hard."

She laughed at the old joke and slipped into the passenger seat. He only drove as far as the employee parking lot, so he had no plans of running off with her.

Not yet, anyway.

"Okay," she said when he parked. "Talk."

"I'm not here to discuss Dr. Knowles, or you or me."

"Then what? What's so important now that you couldn't have told me earlier today?"

"Josh." He paused, knowing he had her full attention. "He's been calling me. A lot."

She had given Josh her old cell when she got her iPhone so that he could call her when she was at work. He didn't take it to school, but liked to have it near him at night.

"I knew you two had spoken a few times, but I made him promise not to call you again."

"Well, promise or no promise, the boy calls me every night before he goes to sleep." He glanced out the window, then back at her. "I've tried to discourage him."

"I didn't know." Lauren's hand flew up to her throat. "I should have known." She glanced at him. "What does he say to you?"

"You know how he feels. He keeps asking me why he can't see me anymore, and don't I want to see him." Shane scratched his head. "It's painful. Poor little guy. He said, can't I get well and be his dad?"

"Oh, Shane." Heat rushed to her face, and her heart beat like a bird's wing inside her chest. "I feel awful. He loves you, I know he does. This is breaking his heart. And mine."

"Mine too. I don't know what to say to him. What do you want me to say?"

She opened her mouth, then closed it again. "I don't know. I've explained to him as well as I can. I've told him this is not your fault, that you have a sickness inside of you, and until you're healed, we can't see you. Am I doing the right thing? Tell me, Shane. Is keeping Josh away from you right or wrong?"

He hesitated, then cupped her face in his one hand. "I don't have an easy answer. I swear I can control this disease and not let it get the better of me. I will, Lauren. It would be easier if I had you at my side, but with you or without you, I'm not going to drink again. Ever. I have too much to lose." His fingers stroked through her hair. "I can only control one day at a time, and I shouldn't make promises, but just the thought of a drink makes me sick."

She swallowed hard. "You frightened me, Shane, and I can't allow Josh to see you like that. I have to protect him, even if it means breaking his heart."

Shane dropped his hand and straightened, staring out the windshield. "I won't answer the phone again when he calls. I won't encourage him."

She nodded, even as disappointment threatened to drown her. "That's probably best. It's going to upset him of course, but I'll tell Julie to take his phone away at night when she puts him to bed. And I'll have a talk with him and explain why. We're not punishing him, but he'll think we are." She brushed a tear from her eye. "Why does life have to be so tough? He lost his father when he was only three. He's lost enough."

Shane turned to her again. "Kids are resilient, you know that. He'll get over it soon, but it would help if he could make some new friends. How's it going at school?"

She told him about her most recent talk with the school counselor, how Josh was instigating fights. "That's not like him, Shane. He's always been a good boy. Sensitive."

"You're right. He is a good boy, and maybe I was wrong to try to discourage you from seeing George. If you really like him, I'll stay clear. Josh needs a man around. Even if you don't," he added with a sad smile.

"It's not that I don't," she said quietly. "But nobody is perfect, and I don't want to compromise."

"You shouldn't have to."

"Thanks for telling me this tonight. I'll have a talk with Josh." She opened the car door. "I believe in you, Shane. I know you can beat your addictions and be the man you want to be. I'm betting on it."

He gave her a long look. "So am I."

~

Two nights later, Josh ran away.

Lauren was at work when Julie called the hospital to say there was an emergency at home. She raced out of the ER to make the call home. "What's happened? Is Josh all right?"

"He's not here! I put him to bed as always, and took away his phone, like you said." She heard Julie sniffle and blow her nose.

"He's gone? He ran away?" Lauren grabbed her stomach, feeling like a cannonball had shot right through her.

"I'm sorry," Julie said, "but when I left him, he didn't seem upset. He was just kind of quiet. I waited a while and when I didn't hear anything, I opened the door a crack to see if he'd fallen asleep. I do hate to hear that boy cry."

Lauren listened to her words, feeling like her life was slipping away. If she lost Josh . . . no, she had to hold on tight. Control, she needed control.

"Julie. Did you check the house? Maybe he's hiding somewhere."

"Yes, I did. He's not here."

"Have you called the police?" Panic made her voice unusually hard.

"Not yet. I wanted to call you first."

"How could he have gotten out?" She fought to stay calm, but the walls in the corridor seemed to be closing in.

"I was in the family room watching TV. He must have tiptoed right behind me and left by the front door. I don't know why I didn't hear him."

"Did you go outside and look around? Maybe he's out in the garden or down at the park."

"I ran out first thing. I looked all around the yard, and up and down the street. Then I came back inside and called you."

"You need to hang up now and call 911." She drew in a deep breath. "I'll be home soon. I just have to make sure they have someone to cover for me, and then I'll be on my way. Probably thirty minutes tops." She wiped away a tear. This was no time to fall apart. "Don't worry. We'll find him."

"I hope so, Dr. Reynolds. I sure do."

"I'll call Shane. It's possible that Josh has headed there."

"Good idea. I bet you're right. He's probably gone to find Shane." Julie suddenly gasped. "Oh no! He doesn't have his cell phone with him. I have it right here."

Lauren's heart tightened and squeezed. She felt dizzy. "He won't know where to go," she whispered. "Shane lives thirty minutes away, and he's never been there." She shook her head to clear it. "How could I not have seen this coming?"

"You can't blame yourself. You were doing what you thought was the right thing for the boy."

"Buy why did he run away, instead of turning to me?"

A mistake in judgment had resulted in her husband's death. If that happened to Josh…No! No! She mustn't think like that. She could bear anything, but not that.

CHAPTER THIRTY-SEVEN

Shane picked up the moment he recognized Lauren's cell number. "What's up?"

"Josh. He's missing. Julie called me at work, and I told her to call 911." Lauren rushed on, "He's probably trying to come to you, but he can't call. We've been taking away his cell phone at night."

Shane grabbed his keys, heading for the door. "You go home and I'll start searching the neighborhood. Call my cell phone as soon as anything changes."

"I will. Please hurry. We've got to find him."

"We will. I promise, nothing bad will happen to him. We'll find him."

"I can't believe he did this." She made a fist with her hands. "I should have let him see you."

"Don't start panicking." He kept his voice calm. "He doesn't know where to go, so I'm sure he hasn't gotten far. We'll get him, I promise."

They hung up, and Shane shooed Major out the door. "Come on, boy. We've got a job to do." On the way to his car, he called the EMTs, asking if they'd look out for a six-year-old boy. "He was in bed when he went missing, so I don't know if he's roaming the streets in his PJs or wearing street clothes. But he's tall for his age, skinny, with straight strawberry-blond hair that he wears past his ears. He's got blue eyes and a mole on his left cheek. A cute kid. And he might be looking for me."

"Got it," the dispatcher answered. "We'll keep our eyes and ears open."

"Thanks." Shane and the dog headed over to Belmont Shores, driving up and down the beach, hoping to spot Josh on the bike path. Several couples strolled hand in hand, and a few people were out walking their dogs, but no sign of Josh. He got out of his car and ran down the pier, but it was dark and deserted.

"You got a drink?"

Shane turned to see an old drunk sitting on the pier, his back against a wooden rail, a brown bag between his legs. "No. No drink. You seen a boy about this high?" He indicated Josh's height with his hand.

"What if I have?" the grizzled man answered. "What's it worth to you?"

Major whined and sniffed the old man.

"You seen a kid or not?" Shane had no time for games, and no patience either. "Ten dollars if you know where he is."

"I saw a boy down by the liquor store. On 2nd Street. About an hour ago." Major was now sniffing the man's crotch, and the old geezer pushed the dog's head away.

Shane whipped a twenty out of his wallet and dropped it in the man's lap. "Don't drink it all. Get a meal."

"I'll do that." He put the bottle to his lips and drank the last of it. "You're a generous man."

Shane left his car and ran up and down 2nd Street, with Major racing along beside him. Unlike the pier and the beach walk, it was lively this time of night. A four-block stretch had popular restaurants, shops, boutiques, and coffee shops. He headed for the local ice cream shop first, trying to think where Josh would hide out.

If a boy were alone and frightened, where would he go? Josh didn't have any money or a phone. He couldn't even call home.

Something caught his eye under a bench on the sidewalk. Looked like a backpack, and sticking out of it was Woody, from *Toy Story*.

He had no idea if this was Josh's bag, but if it was, where was he?

~

By the time Lauren got home, the police had come, questioned Julie, and gone.

"Are you okay?" Lauren asked, noting with concern Julie's stricken expression. Her eyes were red from weeping, her face pale, and she was visibly shaking.

"I will be. Once we have Josh back home." She dug a tissue out of her pants pocket and wiped her eyes. "I'm so sorry this happened. I feel terrible."

"I know you do, but it's not your fault. You're not responsible for this." She gave Julie a hug, then paced the room. "What did the police say? Are they out looking for him?"

"Yes. They told me that they sent Josh's description to all the patrol cars in this area, but they haven't entered him into the nationwide databases because he left voluntarily. If he'd been kidnapped, it would have been different."

"I see." She was doing her best to remain calm and not be overwhelmed by the towering wave of fear building inside her. She felt suffocated, as though oxygen couldn't get through her bloodstream.

"I should have known Josh would do something extreme. He's been unusually hyper, acting out in school, not listening to me." She ran her hands up and down her arms, trying to warm herself. "Should have seen this coming."

"Don't say that. Blaming ourselves only makes things worse." Julie put a comforting hand on Lauren's shoulder. "He'll come home. I know he will." She glanced at the clock. "Its half past nine, and he's got nowhere to go."

"Wait by the phone, Julie. I'm going to look around the neighborhood and check in with Shane." Once she hit the street, she called him, but he didn't pick up.

Why wasn't he calling her? Had he found something? Her worries escalated to full blown panic. If he'd found Josh's body, he'd have to tell her face to face. He wouldn't answer her text messages. He wouldn't call her on the phone.

She ran around the neighborhood, knocking on people's doors, stopping cars as they passed, then limped back to the house. She sank into a chair as her legs gave way. "Josh, oh Josh, please come home. Please, God."

Julie entered the room. "Nothing? Did you hear from Shane? Has he found our boy?" Tears ran down her cheeks. "What is it? You're scaring me."

"No, Julie. I couldn't get Shane on the phone. Why wouldn't he answer it?" She didn't wait for a reply. "I'm so scared, I can't think straight." She put her shaking hands to her lips. "I was just about to pray. Would you pray too?"

Julie sat on the sofa, near enough to reach over and pat Lauren's knee. "Believe me, I've been praying real hard. I want to see that boy nearly as much as you."

Lauren called Shane again. When he didn't answer, she jumped up from the chair, and paced the room. "Why won't he answer the damn phone?"

Her fears took on a life of their own. Every mother's nightmare exploded in her mind. He could be lost, or hit by a car, or meet the kind of people who harm little boys.

CHAPTER THIRTY-EIGHT

Shane ran up and down the area, shouting Josh's name. Major barked madly, overly excited by all the drama. After several minutes of this, Shane stopped and called Lauren.

"Haven't got him yet, but there's a blue Nike backpack under a bench with a Woody toy sticking out. Is that his?"

"Yes, yes, but where is he? If the bag's there, what happened to him?" Lauren cried, "Shane. You've got to find him before something terrible happens."

"I will. Hang in there." Shane put his phone away and retraced his steps to the place he'd seen the bag. For the first time that night, Shane feared the worst.

Long Beach was a quirky, unorthodox community, which made the beach town an interesting place to live. But right now, all he could think about was the possibility that a pedophile might have gotten to Josh first.

He found the bag and gave Major the toy to catch the boy's scent. "Gotta find Josh. Come on Major. Focus. This is important."

Major ran around in circles then put his head in the air, nostrils twitching, and raced up and down the street. Shane chased after him, breathing heavily.

"Focus, Major. This isn't a game. We've got to get Josh." He wagged the toy in front of the dog's nose. "Now do it."

Shane thought he heard a whimper. "Did you hear something?" he spoke aloud. "Come on. Let's find him."

The dog slowed down, sniffing every bush, running from one to the next, then he lifted his head, his ears twitched, and he began yipping and jumping all over the place.

Shane was a few steps behind. "Josh? Josh! Are you there?" He pulled back branches, trying to uncover the small shape that hid from sight.

He heard the boy sniffle and cry. "Mommy's going to be so mad. I ran away and I got lost."

"You're not lost anymore. I found you, son." He pulled Josh out of the bush, not giving a damn if they were both covered in scratches. He held the small body tight to his chest and kissed the top of his head. "Oh, Josh, you had us so worried."

Major had to greet him too. He stood on his hind legs to lick the boy's face.

Josh giggled, then a sob ripped out. He had his little arms wrapped around Shane in a stranglehold. "I was so scared I wet my pants. Some weirdo offered me a drink for my bag. I ran like crazy and dropped my bag, but I didn't go back. I hid in the bushes."

"That was very smart of you." He moved slightly away so he could see the boy's face. "Your mom is going to be so happy to see you. She's waiting for you at home. What do you say?" He kissed the boy's wet cheeks. "Shall we go home now and see your mom?"

"Will you come too?" he asked in a small voice. "Please, please come too."

"Of course, I'll come." He hit redial, and Lauren answered immediately in a breathless voice. He could picture her, a total wreck on the inside, but holding it all together on the outside, putting on a brave front for the world to see.

"I have him. He's safe."

"Oh, thank God." A sob ripped from her. "Shane, Shane, how can I ever thank you enough?"

"You just did." Shane held the phone out to Josh. "Say hi to your mom."

"Mom, I'm sorry." His little face crumpled, and tears slid down his face. "I'll never do it again. Promise."

Shane recaptured the phone. "I'll have him home in a few minutes. He's fine, Lauren. Just fine."

~

"Shane." Tears filled her eyes, and she couldn't speak. The phone slipped out of her hand.

Julie picked it up and stood watching her, anxiously waiting to hear. Lauren nodded and swallowed a rather large lump. "Josh is safe. Shane's bringing him home."

The moment Shane pulled up the driveway, Lauren flung the door open and ran outside. She threw her arms around her son, laughing and crying.

"Josh, oh baby, thank God you're safe."

"Are you mad at me?" Josh asked in a small voice, rapidly blinking back tears. "I'm sorry I ran away. I didn't have my phone."

He let out a heart-wrenching sob. "I wanted to call, but I couldn't."

Lauren cried too. "I know, honey. I promise I'll never take your phone away again. Never, ever." She pulled Josh into her arms and grabbed Shane's hand. "You were very lucky tonight that Shane found you, but what you did was a terrible, scary thing. You must never run away again, no matter how bad you feel, and how angry you get." She kissed his cheeks and wiped his tears. "Promise me, sweetheart. Something terrible could have happened to you, and I love you so much."

"I won't, Mommy. I promise."

She turned her eyes on Shane. "We will talk later, but I'll never forget what you did tonight. I can never thank you enough."

"I don't need your thanks," he said quietly. "I love Josh, and he had me worried too." He ruffled the boy's hair. "You won't ever do this again, will you? Your Mom has good reasons for the things she does and your best interests at heart."

"But I wanted to see you."

Shane and Lauren exchanged a glance. She bit her lip and sucked back tears. "Maybe you can. But this was a bad way of going about it," she said sternly.

Shane just looked at her, and she knew he was thinking about their relationship. But she had no answers for him right now. She loved him, she wanted him back in their lives, but tonight was not a night to make those decisions.

She kept her fingers entwined with his, but glanced away. Her emotions were on overload, and she needed a clear head to answer the question in his eyes.

"Shane, Josh, are you hungry? I put on a pot of coffee, and Julie made a raisin zucchini loaf this afternoon."

Shane answered first. "I've got Major with me." He glanced at the dog, who had his head out the window, tongue hanging out, and spittle running down the side of the car. "He doesn't look like much right now, but he was the real hero tonight. Sniffed out Josh, didn't you boy?"

Lauren smiled. "Bring him in too."

Josh laughed. "Yeah. I want a dog just like him. Can I, mom?"

"We'll talk about that later." She put an arm around his shoulders. "First let's get you cleaned up and put something in that stomach of yours."

"Good. I'm so hungry, I could eat a whale."

"A whale?" Shane laughed, then rescued Major from the car, and they all walked together toward the house. "I'll stick to Julie's loaf, if that's all right."

When they were washed up and seated at the kitchen table, Lauren couldn't take her eyes off her son. She wanted to gobble him up. He was laughing and talking to Shane, and he hadn't looked so happy since…since the last time Shane had been there.

Her gaze lifted from her son's face to Shane. She wanted him in their life as much as her son did. Maybe she had made a serious mistake by not giving him another chance. Being an alcoholic was an illness, but one that could be managed. Millions of people around the world had this disease but had kicked the addiction and lived happy, successful lives. If there ever was a man she'd bet her money on, it was Shane.

Besides, who was she to judge? She had more to atone for than this brave wounded warrior who sat before her.

She smiled at him and felt warmed all over when he smiled back. "More coffee?" she asked, getting up to refill his cup.

He took her hand when she reached for his cup and looked deep into her eyes. She felt a sudden flash of heat and a powerful yearning deep inside, a physical reaction so strong it took her breath away.

"I've had enough," he said. "I don't want to overstay my welcome."

"You could never do that," she answered, pouring him another half cup.

He raised an eyebrow, and she flushed. "Josh and I want you here. It was wrong of me to keep you apart." Her eyes were steady on his. "You're strong. You can beat this. I know you can. I know."

He glanced away and shrugged. "You did what you had to do."

Although obviously happy to be with Shane again, Josh was falling asleep at the table. Lauren told him she'd tuck him into bed, and then looked at Shane, asking if he could stay for a few more minutes. He agreed, much to her relief.

Josh climbed right into bed, and Lauren was still giving him a good-night hug when he fell asleep. She sat on his bed for a few minutes more, watching him sleep, thanking God that he was home with her again.

When she returned to the kitchen, she found Shane standing by the front door. A new anxiety gripped her. He seemed in a hurry to leave, and she very much wanted him to stay.

"Do you have to go?" she asked quietly. "There are so many things I need to say."

"Not now. I know what an emotional night it's been. Whatever you feel that you need to say can wait until you are in a more rational frame of mind."

"No, it can't. I need to make this right with you."

"Not now, Lauren." He opened the door. "I really have to leave."

"Shane... you're not going to do anything you're regret, are you?"

"No, Lauren. Never again. You don't need to worry about that."

"Then why?"

He didn't answer, just shook his head, his eyes skittering away from hers.

The door closed behind him, and feeling as though her heart had been ripped right out of her, Lauren let him go.

CHAPTER THIRTY-NINE

By the time Shane got home, he had the shakes. Wanted a drink so bad, it was eating him alive. What the fuck had happened tonight to set him off? He hadn't had the urge since he'd fallen off the wagon several weeks ago, when Brent's plane went down.

He put his head in his hands, disgusted with himself. He hadn't wanted Lauren to see him this way. What was his problem, anyway? It wasn't like he wanted a damn drink. He needed one. Would it always be like this? Could he not face a stressful situation without needing a drink?

He looked at his shaking hand and wanted to smash something. Getting up, he looked in the bathroom mirror, seeing the terror and the disgust in his own eyes. Breathing deeply, he forced himself to be calm.

After he'd splashed water over his face, he returned to the living room to call his AA sponsor, Jimmy. "It's Shane here. I'm in trouble right now."

"Give me your address and I'll get there as fast as I can."

He spieled off his address, then sat down to wait, loathing himself, weighed down by shame. How could he be so weak? After all the things he'd experienced in his life, why couldn't he be strong? He'd faced danger most of his adult life.

Spent eight years with CAL FIRE, saving lives amid raging forest fires, putting his own life on the line. Then he'd packed it in and gone off to Iraq, where every minute of every day and night could have been his last. He'd patched up women and men younger than himself, and had lost a great many too. He'd worked on victims whose limbs had been torn off or flesh burned off; held brave soldiers who'd screamed in pain as they died in his arms.

He'd lived through all that without the need for a drink. So why now? Now, when he had a chance for a normal life, why was he screwing up the best possible thing that had ever happened to him? He loved Lauren and Josh, and he knew they loved him.

Hell, when he'd seen the backpack lying there, he'd nearly lost it. If something bad had happened to the boy, he didn't know what he would have done, but it wouldn't have been pretty.

Even though Josh was home safe, all he could think about was a drink. His hands had started to shake while waiting for Lauren to get Josh off to bed. The longing for alcohol had come fast and hard.

He was not much better than that bum he'd met on the pier. Given the right circumstances, it could have been him drinking cheap rotgut out of a brown paper bag.

He might be weak, but he would not drink, not tonight, not tomorrow, not if it killed him. For once, he would do something right, and not screw up again.

~

Lauren woke up the next day, her mind going in a million directions. She loved Shane and so did Josh. If he was riddled with cancer or had some other deadly disease, would she have turned her back on him? Of course not. She was a doctor, and she had taken an oath to save lives. When it came to Shane, it was probably her own prejudice that had made her judge him so harshly. Had her husband not been killed by someone with a DUI, she might have been more understanding with his problem.

Yes, he was an alcoholic, but he was strong, and he could fight this disease. And she would fight it with him.

Her thoughts turned to Josh and she realized she'd made an error in trying to protect him from Shane's potentially recurring problem. By refusing them a relationship, she'd also closed the door on all the good things that could come from it.

After she dropped Josh at school, she drove over to Shane's, determined to put things right. He had a solid reason for keeping her at arm's length after cutting him out of their lives, but she would prove to him that it would be different now.

He answered the door and seemed surprised to see her. "Lauren, hi. Come on in."

Major greeted her by jumping up and down, but she only had eyes for Shane. He was wearing a pair of well-worn jeans and had a knit top that outlined his muscular chest and iron-hard stomach. No doubt about it. He was definitely drool worthy.

She smiled and moved in close, eager to show him why she'd come. "Shane, I thought about you all last night. I couldn't wait another moment to do this." Before he had a chance to react, she put her hands behind his neck and gave him a warm kiss. She rubbed her cheek against him, breathing in his familiar aftershave. There wasn't a damn thing she didn't love about this guy.

"Lauren, I—"

She put a finger over his mouth. "Don't say a word. Not yet. I have so much to tell you first." She took his hand and led him to the sofa, tugging him down to sit next to her.

"I need to tell you a few things too," he said.

She smiled and cuddled up beside him. "Me first." She leaned over to kiss his cheek. "I made a terrible mistake, trying to keep you and Josh apart. By trying to protect him, I also shut out all the wonderful, positive blessings you bring to us. We are so much better with you in our lives."

He pushed away from her. "No, that's not true." He wouldn't meet her eyes. "You were right to kick me out of your lives. I know that now, and I'm going to stay clear. It's best."

"What are you talking about?" She felt a flash of fear. "You can't do that to Josh. Not now, not when I've told him he can see you again."

"You don't get to call the shots anymore." His jaw was set. "I'm calling them."

"Why?" Hurt slammed into her, and the morning's happiness evaporated. "Is this to punish me?"

"You still don't get me, do you?" He got off the couch and began to pace the room. "I would never hurt you or Josh. That's not what this is about." He paused, rubbing his hands over his face. "Believe me when I say it's not you. It's me."

"Did you just give me the worst break-up line ever?"

He turned to her. "Lauren, you're a bright woman. Don't pretend to be dense." He shook his head and spoke slowly. "I'm not breaking up with you. We are not in a relationship and whatever we had is over. It wasn't right for either of us, and we both knew it."

"But that changed. We fell in love." She said with a little more desperation, "I know we have obstacles, but I'm willing to face them. I love you."

"You'll get over it."

His face had closed down, and he seemed emotionless. She couldn't read him at all.

"I don't want to get over it." Her stubborn spirit kicked in. No way was he getting rid of her. "Josh loves you, and I have finally found the man I want to spend the rest of my life with."

"You don't mean that, and if you do, it's time I set you straight."

His jaw muscle twitched, and she knew he was fighting his feelings for her. What she didn't understand was the why. "There is nothing you can say that'll change my mind," she told him.

"Oh, yeah? Try this." He ran a hand through his hair, took a deep breath, and exhaled loudly. "I had to call my AA sponsor last night to come over and sit with me. He just left a few minutes before you showed up."

"Why?" Dread filled her. "Why did you call him?"

"Because I didn't trust myself. Sitting in your house last night, I didn't want coffee, I wanted a drink."

"That's why you left the way you did?"

"Yes." He looked angry now. "I'm an alcoholic, Lauren, and that will never change."

"I know you are, but you can handle this. You can change your life around." She jumped off the couch and put her arms around his middle. She leaned her head on his chest. "You didn't have a drink, did you?" She looked up into his face. "Did you?"

"No, but the next time I might. It's an incurable sickness and I'll never get rid of it. God knows, if I could, I would."

"Shane, so you're not perfect. Neither am I. But you are worth fighting for, and I'm not giving up on you. Don't you dare give up on yourself."

"This is pointless." He prowled the room, and she could see the frustration in the lines of his face. "I've told you I'm no good. You and Josh can do better."

"I have my own pains, my own devils to fight."

"Lauren, I know you're trying to help, but..."

She reached a hand toward him, hoping he'd take it. "You're the best person I know. And you're the only person I want." When he didn't move, she folded her arms and sighed. "More importantly, I'm confident that you'll succeed in AA. You have the strength. More strength than me, that's for sure."

"That's not true," he said stubbornly.

"Will you please sit down, so I can tell you something?"

He finally took a seat on the couch, as far away from her as he could get. "Okay. Shoot."

"You know how my husband died. That he was on his way home from work and was killed by a drunk driver. What you don't know is that he called me on his cell. Josh had been acting up all day, and instead of waiting until Jeremy got home, I got into it right then and there." She paused for a second, remembering her role clearly. "I told him I wanted to have

Josh tested for ADHD, and he got really mad. Told me to do whatever the hell I wanted. Said that I always did anyway."

Shane didn't say anything, so she rushed on. "Well, that was the start of a really big fight. Jeremy refused to believe that Josh had a problem, telling me he was just an active little boy. But I knew differently. I was around him all the time and I suspected that he had a learning disorder. Jeremy was totally in denial."

"Having a disagreement on the phone doesn't mean you were the cause of his death."

"You're wrong. It was raining, and he was on a busy highway. I got him angry and distracted."

"You can't blame yourself for what happened." He reached across the distance between them and caught a lock of her hair, twiddling it with his fingers. "You weren't in the car with him. He was the one driving. It was his responsibility to stay focused."

She shook her head, forcing him to drop his hand. "I've had this on my conscience since the night he died. It was easier to put all the blame on the alcoholic than to admit I might have had something to do with it."

"You didn't. That's ridiculous."

"Is it?" She angled her body so she could watch his face. "Shane, I've never told anyone this story, and I don't ever want Josh to know. But you need to know the truth about me. I'm stubborn, impatient, and nearly always right. Even when I'm not."

He gave a wry smile. "You forgot bossy."

"Yes, I did. I'm bossy too."

"Well, sugar pie, it seems like we are both quite a mess." He leaned into the corner of the sofa, again as far away as he could get. "Now that we're in a confessing mood, I'll tell you my deep, dark secret."

"I'm all ears."

"When I was a prisoner in that guerrilla camp, I was forced to perform surgery on a high-ranking Iraqi officer. A grenade had exploded near him, and when they brought him into the camp he was barely alive. His torso had been blown up, exposing his organs. Very little of him was left intact. I told them I couldn't save him, but they didn't have a real doctor, only me."

He closed his eyes and drew in a long breath. "He lived for nearly a week and then died from an infection."

"So you did the best you could."

"It must have been a hundred degrees in that shack that was my operating room. Flies were always buzzing around and the sweat poured off me. I remember swatting at the flies, and then I returned to patching up the patient without washing my hands." He shook his head. "My hands and instruments weren't sterile."

"You were forced to perform surgery under threat of death, and you said yourself that he was beyond repair."

"I should have refused. Let them kill me. I never should have given in to the buggers in the first place."

"You chose to survive. There's no shame in that. And from what you tell me, you performed some kind of miracle keeping this officer alive as long as you did."

"Guess they didn't see it that way, and neither did I."

"So that's it? That's your deep, dark secret? That's the best you've got?"

He looked angry. "I was weak, frightened. Pathetic. No damn hero, that's for sure."

"I see it differently. I think you're extremely brave, and you did something really heroic. You performed surgery, something you were not trained to do, with guns pointed at your head and men only too eager to blast you to kingdom come, and you kept him alive. He didn't die on the table. That's amazing. I'm proud of you."

He shook his head again, but she caught a hint of a smile. "I think you're just saying that because you're too stubborn to give up on someone like me."

She slid over to him and cupped his face in her hands. "Not someone like you. Just you! Shane Dawson, you are going to be a great doctor. I've seen you in action, and you're confident, capable, and have a quick mind and good dexterity. You have the makings of a great physician. I'm going to see that you become one."

"You forgot one little problem. I'm a drunk."

"Don't make me hurt you." She leaned over and kissed his lips. "If you continue to talk trash about yourself, I might have to do something drastic, like wash your mouth out with soap."

She definitely saw a smile now. "Do people actually do that?"

"I don't know. I hope not."

"So what's going to happen the next time I have a major crisis in my life and go for the bottle? You going to stick around then?"

"Yes. I'll be your lifeline." Tears filled her eyes. "From here on in, Shane, I've got your back. You hear me?" She gave him little kisses all over his face. "I've got your back."

He pulled her into his arms. "Lauren, that's a helluva chore." He tilted her head to look into her eyes. "You're one stubborn woman, but I might be too much even for you."

"There is nothing you can do to stop me from loving you." Tears filled her eyes. "I will never give up on you. Not ever."

He kissed her lips softly. "Don't cry. I don't ever want you to shed a tear for me."

"Then stay with me."

"I will for now, but if there ever comes a time when you can't be around me anymore, I want you to take Josh and go."

"That won't happen. I lost one good man, and I don't intend to lose another."

He smiled, but it was a sad smile. "You win." He pulled her close. "I can't fight you any longer, and I want you too much to try."

She put her arms around him. "Good, but I still have one request."

"Anything." His lips grazed on her earlobe and then trailed down her neck.

"Will you make love to me right now?"

He chuckled. "With great pleasure." His hand slid under her top and found her breast. "I feel your heart beating. I want you naked, your heart beating with mine."

"Oh, Shane. I have been alone so long, and now I will never feel empty again. You complete me."

He smiled. "Now who's using the corny lines?"

She laughed and stood up. "I'll give you about two seconds to get me undressed, and then I'm coming after you."

"Bossy woman." He lifted her shirt and pulled it over her head. His fingers flew to her zipper, and he tugged her pants over her slim hips. She wiggled out of them.

When she was gloriously naked, she watched him with half-closed eyes. "Take your clothes off. I want you inside me."

When he was undressed, he laid her on the couch and poised himself over her. "Give me your last command, and then I'm going to do whatever the hell I want."

She touched him, feeling him shiver, and guided him into her. "Make love to me and never stop."

"Last chance to walk away." He slid halfway into her. "In another second, I'll never let you go."

"I'm not going anywhere. There is no place I'd rather be." She kissed him deeply, giving him all the love she had stored up inside. "I've found my home. With you."

EPILOGUE

One Year Later.

Shane strolled into the kitchen in flip-flops and his boxer shorts. He pecked Lauren's cheek, and gave her bottom a friendly pat.

"Hi hon," she murmured, breathing in his familiar scent. After living together for six months, she still couldn't get enough of him. "Sleep well?"

"Not really. I laid awake and watched you sleep until around three or so, then drifted off. I didn't hear you get up." He glanced at the clock. "It's after eight. I'm sorry, I missed seeing Josh off."

"I know, but I didn't have the heart to wake you." Noticing the empty cup in his hand, she put a fresh pot of coffee on to brew.

"You should have. I like taking him to school."

"His friend's mother picked him up. Remember? We've decided to car pool. It's easier all around."

"Oh, yeah." He rubbed the stubble on his chin. "I forgot about that, but I've had some things on my mind."

"Yeah? Like what?"

"Well, for starters, when you were working yesterday, I interviewed a young woman who's going to take care of Brent."

Shane ignored the look she gave him, and continued his story. "He's going to flip out on me, but what the hell. Until he gets his eyesight back, he can't possibly live alone."

Brent had been successfully evacuated out of Afghanistan; his burns had been bad, but losing his sight had been far worse. Now, after a second operation, the doctors were a little more hopeful that he'd soon see again.

"You did what?" Lauren cracked a couple of eggs into the frying pan, and popped two English muffins into the toaster. "You hired her without consulting him first?"

At his nod, she sucked in a breath and released it slowly. "You're in for it now. So how did you find her?"

"Called an agency and they sent her for an interview."

"You checked her references, I hope?"

He grimaced. "Not exactly. She just moved here." He didn't look at her when he added, "I felt sorry for her. She looked kind of desperate."

She smiled fondly. "You and your strays. You'd take care of the whole world if you could."

"The only one I want to take care of is you."

"You can do that once you're done with your residency." She stood on her tiptoes to give him a quick kiss. "Now that you're in med school, your life is going to get a whole lot busier."

"Speaking of which. We have the house to ourselves, right?"

"Right."

"So that means we have a couple of hours to be alone."

She smiled. "Uh-huh. What do you have in mind?"

His eyes roamed over her. She was wearing a short robe, and nothing underneath. "Oh, you know. You and me. We need to keep practicing, in order to make a perfect baby."

She laughed. "Don't we have enough on our plates? I can't get pregnant now. I'm going to be the main breadwinner for the next few years. You can support me once you're Doctor Dawson."

"I don't want to wait six or seven years to start a family. Josh wants a brother or a sister. Now. So, Mrs. Dawson, what do you say we give it our best shot?"

"I think I like this honeymoon phase. We've been married for six months, you haven't had a nightmare or a drink." She smiled fondly at him. "Every day seems like a beginning." She stood on tiptoe, and kissed his lips softly. "I don't think I'll ever take you for granted. You make me breathless, Mr. Dawson."

They had been married in a simple service with only his family and hers, and a few close friends including all the Harrington clan. Brent had been the best man and Shane's partner Rick and his wife Linda were in attendance. Lauren had invited Julie, Margaret, and Trish. Margaret brought her new boyfriend, a young intern, and Trish came with her husband, and that completed the short list.

They'd been married at a quaint B&B near the beach and the wedding had been held outdoors in the garden. They'd said their vows next to a gazebo decorated in pink and red roses, followed by a moonlit dinner. Along with her father, Josh had handed her over to Shane.

The beautiful memory made her eyes sting.

She turned off the burner and moved the eggs off the stove. Then she slipped her arms around his neck, and moved in closer. "Have I told you lately that I love you?"

"Yes, but I never get tired of hearing it." He reached for her hand. "I can afford to feed our family while you're on maternity leave." He nuzzled her neck. "Come on. Humor me."

"With pleasure." She undid the knot on her robe and pulled him toward the bedroom. "I'm not sure how we can afford a baby now with your tuition fees, and me not working, but there is one thing I do know."

"What's that, my love?"

"Whatever life brings us, we can handle it together."

ABOUT THE AUTHOR

60 Minute Photos

Patrice Wilton was born in Vancouver, Canada, and knew from the age of twelve that she wanted to be a writer. She also knew that she had to grow up first and see the world that she wanted to write about, so she became a flight attendant and for seventeen years traveled the world. At the age of forty, she sat down to write her first novel—in longhand!

She is the proud mother of two, with four lovely granddaughters and a wonderful, supportive man at her side. They live in West Palm Beach, Florida, where he teaches her golf, and she teaches him patience.

Kindle Serials

This book was originally released in Episodes as a Kindle Serial. Kindle Serials launched in 2012 as a new way to experience serialized books. Kindle Serials allow readers to enjoy the story as the author creates it, purchasing once and receiving all existing Episodes immediately, followed by future Episodes as they are published. To find out more about Kindle Serials and to see the current selection of Serials titles, visit www.amazon.com/kindleserials.

Made in the USA
Charleston, SC
16 August 2013